Michael Moorcock was born in London in 1939 and published his first novel in 1961. From 1964 to 1980 he edited the seminal imaginative fiction magazine *New Worlds* where he remains consulting editor. He has written for and performed with the rock groups Hawkwind and Blue Oyster Cult. He has written more than eighty books, fiction and non fiction. *The Condition of Muzak* won the *Guardian* Fiction Prize and *Mother London* was shortlisted for the Whitbread Prize. Based in London, he also travels for significant parts of each year in the USA, Europe and North Africa.

ALSO IN PHOENIX PAPERBACKS
BY MICHAEL MOORCOCK

Gloriana; or, The Unfulfill'd Queen

The Brothel in Rosenstrasse
An Extravagant Tale

MICHAEL MOORCOCK

PHŒNIX

A PHOENIX PAPERBACK

First published in Great Britain by
Britton and Butterworth in association with
New English Library in 1982
This paperback edition published in 1993 by Phoenix,
a division of Orion Books Ltd,
Orion House, 5 Upper St Martin's Lane,
London WC2H 9EA

A CIP catalogue record for this book is available from the
British Library

ISBN 1 85799 052 8

Printed and bound in Great Britain by
The Guernsey Press Co. Ltd, Guernsey, Channel Islands.

For Angela Carter – one of the great, generous
hearts of our age – with respect and love

Romanesque, Gothic and Baroque crowd together: the early basilica of St Vaclar stands between the sixteenth-century Chemnitz fortress and the eighteenth-century Capuchin monastery, all noteable examples of their periods, and are joined just below, in Königsplatz, by the beautiful new Egyptianate concert hall designed by Charles Rennie Mackintosh. It has been fairly said that there are no ugly buildings in Mirenburg, only some which are less beautiful than others. Many travellers stop here on their way to and from the Bohemian spas of Karlsbad, Marienbad and Franzenbad. Mirenburg is joined to Vienna by water, rail and road and it is common to change here from one mode of transport to another, or merely to make the appropriate train connections. The station is by Kammerer: a Temple to Steam in the modern 'Style Liberty'. From it one may progress easily to Prague or Dresden, to St Petersburg or Moscow, to Wroclaw or Krakow, to Buda-Pesht or Vienna, and beyond to Venice and Trieste, which may also be reached by canal.

Mirenburg's wealth comes from the industry and commerce of Wäldenstein, whose capital she is, but it is enhanced by the constant waves of visitors, who arrive at all seasons.

The revenues from tourism are used to maintain the older structures to perfection and it is well-known that Prince Badehoff-Krasny, the hereditary ruler of Wäldenstein, spends a considerable proportion of his own fortune on commissioning new buildings, as well as works by living painters, composers and writers. For this reason he has been fairly called a 'present-day Lorenzo' and he is apparently quite conscious of this comparison to the great Florentine. Mirenburg is the quintessential representation of a Renaissance which is at work everywhere in modern Europe.

R.P. DOWNES, *Cities which Fascinate*,
Kelly, London, 1896

CHAPTER ONE

Mirenburg

I am at last able to move my right hand for extended periods of time. My left hand, although still subject to sudden weakness and trembling, is satisfactory. Old Papadakis continues to feed me and I have ceased to be filled with the panic of prospective abandonment. The suffering is now no worse than anything I knew as a small boy in the family sickroom. In fact minor discomforts, like an irritated groin, I welcome as wonderful aids to memory, while I continue to be astonished at my difficulty in recalling that overwhelming emotional anguish I experienced in my youth. My present tantrums and fits of despair cannot bear comparison: the impotence of sickness or old age at least reconciles one to the knowledge there is nothing one can do to improve one's own condition. Those old wounds seem thoroughly healed, yet here I am about to tear them open again, so possibly I shall discover if I have learned anything; or shall find out why I should have suffered at all.

Mirenburg is the most beautiful of cities. Great architects and builders have displayed their best talents here since the tenth century. Every tenement or hovel, warehouse or workshop, would elsewhere be envied and admired as art. On a September morning, shortly before dawn, little paddle-steamers begin to sound their horns in the grey mist. Only the twin Gothic spires of the Cathedral of St-Maria-and-St-Maria are visible at this time, rising out of the mist as symmetrical sea-carved rocks might thrust above a sluggish silver tide.

I was completely alive in Mirenburg. Ironically, during the days of the Siege, I feared death far more than I fear it now when death exhibits itself in every limb, in every organ; an unavoidable reality. Life was never to be experienced so fully. For years I yearned for the dark, lifting sensuality, that all-embracing atmosphere of sexual ecstasy I had known in Mirenburg. To have maintained that ambience, even if it had been in my power, would have led to inevitable self-destruction, so I have not entirely regretted living past the Mirenburg days. I have made I think the best of my life. Since I retired to Italy it has been simpler of course and I have been forced to review many habits I had not much questioned. Friends visit; we have memories. We relive our best times and usually joke about the worst. Changing events have not greatly disturbed us. But there is no-one who shared the Mirenburg period and few believe me if I speak of all that happened. There was so much. Alexandra. My Alice. She is still sixteen. She lies surrounded by green velvet and she is naked. I have arranged blossoms upon her skin, pink and pale yellow against her tawny flesh; flowers from a Venetian hothouse to warm her in our early autumn days, while in the ballroom below we hear the zither, the Cafe Mozart Waltz, and I smell my sex mingling with her scent, with honey and roses. Her eyes are heated, her smile is languid yet brilliant in the dark curls which surround it. She spreads her little arms. Alexandra. She called herself Alex. Later it will be Alice. I am enchanted; I am captured by Romance. Beyond the window the spires and roofs of Mirenburg glitter like a mirage. I am about to be betrayed by my own imagination. Those huge eyes, the colour of ancient oak, seem to give me all their attention and I am flattered, overwhelmed. My Alexandra. Her head moves to one side, her shoulder goes up, she speaks my name:

'Ricky?'

I am tempted to put down my pen and push myself higher in

8

my pillows to try to peer over the top of the writing-board and look to see if I really did hear her; but I continue to write, glad to touch just a little of that ambience again.

As a child, when I played with my toy soldiers, arranging battalions, positioning cavalry and artillery, I would sometimes receive an unexpected thrill of intense sexual pleasure, to the point of achieving not only an erection but often an orgasm. Even now, when I see a display of toy soldiers in a shop, I may be touched by that same sensation, almost as poignantly as when I was twelve or thirteen. Why I experienced it then and why I continued to experience it I do not know. Perhaps it had something to do with my complete power over those little men which, in turn, released in me all the power of my sex, full and unchecked by convention or upbringing. Certainly I had very little power as a boy. My brothers and sisters being so much older than I, I had a relatively solitary childhood. My mother was never mentioned. I was to discover she was in disgrace, somewhere in Roumania, with a Dutchman.

Shortly before her death, I met her briefly, by accident, in a fashionable restaurant off the Avenue Victor Hugo and recognised her from her photograph. She was small and serene and was very polite to me when I pointed out our relationship. Both she and her Dutchman were dressed in black. My father's interest was in politics. He served the government and was close to Bismarck. At our estates in Bek I had been brought up chiefly by Scottish governesses, doted on by pretty housemaids who, when the time came, had been more than willing to educate me sexually. I have been in the power of women, it seems, all my life.

Dawn comes and Mirenburg begins to rattle like a beggar's cup: the first horses and trams are abroad. The shutters are being raised, windows are being opened. The sun is pale brass upon the mist which thins to reveal a sky of milky blue. White and grey stone shimmers. She speaks the affected 'English'-accented German of fashionable Vienna; she pronounces R as W. She is captivating, artificial, an object to treasure. From some secluded tree-lined square comes the tolling of a Catholic

9

bell. At certain heights it is possible to see most of Mirenburg's antique turrets and gables, her twisting chimneys, her picturesque steeples and balconies, her bridges built by old kings, her walls and canals. The modern apartment-houses, hotels and stores, as noble and inspiring as the palaces and churches which surround them, are monumentally designed by Sommaragu and Niermans and Kammerer. She is a symphony of broad paved avenues and cobbled alleys, glinting spires and domes and stained glass. She lies staring up into my face, her small breasts held fast against my slow penis. It is warm in the room. The sun cuts between the heavy curtains and falls, a single slab of light, upon the bed, across my back. Our faces and our legs are in deep shadow; the white sperm strikes at her throat and she cries out in unison with me; my Alice. I roll to my side and I am laughing with pleasure. She lights me a cigarette. I feel like a demigod. I smoke. Every action is heroic. And she is a spirit, an *erdgeist* out of Wedekind become my very own reality. We joke. She smiles. It is dawn in Mirenburg. We shall sleep later and at about noon I will rise to wrap myself in my black and white silk robe and stand on the balcony looking out at the exquisite view which, to my mind, cannot be matched, even by Venice. I glance at the table and the dark blue leather notebook in which I shall try to write a poem for her; the book was a present from my middle sister and has my name in gold stamped on the front: Rickhardt von Bek. I am the youngest son; the prodigal of the family, and in this part I am tolerated by almost everyone. The senile trees rustle in a light East wind. I smell mint and garlic. Papadakis brings me fresh materials and a little morphine. I can feel myself trembling again, but not from pain or infirmity; I am trembling as I trembled then, with every sense at almost unbearable intensity. I touch the skin of an unripe peach. Down the wide Mladota Steps, also known as the Tilly Steps, carefully descends a single student, still drunk from a party, still in his light blue uniform except that instead of his cap he wears a Homburg hat at least three sizes too large for him. It covers his ears and his eyes. His immature lips are pursed to whistle some misremembered Mozart. He is trying to make his way back to the Old Quarter where he lodges. Two working girls, pink-faced and blonde in shawls and long dark smocks, pass him as they ascend, giggling and trying to flirt with him, but he is oblivious to them, for all the sharp clack of their clogs. He reaches the bottom of the steps and casts himself off across the roadway. The embankment on both sides is planted with firs and cypresses; immediately opposite him are the wrought-iron gates and carved granite pillars of the Botanical Gardens.

These mansions on the very fringe of the Old Quarter were once the residences of the ruling class but are today primarily public buildings and museums. They retain their grounds and their imported trees and shrubs. The largest house which the student, now clinging to the railings, would be able to see if he lifted his hat, was the summer place of the Graf Gunther von Baudessin who said he loved the city more than his own Bavarian estates. He was for a while special ambassador for his homeland and did much to help Mirenburg retain her independence during the expansionist wars of the mid-eighteenth century when three enemies (Russia, Saxony and Austria) converged on Wäldenstein's borders, then failed to agree who should own the province.

From the Gardens come a thousand scents: autumn flowers and shrubs; the small, scarlet deeply-perfumed rose for which Mirenburg is famous blooms late and sometimes lasts until December. There is still dew on the grass. The student steadies himself and continues, turning back up the broad avenue of Pushkinstrasse. He is alerted momentarily by the cry of some exotic beast awakening in the nearby Zoo. A milkman's cart, decorated in blue, red and green, passes him, its cans jingling, its boney horse rolling her old eyes in the shade of her blinkers as she takes her familiar course. He reaches the Lugnerhoff at last, where the Protestant martyrs were burned in 1497. Here the houses are suddenly close-packed, leaning one upon the other like a crowd of old men around a game of bowls. In the centre of the cobbled court is a baroque fountain: the defiant Hussites about to mount their pyre. The student crosses

11

Lugnerhoff to reach the narrow entrance to Korkziehiergasse and sunlight touches a green copper roof. Only the upper floors on the right-hand side of the alley are so far warmed by the sun; all the rest remain in deep shadow. The student opens a door into a courtyard and disappears. His feet can still be heard climbing the iron staircase to the room over what was once a stable now used by Jewish street-traders to store their goods.

Further up Korkziehiergasse, ascending the steep grey serpentine slope which leads from here to Cutovskiplatz, her knuckles blue as her fingers grasp inch by inch the metal bannister, the old candy-woman is a threadbare silhouette in the morning light. This hunched, exhausted and vulnerable little creature was once the darling of the Schoen Theatre: 'a spark of true life-force surrounded by the putrescent glow of simulated vitality', as Snarewitz described her fifty years ago. Marya Zamarovski lived for love in those days and gave herself up to the moment thoroughly and generously. Her men, while they continued to be attractive to her, had everything they desired. With every lover, she discarded houses, jewels, furniture and money, until almost simultaneously her wealth became exhausted together with her beauty and her public success. She opened a chocolate shop, but was cheated out of it by the last man she loved. Now she sells her sweets from the heavy tray about her neck. She will stand in Cutovskiplatz until evening, not far from the theatre where she used to perform (it continues to put on popular melodramas and farces). I buy candied violets from her for Alexandra who nibbles at one and offers it to me. I bite. The scented sweet mingles its strong perfume with her subtle cologne and I resist the urge to draw her to me. There is a noise from the river. On the quays the coal-heavers carry sacks to the little steamers. The docks of Mirenburg are sometimes as busy as any seaport. In winter the merchants, wrapped in overlarge fur coats which will give them the appearance of so many sober fledgelings standing in concourse, will supervise their cargoes. It is now seven o'clock in the morning and the express from Berlin is steaming into the station. The workman's cafes, bristling with newspapers in German, Czech and Svitavian, fill with smoking red sausages and dark coffee, purple arms and blue overalls, the smell of strong cigarettes, the sound of cutlery and argument. Waiters and waitresses, their big enamel trays held above their heads, move rapidly amongst the crowded marble-topped tables. We hear a bellow from the Berlin train.

On the balconies of the hotels above Cutovskiplatz a few early risers are breakfasting. One can locate a hotel at this hour by the distinctive aura of café-au-lait and croissants. Soon the English tourists in their Burberrys and Ulsters will emerge and make for Mladota where they will disdain the little funicular car running up beside it and insist on trudging all one hundred and twenty steps, irrespective of the weather; then they will head for the Cathedral of St-Maria-and-St-Maria, or go to the Radota Bridge which spans the Rätt. The balustrades of this bridge are supported on both sides by Romanesque pillars representing the famous line of Svitavian kings whose power was broken in 1370 by the Holy Roman Emperor Charles IV who, by diplomacy and threat, set his own candidate upon the throne and insisted Svitavia be called by its German name of Wäldenstein and Mirov-Cesny become Mirenburg, with the effect that Svitavian is now only spoken fluently in the rural districts.

The Rätt is a fast-flowing river. Upstream is the Oder and downstream the Danube. She is loved by barge-men as a good, safe river, spine of the most sophisticated canal system in the world. The Rätt is the chief contributor to Wäldenstein's prosperity. Several hundred yards from the Radota Bridge, beside older cobbled quays, are cramped coffee-houses and restaurants, covered in hand-written advertisements and posters so that it is almost impossible to see through windows where weathered barge-captains and pale shipping clerks drink thick Rättdämpfen soup from Dresden crockery and wipe their lips on Brno linen. The conversation is nothing but lists of goods and prices in a dozen currencies. Steam from tureens behind the counters threatens to peel placards from the glass

13

and on a misty evening one can go outside and scarcely notice any difference in visibility from the interior.

In the tall white and brown café on the corner of Kanalstrasse and Kaspergasse, underneath the billboard advertising a brand of Russian tea, sit drinking the Slav nationalists. Many have been up all night and some have just arrived. They argue in fierce but usually inexpert Svitavian or Bohemian. They quote the poetry of Kollar and Celakovsky: *Slavia, Slavia! Thou name of sweet sound but of bitter memory; hundred times divided and destroyed, but yet more honoured than ever.* They refuse to speak German or French. They wear peasant blouses under their frock-coats. They affect boots rather than shoes and rather than cigars they smoke the yellow cigarettes of the peasant. Though most of them have been educated at the universities of Prague and Heidelberg, even Paris, they reject this learning. They speak instead of 'blood' and 'instinct', of lost glories and stolen pride. Alexandra tells me her brother was for a while of their number and it is the chief reason her parents decided to take him to Rome. I tell her I am grateful to her brother for his radicalism. Her little stomach is so soft. I touch it lightly with my fingertips. I move my hand towards her pubis. She jumps and gently takes hold of my wrist. What yesterday had been of peripheral interest to me today becomes central, abiding, almost an obsession. I take as keen a delight in the contents of jewellery shop windows, the couturiers, the fashion magazines as I once took in watching a horse-race or reading about exotic lands. This change has not been gradual, it seems to have occurred overnight, as if I cannot remember any other life. Alexandra has me. My blood quickens. Now I am remembering the detail of the pleasure. I wave Papadakis away. I cling to the sensation. It becomes more than memory. I experience it again. What have I invented? Is she my creation or is she creating me? Commonplace events are of no consequence. The room darkens. A background of red velvet and roses. Her passivity; her weakness. Her sudden, fierce passion and her sharp, white teeth. She becomes strong, but she remains so soft. The cathedral bells are chiming. We are

14

playing a game. She understands the rules better than I. I break away from her and stand upright. I go to the window and part the curtains. She is laughing from the twisted sheets. I turn towards her again:

'You are hopeless.'

Papadakis is at my shoulder, asking for instructions. I tell him to light my lamp. She pushes her head under the pillow. Her feet and calves are hidden by the linen; her bottom curves in the brown gloom and her vertebrae are gleaming. She comes to the surface, her dark curls damp with sweat, and I return to her, forcing her down on her face and laying my penis in the cleft of her rear, denying myself the heat of her vagina: I have never known such heat, before or since, in a woman's sex. She bites at my hand. Traffic is noisy in the square today; a political demonstration of some kind, Papadakis says: he is contemptuous. 'Communists.' We hire a carriage and driver to take us east to Staromest, the hilly semi-rural suburb of Mirenburg where proud-eyed little girls watch over goats and chickens and shoo off strangers as if they were foxes. Here, amid the old cottages and windmills, we shall stop at an inn and either lunch there or ask them for a picnic. One or two fashionable 'Resting Houses' have been built in Staromest. They are frequented by invalids and the elderly and are staffed by nuns. Thus the peace of the hills is somewhat artificially preserved from the natural encroachment of the city. The apartment blocks stand below, silent besiegers who must inevitably conquer. We pass a small convoy of vivid gypsy wagons. Alexandra points at a brown and white pony as if I could buy it for her. The earth roads are still dry. From the dust the plodding gypsies do not look at us as we pass. We stop to gaze on the rooftops.

I point out, in the curve of the river, the old dock known as Suicide Bay. By some trick of the current most of those who fling themselves off the Radota Bridge are washed in to this dock. We can also see the distant race-track, dark masses of horses and spectators, bright silks and flags against the green turf. Closer to us is the cupola of the great Concert Hall where

15

tonight one can hear Smetana and Dvorak on the same programme as Wagner, Strauss and Debussy. Mirenburg is more liberal in her tastes than Vienna. Not far from the Concert Hall is a gilded sign, by Mucha, for the Cabaret Roberto, which offers popular singers, comedians, dancers and trained animals in a single evening's entertainment. Alexandra wishes to attend Roberto's. I promise her we shall go, even though I know she is as likely as I am to change her mind in the next half-hour. She touches my cheek with warm lips. I am enraptured by the city's beauty. I watch a green and gold tramcar, drawn by two chestnut horses, as it moves towards Little Bohemia, the Jewish Quarter, where from Monday to Thursday a market flourishes.

The tramcar reaches its terminus, near the market. The core of the market is in Gansplatz but nowadays it has spread through surrounding streets and each street has come to be identified by its stalls. In Bäverninstrasse is second-hand clothing, linen, lace and tapestries; in Fahnestrasse antiques and sporting-guns; in Hangengasse books, stationery, prints; and in Messingstrasse fruit and vegetables, meat and fish; while the main market has a little of everything, including Italian organ-grinders, gypsy fiddlers, mimes and puppeteers. Stall-holders and their customers haggle beneath bright stripes of the awnings, all in the shadow of the Great Synagogue, said to be the largest in Europe. Her rabbis are amongst the world's most famous and influential.

Dignified men, dark and learned, come and go on steps where gingerbread sellers rest their trays, where little boys sell cigarettes out of inverted drums and their sisters, in pretty tinsel, perform simple dances to attract attention to their cakes and sweets.

The stalls are crowded with toys, tools, jams and sausages, musical instruments and domestic wares. Vendors shout their bargains, and sardonic hausfraus challenge them above the noise of guitars, accordions, violins and hurdy-gurdies.

At the far end of Hangengasse a large crimson automobile, imported from France, bucks and rumbles on its springs, its

16

driver seated high above his passengers and wearing the cap, goggles and overcoat of his calling so he resembles a comical lemur in his profound sobriety. The chaffeur's gloved fingers squeeze a horn: a tin trumpet blown by a mouse announces the progress of Juggernaut. The crowd divides, from curiosity rather than fear, and the crimson machine is on its way to more fashionable parts, to Falfnersallee, the Champs Elysees of Mirenburg, and the Restaurant Schmidt, all silver, mirrors and pale yellow. Here the nouveaux riches display themselves, to the chagrin of waiters who until a year or two ago served only Mirenburg's aristocracy. The upper classes, they say, have been driven out by the vulgar owners of steamships and mechanical looms, whose wives wear the pearls of ancient impoverished families about red throats and speak a kind of German hitherto only heard in the Moravian district, the industrial suburb on the far side of the river.

This class has come to be known as 'les sauvages' or 'die Unbebaut', the subject of cartoons in the illustrated papers and mockery in cabarets which these days all but fill Kodaly Square, yet its money allows the journals and entertainments to flourish while its trade, especially with Berlin, increases Wäldenstein's prosperity.

At a large round table near the window, looking out upon the trees, the kiosks and the traffic of Falfnersallee, sits in corpulent well-being, in English tweed and French linen, Pasitch the Press King, a loyal supporter of the government of Prince Badehoff-Krasny and believer in stronger ties with Germany. His newspapers persistently emphasise the Austro-Hungarian threat and pillory an opposition favouring the views of Count Holzhammer currently exiled to Vienna, where he is courted by those who believe firmly in a 'union' between Bohemia and Wäldenstein.

Herr Pasitch eats his Kalbsaxe and discusses international politics with his uncritical sons and daughters. They are expecting a guest. My first memories of Mirenburg are of the Restaurant Schmidt. Father had taken me to the city for a season. I had spent some part of the summer at a private

17

academy before being sent on to school in Heidelberg. I recall skiffs and tea-gardens. Mirenburg had seemed a haven of peace and stability in Europe. I am inclined to resent any politics here. Mirenburg is a retreat; I escape to her. I always expected to find an Alexandra in Mirenburg so I scarcely question my fortune. We drive into the early afternoon.

Herr Pasitch's guest has arrived, seating himself with a flourish and drawing the full attention of the Pasitch daughters. He is Herbert Block, the popular song-writer; selfish, humorous and charming. Without favouritism he has looted the romantic lyrics of antecedents and contemporaries to considerable profit. Few of the victims complain. His charm is such that, although he is now nearing forty, people still regard him as a schoolboy whose pranks do no real harm, and, while he remains witty and vain, he will always have tolerant friends, especially amongst women. His dark eyes are professionally active. His dark hair might now be dyed. He leans back in his chair and flashes an expert smile. Herr Pasitch explains the strategies of Bismarck. Herr Block turns the conversation to the exploits of Count Rudolph Stefanik, the famous Czech balloon adventurer, who was recently forced to leave Zurich under scandalous conditions and narrowly missed having his vessel seized and burned by outraged citizens. They had welcomed him as a hero and he had thoroughly abused their hospitality. 'Caught in the basket!' says Herr Block. 'He is a dear friend of mine. But, O!' This episode, involving a young lady of previously good reputation, was not dissimilar to many others in the Count's history. 'His adventures have spanned five continents.' Getting some wind of the composer's drift, Herr Pasitch firmly steers the topic back to Bismarck. Herr Block smiles at the women as if in defeat. He suggests that they might like to repair later to the Straus Tea Gardens, to the south of Mirenburg, on the river. 'To catch the last of the summer.'

From these gardens, some five miles away, one can watch the trains crossing the long viaduct which spans the valley where the Rätt widens. It has thirty-two arches and was completed in 1874 by engineers from the Rhineland.

According to legend a man lost his life for every arch completed and some of the victims are said to lie beneath the plinths, their ghosts occasionally appearing on the track at night, causing drivers to apply their brakes and bring trains to an alarming halt. Usually these ghosts are discovered to be baffled deer or wolves which have strayed on to the bridge and are unable to escape.

Five minutes from the Restaurant Schmidt, in Edelstrasse, a narrow street running parallel to Falfnersallee, is the Restaurant Anglais. Socialists gather here, followers of Kropotkin, Proudhon and Karl Marx, to debate how much support they have in Parliament and how soon the workers in the Moravia will grow tired of their lot and rise against their masters. They wear grey frock-coats and high collars but only a few have the soft felt hats and loose ties of the conventional radical. In the same street, at the Hotel Dresden, are members of the League of St Ignatz, a little older, on average, but otherwise very similar to the clientèle at the Restaurant Anglais. These strong conservatives are almost as suspicious of the socialists as they are of the Jews, the Jesuits and the Freemasons, whom they term the 'super-national powers', deliberate fomentors of war and rebellion. It is early afternoon. Socialists and conservatives begin to return to offices where they will mingle and conduct the business of Mirenburg with exactly the same degree of zeal shown by their non-political colleagues.

A squadron of cavalry, its bright blues and golds softened by the September sun, rides past one end of Edelstrasse, on its way to guard the Kasimirsky Palace, where Parliament meets (today it debates a new Armaments Bill); and in the other direction goes a closed carriage bearing the arms of Hungarian Archduke Otto Budenya-Graetz, exiled from his own country by relatives who pay him to stay abroad. His reputation is so villainous not even the lion-hunting ladies of the Regenstrasse invite him to their salons. It is said he always has a small revolver with him. So many attempts have been made on his life by jealous lovers or their husbands, he carries the weapon for self-defence. The carriage turns down toward the river, passing the neo-classical Customs House, and heading inevitably for Rosenstrasse. Alexandra's teeth touch the pale flesh of chicken and I raise my champagne glass to her. The shadows already begin to lengthen. I recall my second visit to Mirenburg, the lilacs against a bright blue sky which deepened to violet at sunset; then I had spent considerable time and most of my money at the Casino. I had a passion for roulette and the Circus. Both Casino and Circus still exist, but I have so far visited neither.

Our landau takes us back to our hotel. We smell crisp Leckerli gingerbread in the hands of schoolchildren who file out of the bakeshops on their way home. I tell Alexandra of the summer in the cottage when I was a boy, of my father coming to visit us. I had the impression almost everything was white and yellow, and even now when I recall the cornflowers I am astonished at this sudden infusion of brilliant blue into my memory. I can, I tell her, with effort also re-experience the red-orange of the poppies, but I suspect this might be a false recollection, or at least one from a later period.

The smell of those poppies, however, is almost always with me, whenever I think of them. I am under the impression I am losing Alexandra's attention, but we shall soon be back at the hotel and I know how to recapture her quickly enough. I begin the story of the consumptive twins and their dog, even before we have left the carriage, although my mind is still obsessed with that scent of poppies and I wonder why I should associate it so strongly with sexual passion. Perhaps both are capable of absorbing one's total attention. Yet I could not have been more than seven when we paid our last visit to the country. Papadakis wishes to retire. He asks if he can douse my lamp. I shake my head and tell him to go. I remember, as I escort Alexandra through the lobby, the first woman I became infatuated with. She was married and her husband was abroad in some small German colony. 'You are a sympathetic friend,' she had said to me. 'And sometimes that is the last thing one seeks in a lover.' She had laughed. 'That is the job of the husband.' She taught me an excellent lesson. Once again, as I prepare to bathe, I consider the relationship between passion and power, between sexuality and spiritual fulfillment, the realisation of the Self. I complete the story of the twins. Alexandra begins to laugh and becomes helpless.

Her arms grip my back, her legs encircle my thighs; I begin the slow injection. 'Never stop loving me,' she says. 'Promise me.' I promise. 'And I will never stop loving you,' she says. But I am a fiction. My reality could destroy me. She is a dream and I shall never stop loving her. We are silent now. I move further into that tiny flame, the gateway to a universe of pleasure; beyond her vagina is infinity, immortality, marvellous escape. She is yelling. Her nails stab into my buttocks and my cries join hers. She lies with her curls against my neck and shoulder. I stroke her arm in the long twilight. 'Shall we go to Roberto's?'

'I am too tired,' she says, 'for the moment. Let us have an early supper here and then see.'

In Zwergengasse, once the home of a famous eighteenth-century Italian circus troupe, a knife-grinder pushes his cart over the cobbles. The street is barely wide enough for him and not much more than thirty yards long. It runs up to the old wall of the city. Its lower floors are large and vacant, occupied only by a tribe of beggars who will, when winter comes, move on to warmer quarters near the quaysides; they squat amongst the remains of the circus – painted tin and rotting velvet – discussing their adventures in loud voices while Pan Sladek reaches his premises at last, lowers the handles of his cart and unlocks the doors of his workshop, suspicious as always of the beggars (who would be far too timid to rob him). His grey face shines like a hatchet as he sweats to manipulate his grinding equipment into the shop. His nose is blue and pointed. He has had a hard day. He locks up and enters the doorway next to the shed, climbing the stairs slowly, but two at a time on his spidery legs until he reaches a door painted a fresh and startling yellow. He opens it. The smell of frying comes from the kitchen. Today is schnitzel day. When Pan Sladek remembers

21

this he brightens. He goes into the kitchen and kisses Pani Sladek as he always kisses her. She smiles to herself. Below, as Zwergengasse grows dim, more beggars flit back, rooks to a rookery, their hands full of sour wine and loaves of yesterday's bread. Somewhere close by, students of the Academy and the Polytechnic are fighting again, shouting obscure private battle-cries from street to street and lying in ambush for one another in alleys and shop doorways, brandishing stolen colours, caps and scarves, which they nail to the walls and beams of the beerhalls, their headquarters. Willi's in Morgenstrasse and Leopold's in Grunegasse are respectively strongholds of the Academy and the Polytechnic. Near Leopold's is The Amoral Jew, a cabaret populated entirely by proponents of the New Art, young Russians and Germans with bizarre notions of perspective.

Alexandra likes The Amoral Jew and I have acquaintances there. We arrive at about nine o'clock to watch the negro orchestra which delighted her on our last visit. She is over-dressed and heavily painted for this cabaret but so beautiful that nobody cares. Kulacharsky, barrel-chested and ferociously bearded, in a peasant blouse and clogs, fondles the ostrich feathers in her diamond aigrette and says something wicked to her in Russian which pleases her, though she does not understand a word. It is dark and noisy in The Amoral Jew and Rosenblum himself presides, his goatee twitching as he strolls amongst the tables and glances secretly here and there from mysterious eyes which could be drugged. There are murals on the walls, in gaudy primaries. Were it not for the strange manner of their execution they would be thought indelicate. They were painted by a Spaniard who passed through. Alexandra accepts a glass of absinthe, still the drink of the bohemian from St Petersburg to Paris. Voorman, sweating in his heavy jacket and tweed shooting breeches, begins to talk about his telescope; he is considering giving up painting for astronomy. 'Science is today the proper province of the artist.' Alexandra laughs, but because she finds him attractive not because she understands him. Bodies press around us like

22

mourners at a wake. Alexandra enjoys the attention of the avant-garde. In the old barracks a few streets away, built into the walls of Mirenburg, privates at an off-duty card game drink surreptitiously from illicit jugs while avuncular sergeants turn blind eyes. In the upper storeys of the garrison captains and lieutenants passionately discuss the Armaments Bill which, if implemented, will mean a stronger Wäldenstein. 'Everyone is arming. If we wish to keep our freedom, so should we. We are the prize of Europe, never forget that. We are coveted by all: three empires flank us and the only security we have is that one empire will not risk warring upon another in order to win us. Remember Bismarck's words: "Wäldenstein is the most beautiful bride the masculine nations have ever courted: a virgin whose dowry opens the gateway to power over the entire continent. Whoever wins her shall win the world." The Prince thinks our neutrality is all the security we need. But we must be prepared to defend ourselves from within. There are those who would sell the virgin to the highest bidder.' So says Captain Thomas Vladoroff, a distant cousin of mine, as his batman clears away the cheese. Vladoroff has the pale and misleadingly vacant good looks of his family. 'We must be alert for the agent provocateur in our midst. There are many, in the army and out of it, who support Count Holzhammer.' His friends smile at his zeal. He loosens the collar of his dress tunic. Someone tells him that there could never be a civil war in Wäldenstein. 'We are too sensible, too united, too fond of comfort.' Alexandra dislikes my cousin. He is bloodless, she says, and more interested in machines than in his fellow men. He is leaving now, to visit his mistress in Regenstrasse, the widow of an officer killed some twenty years ago as a volunteer on the Prussian side during their last war with the French. Her name is Katerina von Elfenberg and she was seventeen when her husband died. She told my cousin he could be a reincarnation of that dashing Hussar, who was blown to pieces by a huge Krupp gun he was attempting to recapture. Her other lover is a Baron, a chief of the Stock Exchange, and her advice is making my cousin moderately rich, although he becomes concerned

23

about the nature of the speculation, for it seems to him to anticipate strife. There is a small party tonight. I have been invited but I could not take Alexandra for fear of meeting members of her family. As it is, her servants have had to be heavily bribed to tell callers she is out and to bring messages in secret to our hotel so that she can reply and thus preserve the pretence of being in residence. Her parents write regularly from Rome and she dutifully replies with news of friends and relatives, the weather, expeditions with her friends to museums and the more suitable tea-gardens. She is expected, next year, to go to be finished in Switzerland, but she plans instead, she tells me, to meet me in Berlin. From there we shall discuss the possibilities of Paris, Marseilles and Tangiers, for of course she is below the age of consent.

My cousin is introduced to the members of the Mirenburg Royal Ballet Company, some of the finest dancers in the world. The women offer him controlled hands to be kissed. He will tell me later how he feels uncomfortable, as if corralled with a squadron of ceremonial horses, all of which can pick up their feet and none of which can charge. I look toward the little stage, my arm about Alexandra. She loves the comedy, borrowed from Debureau, she says. Pierrot pursues Columbine and is defeated by Harlequin. A large silk moon ripples in the draught from the door and Pierrot plucks his guitar, singing in French. I am told it is Laforgue. Projected against the backdrop are silhouettes of balloons, trains and automobiles, of factories and iron ships. The song is in praise, I gather, of the machine, for Pierrot's accent is so gutteral I can scarcely understand one word in three. Then on come the novelty dancers; some little ballet of primitive lust and discordant fiddles. In the morning, as soon as there is sunlight a lark will begin to sing from our roof. We touch glasses and sip the heady wormwood. There is no time. I am adrift. I lean towards my ink. I have no pain now. I am full of delight. In Mirenburg's gaslight I call for a cab. Around us is ancient beauty, delicate lacework-stone silent under the deep sky. I resist the temptation to brave Katerina von Elfenberg's salon and we drive instead to the Yanokovski Promenade to marvel at its electrical lights and to listen to the music from the bandstand. I am an old man now and my white suits have become yellowed by the sun; but there is a bandstand in the town, where Italians play selections from Verdi and Rossini. A pleasure boat goes past in the jewelled water. Excited girls and boys of Alexandra's age play innocent games amongst the deck-chairs and the hatch-covers. A flotilla of grim barges passes in the darkness on the other side; a steam-whistle hoots. The pleasure boat disappears beneath the Radota. Mirenburg is the merriest of cities at night. Her citizens belong spiritually to more Southern regions of the continent. In Bachenstrasse, which winds down to the Promenade, Carl-Maria Saratov, his heart broken and his mind desperate for diversion, wanders into the unlit alleys known as the Indian Quarter, perhaps because there was once a cheap waxwork show here with its main tableaux representing the Wild West. Carl-Maria Saratov has come all the way from Falfnersallee where he saw his sweetheart entering the Cafe Wilhelm with his oldest friend, another student at the university. He has heard that opium is to be found in the Indian Quarter and so it is. The den would be unlikely to welcome him. It is typical of its kind, but unlike the one Carl-Maria has heard about from a friend. Mirenburg's best opium-den is not the sordid hovel one finds in Hamburg or London. Even the Chinese attendants at 'Chow-Li's' are not really Chinese, but Magyars dressed in elaborate robes. The place is awash with blue silk and golden brocade. The couches are deep and thickly padded and the owner is British, an exile, James Mackenzie, the Scots military engineer, who committed some crime in the Malay Archipelago and dare not enter any country of the British Empire, yet runs his den with all the tact, discretion and lavish decoration of a fashionable restauranteur. Archduke Otto Budenya-Graetz is there tonight, with two young friends from the military school. Mackenzie will not refuse him entrance, but makes sure he is sent to a remote room and that the pipes are paid for before they are smoked.

25

The Archduke has not enjoyed his visit to Rosenstrasse and swears the place is overrated and he will never return. He complains of his entrapment in 'this provincial town' and speaks to the fascinated students of the glories of Vienna, Buda-Pest and Paris, of the women of St Petersburg, where he was very briefly an attaché, of the boys of Constantinople, and he hands them their pipes with his eyes on their serge thighs and takes a deep breath to relax himself before inhaling. He lets himself remember his days in the service of the Mexicans; that splendid time of unchecked satisfaction when the air was so full of fear one had merely to wave a sabre to fulfill one's grossest needs. 'I can still smell the blood,' he murmurs. 'There is nothing like it to enliven any sport, say what you will.' He takes his pipe as if it were a crop and his eyes, full of pagan Asia, brighten and then cloud. 'But the Jews have robbed me of my birthright . . . ' Alexandra is growing bored. She asks me to take her to 'some secret place' and so we, too, head for 'Chow-Li's' for I must grant her everything she asks. Here she will cough on the smoke and complain it has no effect, but later she will ask me about my women and will lick her lips while I describe their charms and become terrifyingly passionate so that my dreams will be of some transfigured Mirenburg, some Mirenburg of the soul, where tawny young lionesses purr above the trembling corpses of handsome baboons. Now, just when I have awakened from a thoroughly restful sleep for the first time in weeks, it seems that Mirenburg is all around me. I can see her austere Gothic spires in the mist of the September morning. She is completely alive again. On the river a line of rowing boats drifts gradually to rest against the Hoffmeister Quay. The smell of baking comes from Nadelgasse, seemingly from every window there drifts the odour of fresh bread, of cakes and pastries. As a child I dreamed frequently of a golden-haired young girl, whom I loved. I had carried her away from harsh parents in an open-boat and we had been captured by Norse pirates, but again I was able to save her. She loved me as wholly as I loved her. I used to think of her more than I thought of any real person, as I lay awake in my room in daylight, trying to sleep, but knowing that the rest of the world was still awake, hearing my sisters' voices from below. Must we always seek in lovers to satisfy the frustrations we have experienced with parents? An 'echo'. Unable to ease the cares of those who have given birth to us we attempt to improve the lot of a mistress, a husband or a wife. So many women have tried to make me into their ideal father and in resisting I have frequently lost them. Alexandra would rather I were a demon-lover and this role is almost as difficult, but I play it with more relish, for it entails very different responsibilities. My ideal is fair-skinned and blonde, so why should I sense this 'echo' in my little Alexandra, this resonance in the soul which entwines me to her as if we were a single note of music? We speak again of Tangiers. I would take her there now, for fear of her escaping me when she tires of this game, but it is impossible. Instead I acquiesce to every adventure.

She requests instruction. I am inventive. I bring to life every dream. I add all experience to my repertoire, I tell her. I resist nothing. I forget nothing. Sexually I am a chameleon. 'You have the disposition of a whore,' she tells me, laughing. I cannot deny it. We visit my old friend, Professor Eckart, who teaches at the University now and continues his experiments. He is obsessed with Count Rudolph Stefanik and the possibilities of heavier-than-air flight. He shows us his own designs. His room is almost bare, save for drawings pinned here and there upon the panelling. The large window looks out onto geometrical gardens, full of evergreens and Mirenburg's famous roses. He tells us that he has personally entertained Stefanik. Alexandra, who has been bored, asks what the Count is like. 'The man is a rogue,' I say. 'And you are not?' she asks. I have forgotten my part. 'But a genius,' says Professor Eckart, tugging at his sleeve and casting about for the wine he has offered us. Professor Eckart looks like a countryman. He is round and bucolic; he might be a huntsman on some Bavarian estate. 'Would you care to meet him? I am giving a dinner-party next week.' 'We should love to,' says Alexandra. Privately I decide to discover the names of the other

27

guests before I accept. I am suspicious of Alexandra's curiosity; I have some measure of how far she will go to satisfy it. Papadakis brings me my oatmeal gruel. I breakfast on champagne and smoked salmon with my Alexandra. Not long ago even the gruel was painful to my palate and would sometimes seem over-flavoured, but now I disdain its blandness. Papadakis suggests he should have the doctor in today. Angrily I resist the idea. 'I have not felt so well in two years,' I tell him. He leaves to collect the post from the town. I visited my brother Wolfgang at his place in Saxony about a year before I arrived again in Mirenburg. He had just recovered from tuberculosis. 'My cure was sudden and miraculous,' he told me. 'The disease appeared to be killing me. I was its slave. Then, within a matter of weeks, it had released me. I grew steadily stronger, but as I did so I knew enormous regret for the passing of that warm and permanent eroticism which had attended my illness for over forty months. As I returned to normality I experienced the acutest depression and sense of descent into a world whose familiar delights were no longer pleasurable to me.' At the time I had scarcely understood him. Now I know very well what he meant. There is a kind of debilitating insanity which a person will cling to desperately for as long as it possesses them. Only when it has given them up will they begin to describe it as an aberration. 'The world is a dull place now, Ricky,' my brother had said. He had taken to drinking heavily. If it had not been for the threat of dismissal from the diplomatic service he might easily have become a permanent drunkard. But until he died his face held the look of a man who had once known Heaven. Papadakis returns and helps me to the WC. Today the agony of urinating is not so great and I realise that I had grown to look forward to the pain as preferable to any of the other sensations which my disease offers me. But I hurry back to Mirenburg, urging Papadakis on as if he were a coach-horse and I flying for the coast in fear of my life.

At night Mirenburg is both peaceful and mysterious: a perfect mistress. Her shadows do not seem dangerous and her lights do not reveal any ugliness; her desperate aspects are contained; she is tranquil. She is an intelligent city, willing to accept novelty. She is secure and self-possessed. The secret police of three empires conspire in her, observe each other, play peculiar games of intrigue, and she permits it, a tolerant stepmother; the political exiles make their speeches, publish their broadsheets; she does not discourage them so long as her own peace is not disturbed. In the white and brown café on the corner of Kanalstrasse and Kaspergasse, The Café Slavia, the young nationalists have a guest. He is Rakanaspya, an anarchist of uncertain origin; a friend of Kropotkin and Bakunin.

Many believe him to be well-connected in aristocratic circles. Tonight he speaks passionately against privilege, against nationalism, and debates with the youths the virtues of internationalism, mutuality and self-reliance, while in other parts of the café two spies, in the employ of Austria-Hungary and Russia respectively, take surreptitious notes. They are commissioned to report on all agitators. Rakanaspya wears a greatcoat with a fur collar, a bearskin cap; one hand rests on a silver cane. The other hand lifts glasses of brandy to his lips. His voice is unusually thick and husky and is not natural; it was obtained in a duel when his palate was shot away. His imperial hides most of the scar on the left side of his face. He chain-smokes papyrussi so that his fingers, moustache and teeth are stained as yellow as the abandoned tubes which litter his surroundings wherever he stops for more than half-an-hour. They are made for him by an old Russian woman who works for the British Tobacco Company at No. 11 Kanalstrasse. His thin face is pinched and drawn, he has keen, unquiet eyes behind large round glasses and his emaciated, nervous frame speaks of despairing poverty assuaged by fanaticism, perhaps an inheritance from his days in Siberia. Yet when he smiles his face becomes suddenly innocent; it is sympathetic. He speaks several languages fluently and is well read in every European literature. As a go-between for the emigrés and the Wäldenstein authorities he has become almost an official representative. He manages to conciliate both sides (who trust him). He keeps even the fiercest Bohemian or Russian expatriate from expulsion, in spite of constant pressure on the authorities. Austria in particular would welcome any excuse to go to war with Wäldenstein; but she will not risk war with Russia, Germany or both. Wäldenstein lies balanced between the spheres of these empires, as a small planet might be supported by the opposing gravitation of larger ones, and it is thought to be in nobody's interest to disturb that balance. Rakanaspya has momentarily forgotten his politics. Someone has mentioned Odessa, his home. 'I sometimes feel,' he says, 'as if I am the emissary from one magic city to another.' As he becomes drunk Rakanaspya begins to talk of the sea, catching bullheads off the Odessa rocks as a boy, sailing in flat-bottomed boats around the lighthouse, of the foreign vessels lying at anchor on a turquoise ocean, the sailors in the harbour taverns. Many by now know Rakanaspya himself has never been, and probably never will go, to sea; he is fascinated and comforted by the romance of it. His face becomes completely human only when the conversation is turned to salt-water. He never claims experience of sailing, yet believes himself an authority on naval matters and the ways of the world's great ports. The spies are puzzled by this turn in the conversation, wondering at the significance of it. Rakanaspya describes Odessa for his listeners, the smell of the spices in the harbours, the little tramp steamers which ply the Black Sea, the great military ships. Alexandra, wrapped in a coat which hides the extravagant gown I bought her this afternoon, whispers that she finds Rakanaspya intriguing and boring at the same time. 'Are all men so full of talk? Such general stuff?' We slip away from The Café Slavia. She seems angry Rakanaspya did not notice her. We walk beside the river. Men in donkey-jackets stand and smoke their pipes, talking in small groups, glancing at us as we pass. Two Customs officials stroll by. They wear dark blue uniforms, their coats belted at the waist and supporting swords; both have large, carefully-grown moustaches and their caps are at identical angles on their round heads. Papadakis frets over me. He believes I am feverish. He is becoming too insistent. I indicate the paper. 'I am writing again,' I tell him. 'Is that not a sign of my spiritual and physical recovery?' He goes mumbling from the room. He must forever be simplifying experience. He irritates me. I run my thumb-nail down the flesh of her back. She gasps and clutches at bedding but insists I do not stop. I suppose men can learn from women that capacity to make a positive virtue of pain and despair. Women frequently through self-deception and lack of power believe that pain and desperation have meaning in themselves. I tell her she should always seek pleasure and optimism; to seek pain as a form of salvation is to destroy oneself. When we suffer the pain of solitude (as I have done in prison, for instance, or in exile) we are fools if we regard this state as preferable to the ordinary vicissitudes of the world, though we can make of solitude a habit of self-reliance which when needed can stand us in good stead. Pain offers us certain kinds of knowledge which enable us to live in greater harmony with our complex world. An animal which seeks out pain, however, is a mad animal, just as a hermit, who will avoid it, is a mad animal. She is asleep. I rise and go to the window and part the curtains. The square is quiet. I regret, as I smoke a cigarette, I shall not be able to attend the reception being given tomorrow at the Palace.

I met the amiable Prince Damian von Badehoff-Krasny only once, three years ago at a concert given in Munich by his cousin Otto, an old friend from my early years at the Academy. The Badehoff-Krasny family are of Slavonic as well as Teutonic ancestry and came originally from the Ukraine. The province of Wäldenstein was an inheritance, achieved through marriage, and in the seventeenth century, when the family had fallen on hard times and everything else was sold or stolen from them by a variety of warring monarchs, the people asked the Prince's ancestor, who was still an Elector of the Holy Roman Empire, to become their ruler. The family maintained its independence of Germany, Russia and the Hapsburg

31

Empire partly by chance and partly through clever diplomacy, by playing one faction against another and by continuing to marry well. Their intellectual and artistic interests had made them at some time patrons to almost every famous painter, composer and writer in Europe. They had in their possession a thousand mementos of the scholars and actors who had sampled their hospitality. Indeed, my own little Alexandra is a cousin twice removed of the present Prince. I believe her interest in me was aroused when I mentioned at our first meeting, during the dinner-party given by Count Freddy Eulenberg just after my arrival in the city, that I had published one or two small volumes of verse and reminiscence. There is a traditional rivalry in her family for the patronage of any academic or artistic lion, however small and provincial, and I think even Alexandra saw me as something of a kitten, but as the only catch of the season not wholly demeaning. This is not, of course, the chief quality which makes me attractive in her eyes. I have been the subject of gossip both in Mirenburg and in Munich and have acquired that sort of exaggerated reputation which so fascinates young women and so greatly facilitates their seduction. Alexandra speaks of her uncle with considerable affection and some impatience (plainly imitated from her elders), telling me that he lives with his head in the clouds, refusing to be alarmed either by Bismarckian ambition or Austro-Hungarian arrogance, convinced that the likes of Holzhammer mean no great harm and are as content as himself merely to play at politics. I know that soon there must be a scandal; our deception can last only a few more days, but I refuse to confront the problem, as does she. Papadakis hovers at my shoulder. Alexandra breathes deeply. I tell Papadakis to leave me alone. The door closes. The inkwell is crystal. It reflects the light from the window. It is quieter today. The political meeting has dissipated everyone's energy.

Is Wäldenstein, I wonder, too complacent as my cousin Thomas suggests? Should she not defend herself better? I think about that mixture of sentimentality, romance and self-deception which sustains a nation in its myths and which

32

enables it to act in its own immediate self-interest. We are most of us a characteristic segment of the nations from which we spring and it can almost be said we measure our individuality by the degree to which we free ourselves from our inherited prejudices. Many of us talk about it; but talk, I think, is not enough. Words and actions must coincide. Wäldenstein's myth is that because she has for so long been free she can never be enslaved. I turn to look at my Alexandra, who has captured me so thoroughly. I have been swayed by lust before. I have taken considerable risks to fulfill it. But now I am not sure that I am any longer moved by simple lust. It is desire which moves me and I do not understand the origin or the nature of that desire, even though I am obsessed by it.

I deny all reality in order to maintain it; I am even prepared, I know, to relinquish lust, to ignore affection, normal companionship. I feel contempt for the ordinary yet I know this state of mind is self-destructive. Such desire is incapable of ever being satisfied. I believe I have aroused the same terrible energies in Alexandra. With it comes a fierce carelessness which considers no-one: be it myself or the object of my desire. There is only the present, here in Mirenburg. I erase the past; I refuse the future. I tear off my robe and stretch my naked body against hers, turning her towards me and kissing her startled, still sleeping mouth. I remember being sent on a ludicrous errand by my sister who wished her brother-in-law to put an end to an unsuitable courtship. He had received me in his study. He was not defiant, yet his attention had hardly been on me at all. He was a good-looking man of the conventional, military sort. 'I see her three times a week,' he had told me. 'She gives me no more and no less. My life is ruled by this routine. I let nothing interfere with it. I live in terror that it will be broken. I will go to any lengths to sustain it. She has a husband, you see. He is old but she feels affection for him. Her consideration of his sensitivities drives her to elaborate strategies in her deception of him, even though he acquiesces and even encourages her in her affair with me, whom he has never met. This consideration somehow gives dignity to a life which on the surface is sordid

33

enough. He offers her security. In return she allows him to live in the ambience of her wonderful sensuality. It seems enough for both. She will not, naturally, permit me to possess her completely, but she is equally considerate of me. She rarely fails to keep an appointment. When she does I am in agony until she communicates with me. She will never leave him. So long as she acknowledges his feelings and thinks of his well-being he is content. She is a wonderful creature. She would not harm either of us.

'And you can stand this stasis?' I had asked.

'It is the best I can hope for,' he had said. A bell had rung then. He had risen. 'If you wish to call on Friday, I shall be able to see you again.' He walked sadly with me to the landing and watched as I descended the stairs. 'Please give my warmest regards to your sister and tell her how much I appreciate her thoughtfulness.'

There is an evening service at the Cathedral. I leave a note for Alexandra and walk the long cobbled way, up the hill, to listen to the music. I cannot argue with Alexandra. She robs me of logic. When last in Mirenburg I had described to a young lady, with whom I had been having an affair, my state of mind. How, amongst, other things, I had been confused for several years, since my wife had left me for a ship's officer in Friedrickshaven only three months after we were married, about whether or not I should marry again. The young lady had smiled: 'You do not think I wish to marry you?' I said that I had wondered. 'But I assure you . . . ' She had begun to laugh. She had pretended that her laughter was uncontrollable. I had waited until she had finished. 'There is no question,' she had said.

'Excellent.' I had stood up, wondering at that time why she should have denied what had evidently passed through her mind and why I had not the courage to make a direct proposal, for I had been in the mood to do it. That evening, having disappointed myself so thoroughly, I had taken a cab to Frau Schmetterling's and requested a room and a girl – my habit, twice a week, for nearly a year. This, however, had been a third visit in the week and caused Frau Schmetterling some amusement. As I had taken the key from her hand I marvelled at my ability, without intention, to make women laugh. I had seen no reason to suspect that I was held in contempt by them or even that I was unpopular with them, yet I could not fathom how I aroused their humour.

Why do women seem to triumph so often in men's misery, even when they love them? Again I find myself considering the nature of power and of love. Only a few weeks after my failure to propose to the young lady I had occasion to inform another that I no longer wished to see her. 'But I love you,' she had said, 'with all my heart and soul. I will love you forever. I wish to be yours, whatever you want me to be. I want to help you in any way that I can.' And within a week (I think it was six days) she had fallen in love with an official in the Revenue Service to whom she was, by all accounts, a loyal and faithful companion. The trees thicken as one nears the Cathedral. It is almost rural. There are wild flowers amongst the grass. In the spring and summer cherry- and apple-trees blossom here. I mount the uneven pavements. The spires of the Cathedral are high above my head. The choir is singing from within: *Gospodi pomiluj ny – Lord have mercy upon us.* I turn and go back. There is other music to be heard, from the cafés, from the street performers. I pause on the corner of Falfnersallee. The last No. 15 tram is on its way to the terminus in Radoskya. I have known Mirenburg in all her seasons, but this is the one I have always favoured. I pass by the statues of Wäldenstein's great men and women. I find myself craving the famous bortsch to be found in the Mladota district. It is made with beets and ham-bones, in the traditional way, but to it is added a dash of a particular Tokay which for some reason affects the palate and makes it sing. I remember Alexandra telling me it even makes her ears tingle. It is delicious: a drug. I decide to return to the hotel, to rouse her and ask if she will join me in a plate. As I turn into Mirozhny Square a group of beggars comes by. I give them all the coppers I have. They are returning to the Schlaff estate, to the old fever hospital and desolate graveyards. Only

35

the railway track brings any kind of life to that area. It is a goods line. Not even local trains to the northern suburbs and outlying villages take passengers through. This estate is all that is left of the Schlaff family lands. The family has lived exclusively in Paris and Berlin for three generations but refuses to lease the estate to anyone who would make use of it. Thus houses, mills, churches and workshops are occupied only by the homeless and the lawless. Orphans and old men climb amongst the ruins and the neglected graves and more respectable citizens pay to have their garbage and other embarrassments they wish to discard transported there. Strange fires burn in this contradictory wasteland; the flames are unhealthy in colour and mysterious in shape. It is Mirenburg's shame. 'Only a little shame, compared to most,' an ex-Mayor of Mirenburg will later insist to me. I will be bound to agree with him. In daytime even the Schlaff estate looks picturesque, overgrown as it is with wild flowers, but at night it must be sought to be seen. It is almost dawn. I hurry back to Alexandra, suddenly afraid she will awake and leave because I am not there to help her maintain our dream.

It was during a particularly drunken expedition to the Schlaff that I had met Caroline Vacarescu, the Hungarian adventuress, who also currently stays at the Hotel Liverpool and whom I pass in the lobby as I make my hasty ascent to our suite. If Alexandra wakes, realises her predicament and decides to go I shall be unable to reclaim her. She might, of course, have similar fears, but if so she does not exhibit them. Caroline Vacarescu smiles at me. She is doubtless keeping an appointment with Count Mueller, her lover. A wonderful mixture of Magyar beauty and English delicacy, her furs and silks exotically scented, she is the illegitimate daughter of an English duke and a Hungarian aristocrat, born in Pesht. Her father was attached to the Foreign Office, her mother, until her pregnancy, was a lady-in-waiting to the Princess. She received a superb education in Vienna, England and Switzerland and at the age of eighteen married Christoff Béraud, the financier. When Béraud crashed as a result of the Zimmerman scandal of

1889, he shot himself, leaving his wife penniless and having to seek the protection of the man who was already her lover, Hans von Arnim, the successful pianist. Unable to be seen with von Arnim in public, Madame Vacarescu grew bored and eventually left Berlin for Danzig with Count Mueller, who describes his occupation as 'freelance diplomat' but who is known as 'the Messenger Boy of Europe', a spy, an arms-dealer and a blackmailer. Mueller will die this year and it will be rumoured that Caroline Vacarescu has rid herself of a man who had in a dozen ways compromised and humiliated her. She is a warm-hearted, rather detached woman; a very cold lover with me. Alexandra is awake and my terrors vanish; she complains breakfast is late. Perhaps it is my own lack of resolve I mistakenly bestow upon her. The breakfast comes and goes. As we make love I have an intense vision of that massive stone Cathedral; her flesh contrasts with the carved granite; such opposites and yet so similar in their effect upon the hand and eye. It occurs to me that there may be fewer better pleasures than to make love in the St-Maria-and-St-Maria with the light from the stained glass falling on our bodies as I pass my fingers from youthful flesh to ancient stone while the organ plays some favourite piece of music. And would it be blasphemy? Most would see it as that. But I would thank God for all His gifts and pray more joyfully than anyone had ever prayed before. The violence of Alexandra's passion had almost frightened me at first; now it becomes exhilarating, infectious and I respond in kind. Sometimes, inexplicably, she becomes nervous of me. I ignore her fear, and press ahead until she has again forgotten everything but her lust. But I must be forever controlling, guarding against depressions, against commonalities which threaten our idyll. I do not always reckon with the power of Alexandra's determination. When they decided to go to Rome her parents had left her in the charge of her aunt, who in turn put her in the care of an old housekeeper. She had already begun to dream, to prepare herself for adventures which, inspired by the reading of certain French novels, she had yearned to experience for several years. I still do not know

37

whether she sought me out for her instruction or whether she instructs me. I was unable, in spite of sane reservations, to master my lust. I swiftly gave myself up to her. I do not know how long it has been, but I know that I did not believe for more than a few days that I was fully in control of her as I began that process of subtle debauchery she so deeply desired and which, of course, she also feared, as the laudanum-taker fears the drug which is friend and enemy in one. That she will eventually resist any dependency upon me and break my heart will be a tribute to her determination and a confirmation, finally, of my judgement that I had not only met my match but been beaten at a game I had played half-consciously for years. Alexandra grunts and pants; her eyes are burnished copper. I am familiar, as are most men, with the woman who will translate her own will to power through a male medium, but Alexandra is either more subtle or more naive in her attempts to affect her world. This is partly what fascinates me. It has been several years since any woman obsessed me; now I am surely caught. Eros usurps Bacchus. I rise on that dark euphoria which appears to bring objectivity but in fact produces nothing save confusion, uncontrollable misery and eventual collapse. Papadakis steps out of the shadows with a rattling tray. I can only admit now that I gave myself up to Eros deliberately, in the belief it does a man or woman good to make such fools of themselves occasionally; there are few risks much wilder and few which make us so much wiser, should we survive them. Papadakis stretches out his emaciated arms. I smell boiled fish. 'It will do you good,' he says in his half-humorous, half-insinuating voice; a voice once calculated during his own, brief, Golden Age to rob the weak of any volition they might possess; but it had been the single weapon in his arsenal; he had used up all his emotional capital by the time he was forty. He speaks of the past as if it were a personal God which came to betray him. 'They ruined me,' he sometimes says. In his more egocentric moments he claims deliberately to have ruined himself. Even as we fall into the abyss, we men must explain how the descent was predicted and calculated. When the world refuses to be

38

handled by us, we turn to women. And women, for purposes of their own, usually temporary, help us pretend to a power permitted, in reality, only to the securest of tyrants. Papadakis has become a wizened satyr, a monument to mis-spent juices, keeping me alive from motives of dimly-perceived self-interest. I tell him to leave the tray, to bring me white wine. He refuses. He tells me it is not good for me. He is scowling. Perhaps he senses he no longer has any power over me. Alexandra begins to ask me lascivious questions about my other women. I tell her romantically there are none but her and she seems disappointed.

The heat of her saliva is on my penis; the soft lips close, the teeth touch the skin; her head moves slowly up and down and the future is once more successfully banished. Death does not exist. Playing with her clitoris and wiping sperm from her cheek she asks me again about other women. I am anxious to keep her curiosity. I begin to invent stories for her. I tell her of adventures involving several ladies at a time. She says unexpectedly: 'Would you like me to do that for you?' I am interrupted. 'What?'

'Sleep with other women,' she says. 'With you?' I hesitate. 'Have you slept with girls before?' She smiles. 'With school-friends, certainly. We have all done it. Most of us. I love female bodies. They are so beautiful. Beautiful in a different way.' She touches my penis which is erect again. I laugh. 'Where,' she says, 'can we find another lady?' I have the solution. Papadakis is crooning to himself in the corner near the wardrobe. He is doing something with a screwdriver. He is not in good temper. 'Have you taken your pills?' I ask, mocking him. He becomes furious. 'You should see the doctor,' he tells me. 'I cannot be responsible.'

Caroline Vacarescu boasted to me once that she had slept with five reigning monarchs and thirteen heirs apparent, four of them women. The Age of Kings appears to have ended in an orgy of royal lust. The Dictators, according to established pattern, seem extraordinarily celibate in comparison, perhaps because they are not so casually acquainted with power. But with Caroline it was a question of service, not pleasure. She was adding to Count Mueller's secret fortune. We are looking for some cigars for me. Walking up Koenigstrasse in bright sunlight we see an old woman leaning against a shop window full of soap and popular potions. She has a half-eaten cake in one hand and seems drunk. Her clothing is predominantly dark brown. It does not fit her properly. Her left foot is bandaged to just above the ankle. She tugs up her skirt and pees on the paving stones. Her collection of bundles lies to one side of her and the urine spreads slowly towards it. Nearby a street sweeper brushes at the gutter with polite patience, as if waiting to clean the pavement as soon as she has finished. People pass her without stopping, without looking, although they do not appear to be disgusted or afraid. 'There is nothing we can do,' says Alexandra, pulling at me. The sun shines on white roofs and is reflected in elegant windows.

There is a great deal of traffic in Koenigstrasse today; carriages and carts of all sorts. The street smells like a farm. Papadakis refuses to tell me when he will return. He closes the door with unusual force. I am content. A procession of swaggering lancers, jangling metal and bobbing gold braid, trots by on the other side. 'There are so many soldiers about,' says Alexandra. 'Do you know why?' I do not. 'It could be something to do with the Armaments Bill,' I tell her. The Bill has passed through Parliament. The Prince is expected to sign it today. Alexandra takes a cab for Nussbaumhof to see if her parents have written to say when they are returning from Rome. My earlier fears of losing her have disappeared because we are about to embark on another intrigue; she has set her mind on it. How much of her am I destroying, or allowing her to destroy of herself? I relax with a glass of Alsatian beer and some Cambozola at an outside table of the Café Internationale on the corner of Falfnersallee facing the Radota Bridge and the river. The air is unusually warm: everywhere I look I see beauty, reassurance. If Vienna is gay, then Mirenburg is happy; a sane city whose character may be infinitely explored, and yet she has no real secrets; even her vices are admitted and the subject of common knowledge.

Bismarck says Mirenburg is a feminine city and a natural bride for masculine Berlin. He once said that a marriage with Vienna would be a perversion of everything that was natural. My brother knew Bismarck quite well. Apparently the great Chancellor had a habit of describing nations in terms of their sexual characteristics; he loved France, for instance: 'She challenges us expecting to be conquered, then complains she is a victim, that we have robbed her of her honour. What other country would give herself up so completely to a Corsican adventurer, offering him her liberty, her lifeblood, her fortune again and again, and then continue to love him, even when he has so patently abused and ruined her?' Now Bismarck is dying, caustic and sometimes bitter when he considers the actions of his successors or the policies of his Austrian counterpart, the Graf Kazimierz Badeni, who possesses much of Bismarck's ruthlessness and little of his intelligence. The balance of power is threatened. A detachment of flying artillery makes the bridge noisy with its showy hooves and iron-shod wheels. The sun bursts upon the bouncing metal of the new Skoda field-guns: perhaps this is another deliberate display.

I am resentful of their intrusion into my peace of mind. At the next table a German tourist laughs and points towards the artillery as it turns into Kanalstrasse. His wife looks blank. 'See,' he says, 'the Wäldenstein army!' He glances at me for appreciation. I smile and ask the waiter for a *Mirenburg Zeitung*. He brings me the newspaper and I give him fifty pfennigs, telling him to keep the change. The editorial sings of the greater prosperity the Armaments Bill will bring to the country. There is news of Count Holzhammer. He seems to have made some progress with his Austrian allies. There is a discussion of preparations being made for next year's large Exhibition, which will represent every nation in the civilized world; again, prosperity is the leitmotif. I seek out the stock market reports and am reassured. There is an article by a military correspondent on the relative merits of buying arms from foreign sources or of setting up factories at home. I am astonished by prices given for the Krupp cannon and its ammunition: a hint of the significance of the new Bill, which could involve a considerable amount of taxation. Wäldenstein's landowners cannot be pleased at the prospect. Yet the only alternative appears to be in treaties, 'closer union' with one of the Great Powers and a consequent loss of independence. The British have uprisings in India. I fold the newspaper and put it under my beer glass. Alexandra joins me. She is flushed. She is smiling. She has changed her clothes again. 'They will not be back for ages. I've written. And no one suspects anything. I was full of Marya and our punting expeditions!'

I congratulate her on the cleverness of her deception. Papadakis has returned. I hear him pushing furniture about in the next room. With a rustle of that seductive costume she seats herself beside me and whispering asks me if I have made arrangements to visit Rosenstrasse. I have sent a note to Frau Schmetterling. We shall be expected. In his famous *Pamety* – his memoirs – Benes Milovsky recalls a stream running the length of Rosenstrasse. It had its source in the hills beyond the walls and it fed into the Rätt. This stream became subterranean by the middle of the century. It forms the basis for a sophisticated modern sewage system and can still be heard running beneath the Rosenstrasse cobbles.

In the afternoon we visit the Museum of Antiquities, the concrete traces of fifteen hundred years of history. A diorama represents Wäldenstein's primitive settlers, the Svitavian tribesmen who built their camps in the great valley of the Rätt, between four ranges of mountains, fighting off the Teutonic invaders when they swept in during the ninth and tenth centuries. No Roman ever set foot in any settlement along the Upper Rätt. The diorama gives a lie to the sentimental nationalists. The present descendants of those tribes are no more 'true Slavs' than they are 'true Aryans'; the blood has mingled thoroughly to produce the Wäldensteiner. But blood these days has become another word for ambition, a justification of greed, a rationalisation of those frustrated in their political needs, an excuse for terrible murder, a counterbalance to the Christianity we all profess to cherish and which certainly checks us in any honest, pagan rapacity we still possess. Men need myths to set against myths, it seems. They need the precedent of 'blood' or their consciences could tell them they are ineffectual, ruthless, wicked, and thus deny them what they want. A woman rarely seeks such complicated excuses; the means by which she disguises her desires usually take quite a different form. They say women substitute sentimentality for principle, that a woman's logic is entirely based upon her own immediate physical and emotional needs; yet men display similar logic, couched in terms of the highest ideals, and trap themselves quite as thoroughly when their actions diverge significantly from their words. Alexandra speaks softly of the wonderful past. She leans on my arm. Her body seems to wish to become absorbed in mine. Antiquity is a thing of broken statues and rusty iron. I am quickly bored with it. We descend the wide steps of the Museum and look across the city at the magnificent Greek church. Although primarily a Protestant city, Mirenburg represents many other religions within her walls; one would not be surprised to see a mosque here. I go with relief to the nearby Municipal Art Gallery. Here are paintings by all the masters, by new painters who take such an optimistic delight in form and light for its own sake. I am soon restored and my spirits lift. Alexandra examines paintings of women, showing me the figures she finds attractive and those which do not please her, and I know she is deliberately setting the scene for this evening. I continue to be astonished by her, by the violence of her determination to experience every fantasy she has imagined. It is almost inconceivable she will not have destroyed herself, or at very least her capacity for sensation and emotion, by the time she is twenty. And yet I still cannot determine which of us exploits the other, though I know of course what the world would decide. As we drive back to the hotel through the haze of twilight I see the notices advertising evening newspapers. Count Holzhammer, apparently, has returned to Wäldenstein. The importance of this news escapes

43

me. Papdakis enters the room. I dismiss him impatiently. In the hotel we begin to prepare ourselves for sophisticated debauchery. My body has never felt more thoroughly alive. I almost gasp as the silk of my shirt touches my skin. Both of us seem to glow with power as we leave the Hotel Liverpool in a cab and drive towards the West Bank. Rosenstrasse is near the river across from the Moravian Precinct, on the very fringe of the respectable Jewish Quarter near the Botanical Gardens, and only a couple of streets up from the Niersteiner Quay with its trees and awnings and little cafés, between two streets which lead down to the quay, Rauchgasse and Papensgasse. In Papensgasse an archway is the only means of reaching Rosenstrasse, once a private street owned by a religious order. The monastery still occupies a site here. From Rauchgasse one enters through a narrow gap between two tall, seventeenth-century houses. There is a single gas-lamp at either end of Rosenstrasse's cobbled surface. The plane trees and flowering chestnuts give an air of isolation, of seclusion to what is an ideal setting for Frau Schmetterling's brothel. It is in some ways more like a country courtyard, even a garden, than an ordinary city street. The high houses make it seem even narrower than it is. These are primarily eighteenth-century terraces, apparently the residences of moderately well-to-do tradespeople. On the eastern side is the oldest building, single-storeyed, roofed in red slate, with no outward-facing windows at all and to one side massive double doors set in a Gothic arch. The doors are black wood bound in dark iron; they open directly into the cloisters of the disused monastery. Ivy grows over the roof and up the walls of the terraces from the unseen garden. Opposite the monastery is a short row of shops: a bookbinder's, an artists' colourman, a seller of prints and old books. Dominating these is a mansion, No. 10 Rosenstrasse. It is well-kept, impressive; the town-house of a wealthy family until the middle years of the century. The windows at the front are always covered from the inside by heavy curtains or from the outside by green wooden shutters. It is a big, square, solid building, as reassuring as the street itself. Opposite there is a

44

terrace, some more small shops and the entrance to a large apartment house occupied mostly by students. As the sun sets Rosenstrasse fills out with soft shadows. The lamplighter comes through the archway from Papensgasse and ignites the gas, then continues on his business down Rauchgasse towards the river. In the warm September night Mirenburg grows drowsy.

At No. 10 Rosenstrasse shutters are being opened and curtains are being closed, as if the house prepares for guests. Gentle voices can be heard and some laughter. To many travellers Mirenburg is a synonym for Europe's most famous brothel, whose customers speak of it with unqualified affection and respect. Gentlemen will make a diversion of hundreds of miles to spend an evening here. There are women too who will do the same and the friendship they feel for Frau Schmetterling is apparently reciprocated by the madam whose discretion and tact are a byword, as is the range and breadth of her services. The brothel has been described as Mirenburg's greatest treasure. It has become an institution. Those who live near it are almost proud to be associated with it and the few complaints Frau Schmetterling receives are dealt with intelligently and with considerable charm. Her place threatens only those who are patently prone to such threats. It is protected by every authority and tolerated by the Church; important political assignations frequently occur here: one can only enter the doors if one is armed with the most impressive bona-fides. Papadakis tidies the sheets. 'You are too thin,' he says. 'You are wasting yourself.' I ignore him. Alexandra and I step out of our cab in Rauchgasse and pass between the tall white houses into Rosenstrasse. A soft, sultry wind blows through Mirenburg's baroque facades; she seems singularly quiescent. Alexandra's breast rises and falls and her little hand tightens on my arm. We mount the steps of No. 10. Her eyes have a distant, drowsy look, inturned; at once innocent and secretive. At the end of my bed Papadakis coughs and makes some banal remark. I think he is trying to joke. I shout at him to leave. I lift my arm and ring the bell of Frau Schmetterling's door. It opens. I press Alexandra through and pause, taking a grip on myself. My legs are trembling slightly. The door closes behind us. Trudi, a pretty young woman, perhaps an idiot, with blonde hair and vacant blue eyes, takes our street clothes from us. She curtseys. She is wearing peasant costume. There is distant music. The small lobby is furnished in discreet crystal, with hangings of heavy wine-coloured velvet, some flowering plants on polished wood, a mirror in a modern 'Liberty' frame, and several paintings, chiefly portraits of the last French emperor. The air is heavy with the scent of roses and hyacinths.

Now Alexandra holds back a little, a wary cat. I smile down at her as we wait to be received. She smiles in response, wetting her lips with the tip of her red tongue. Mirenburg has begun to sleep a deeper than usual sleep. Even her bells, when they mark off the hours, seem muffled and distant. A moon rises to touch the purity of her architecture so that it gleams like bone. The waters of the river hardly move. Alexandra makes a small sound in her throat, then looks at me with the adoring expression of a schoolgirl about to have her deepest dreams fulfilled. I steady myself against her violence and find myself, in turn, hesitating. I have a momentary desire to wrench open the door and flee Rosenstrasse, leave Mirenburg behind me, return to the bland formality of Berlin. But then Frau Schmetterling, that dignified matriarch, appears in the lobby and I bow, extending a hand towards her even as a small, swiftly-disguised frown crosses her face. Perhaps she has noticed my hand shaking. She looks towards Alexandra.

'Dear Ricky,' she says, and takes a key from her delicate pocket. 'Everything you desire is ready for you. You know the blue door, of course.' She puts the key into my hand. 'Good evening,' she says to Alexandra.

We climb the dark red stairs, our fingers on the bannister's gilded wood. 'She doesn't like me,' whispers Alexandra. 'She doesn't know you,' I reply. We reach the empty landing and walk on soft carpet towards the blue door. The pen is heavy in my hand; suddenly the paper hurts me when I touch it.

Papadakis comes back to busy himself with pillows and I do not resist him. He puts a glass to my lips. I swallow. Mirenburg enjoys her last tranquil night; she fades. For the moment I let her leave me.

CHAPTER TWO

The Brothel

The brothel in Rosenstrasse has the ambience of an integrated nation, hermetic, microcosmic. It is easy, once within, to believe the place possessed of an infinity of rooms and passages, all isolated from that other world outside. Doubtless Frau Schmetterling creates this impression deliberately, with detailed thoroughness. Reminded of childhood security and delicious mystery, the explorer discovers his cares disappearing, together with any adult lessons of morality or self-restraint. Here he may not only fulfill his desires, but he need feel no guilt or concern for doing so: the brothel can be departed from and visited again at will. Money is all he needs. Here there are anodynes for any kind of wound, there are no sharp voices, no pointing fingers, no complicated emotional involvements. Here a man (and occasionally a woman) may feel himself to be what he most wishes to be. Nietzsche's socially destructive admonitions can be safely followed in this enclosure. The ego is allowed full rein. Yet publicly everyone is discreetly polite and compliant; bad manners are frowned upon and must never be displayed in the salon. A maternal and firm-minded woman, neat and plump, Frau Schmetterling runs her brothel with the skill of the captain of a luxury ship. Most of her working day is spent in her head-quarters, her elaborately-equipped kitchen. This is territory generally forbidden to

49

clients but is a haven for her charges. The kitchen is where Frau Schmetterling interviews new girls and where every day she discusses menus with Ulric, her cook. The room is dominated by a massive oak dresser which stretches from floor to ceiling and displays brightly-decorated plates of outstanding quality from every country in Europe; her collection. What it represents to her nobody knows but she is unquestionably in love with it. She will allow no-one else to handle it or even polish the carved surfaces of the wooden shelves. Shrewd in all other matters, she is easily flattered through her china and the taste she displays in it. She sits in a peasant rocking-chair to one side of the dresser so that she can observe both the long, clean table and her collection. Her servants, such as the simple-minded Trudi (whom Frau Schmetterling personally dresses), make tea, coffee and chocolate for the women as they come and go. Very occasionally Frau Schmetterling will entertain two or three of her special girls here for dinner. Through the barred windows of the kitchen is her garden which she cares for almost as jealously as her china, though she allows 'Mister' to do some of the work. 'Mister' is the enfeebled, grey-haired gentleman with the face of a boy whom she will sometimes describe as her 'protector'. He lives at the top of the house and dotes on her, showing temper only if he feels she has been threatened or insulted. He is in charge of Elvira, the madam's little daughter (who goes to the Lutheran school in nearby Kasernestrasse) when she visits the brothel on Sunday afternoons. Elvira is ten, a demure, dark-eyed creature, and has no idea of the madam's business. If asked, she would say that it had something to do with ladies sewing things, for on Sundays the girls usually gather in the big kitchen after lunch to do their mending. She is, as any child would be, very popular with her mother's charges. 'Mister' must go every day to the house where Elvira is boarded and check that she is properly cared for and has everything she needs. In the brothel he supervises the cleanliness of the rooms; he frequently goes shopping for the girls; he makes sure that fresh flowers are permanently in

50

evidence, that the paint of the shutters and doors is impeccable; that Frau Schmetterling's black chow dogs are walked and fed twice a day. These dogs are not popular with every customer, most of whom have at some time tried to pet and show a friendly interest in them. They seem surly beasts and have been known to nip the odd client. I have always fed them with paté and little pieces of liver and have consequently I believe won their friendship. Frau Schmetterling will often remark to me how much Pouf-Pouf and Mimi love their gentlemen and will add that she judges people very much by how the dogs take to them. This anthropomorphic fiction surrounding pets is a common one of course with many women and it is within their power quite unconsciously to give signals to their animals as to whether they like or dislike a particular person. Therefore I have never really known if I have become popular entirely by means of bribery or whether, for uncertain reasons of her own, Frau Schmetterling finds me attractive. I think I was an early customer of this particular establishment. My father sent me here as a boy to be instructed, so I am often 'her' Ricky and she shows a mother's interest in my career. She possesses signed copies of my little books and seems quite proud of them.

Frau Schmetterling is Jewish. Nobody knows her real name. She is well-educated. She is fastidious in her habits, always wearing simple but beautifully-cut old-fashioned dresses trimmed with lace, and she treats 'Mister' with affectionate formality, a queen to her consort. Their mutual respect for each other is touching. Because of her tendency to plumpness, her comfortable homeliness, it is difficult to guess her age, but I believe she must be close to fifty. She speaks several languages very well, and her native tongue seems to be a Russian dialect, suggesting that she was born in Byelorussia or perhaps Poland. 'My girls,' she says, 'are ladies. I expect them to behave accordingly and to be properly treated. In private with a client they may choose to be whatever they and the client wish them to be but at all other times they must behave with tact and discretion.' The girls, whether on duty or off, are perfectly costumed. Clients are expected to wear evening dress. I myself

51

am clothed as carefully as if I were attending a formal dinner at the Embassy. Alexandra has on rose silk and a deep green cape. I open the blue door for her and follow her in. Our first impression is of subtle perfume, dark polished wood, mirrors and rust-coloured drapery. The room is lit by a single ornamental lamp. From another part of the brothel comes the faint sound of barking. Everywhere is luxury. Everything is soft or heavy or dark and the young woman who waits on the coverlet of the four-poster seems small and delicate in contrast. She is apparently relaxed and rather delighted by the adventure. 'M'sieu.' She rises and walks up to Alexandra, kissing her prettily on both cheeks. 'Are you French?' I ask. I go from habit to the sideboard and pour absinthe for all three of us. The lady shrugs as if to say that it is for me to decide her nationality. 'What's your name, mademoiselle?' 'It is Thérèse'. She has a Berlin accent. Her attention is on Alexandra. 'You are very pretty. And young.'

'This is Alexandra.'

Thérèse is about twenty, with straight black hair drawn back from her oval face. She has light blue eyes. Her skin is pink and her hands are long. In her white undergarments, which are trimmed with peach-coloured lace, her figure is fuller than Alexandra's and tends to puppy-fat. She has a large nose, prominent red lips, and a self-contained way of holding herself. She has small pointed breasts. I stipulated the colouring of the girl and the size of her breasts in my note to Frau Schmetterling. In this familiar ambience I become relaxed and my mood seems to be transmitting itself to Alexandra, who remains, however, a trifle ill-at-ease and begins to move around the room looking at pictures and ornaments. Thérèse hides her amusement. All three shadows are thrown onto the large autumnal flowers of the wall-paper. Alexandra is a little taller than Thérèse. Old Papadakis is scowling at me. 'What is it?' I ask him. 'You should let me fetch the doctor,' he says. 'You are not in your right mind. You are weak. You should rest. You are overtaxing yourself.' Is he trying to persuade me to dependency upon him? He cannot be genuinely concerned. I do not employ him for that. 'Go to the village,' I tell him. 'Get me something with cocaine in it.' He mutters in Greek. 'The doctor will give me morphine,' I say. 'It will dull my brain. I need my wits. Can't you see I'm doing something worthwhile again?' I hold up the pages. 'These are my memoirs. You are mentioned in them. You should be pleased.' He comes forward as if to see what I have written. I close the cover. 'Not yet. They will be published when I am dead. Perhaps when you are dead, too.' Thérèse says to Alexandra: 'Is this the first time you have been here?'

'Yes,' says Alexandra. 'And you? How long have you worked here?'

'Two years this Christmas,' says Thérèse. 'I was an artists' model in Prague, for paintings as well as photographs. Will this be your first time?'

'With a lady?' says Alexandra. The rose silk hisses. 'No. In a brothel, yes.'

'And your first time with both a lady and a gentleman,' I remind her gently.

'Yes.'

An encouraging smile from Thérèse. 'You will like it. It is my favourite thing. You mustn't be afraid.'

'I'm not afraid,' said Alexandra removing her cape. She stares hard at Thérèse. 'I am looking forward to it. The surroundings are new to me, that's all.' She keeps her distance from Thérèse, who makes a kind-hearted effort to be pleasant to her. In the past it was Alexandra who took the initiative with her schoolfriends. 'What are you receiving for your services?' she asks suddenly. Thérèse is surprised, answering mildly. 'M'sieu has confirmed the usual arrangements with Frau Schmetterling, I think.'

'Thérèse is on a fixed weekly income,' I say. 'It is one of the benefits Frau Schmetterling offers to those who want to work here. It is a form of security. Part of the money is paid directly. Part is kept in a savings account.'

'You're looked after well, then,' says Alexandra. 'Safer than marriage, even.'

'Far safer,' says Thérèse. She continues to assume that Alexandra is shy. 'Your dress is lovely. Levantine silk, isn't it?'

'Thank you.' Suddenly Alexandra puts down her glass and crosses to Thérèse, embracing her and kissing her full on the mouth. Thérèse is a little taken aback. Alexandra grins. 'You're lovely, too. You're exactly my type, did you know? Did Ricky ask for you specially?' Thérèse begins to relax, as if she now has a notion of what is expected of her. She makes no further attempts to put Alexandra at her ease. 'I'm glad I appeal to you.' There is a touch of irony, a swift glance towards me, but I refuse a part. 'I've always longed to meet a real whore,' murmurs Alexandra, stroking Thérèse's hair. She puts an arm around the girl's shoulders and leads her to the sideboard. 'Pour us another drink, Ricky. I want you to make love to Thérèse first.' Her tone implores but her stance commands. 'I'll wait here.' She indicates a gilded chair padded with brown velvet. She has the manner of a determined little girl setting out the rules of a dolls' game. Not for the first time I find this aspect of her character faintly disconcerting. She seems almost prim. As I finish my drink Thérèse begins to remove her chemise, her pantaloons, her cherry-coloured stockings. I feel some trepidation, not for the action I am about to take but for the spirit in which I shall commit myself to the performance. Alexandra has discovered a closet. I remove my jacket and hand it to her. I remove my waistcoat, my tie and my shirt. All are neatly stowed by Alexandra. I lower my trousers and these she folds. I take off my socks, my underpants. Alexandra steps back from me and I turn towards the bed. Thérèse is also naked, with her hair loosened and her head propped against the pillows. She has become professional; her pink body waits for me. Her lips are slightly parted, her eyes hooded. There is no apparent difference between her artful desire and Alexandra's blind passion. If I was not aware that Thérèse was a whore I would believe that she yearned for me alone. Her youthful skin might never have known a man's touch. Do all women slide so indiscriminately into lust? How are they taught such things? I kiss Thérèse's cheeks, her neck. She moans. I

54

kiss her soft shoulders, her breasts, her stomach. She shudders. Her calf presses against my penis. I kiss her face again. Her tongue is hot on my neck, her hand finds my penis and testicles and fondles them. I hear silk behind me, but I do not turn. I press my fingers into Thérèse's cunt. It is already wet. I push her legs apart and she draws me into her. Her body is more generous than Alexandra's, but Thérèse cannot reproduce that thrilling urgency, that desperation of movement which removes us entirely from the world of ordinary perception. Several years ago, at the Villa D'Este, or rather in the little ravine which runs below it and where there is an older garden, some ancient Emperor's villa, I came upon a very respectable young couple walking there under the trees amongst the toppled columns and broken marble and was certain that I recognised the modestly dressed wife as a whore I had once visited regularly. Then she had been an unreal creature. Now she was a perfectly ordinary bourgeoise. The transformation was considerable. I lifted my hat and introduced myself, saying that I thought we were acquainted. I was in no doubt that it was she. The couple had given some ordinary Roman name and she had politely denied knowing me. But I had confirmed her identity for myself. She was the same nameless child I had fucked at least a score of times at the brothel in Rosenstrasse. I had paid, moreover, a great deal of money for the privilege. Then she had never spoken and it was said by some that she was dumb. Frau Schmetterling had prized her above her other girls at that time; she had referred to this wonderful beauty as her 'niece' and had offered her only to customers for whom she had a special affection. Whenever one went to her room it would always be the same. The draperies would be of darker than usual material and the only light would come from a large candle in a glass funnel, creating all kinds of peculiar, agitated shadows. The nymph would lie upon grey velvet, immobile and passive. About her waist, on a chain as a necklace might be worn, would be hung a massive insect, at least four inches long and about two inches thick, with a wing-span of five inches. The insect's body was carved out of morbid green obsidian, and its wings gave the impression of transparency, being made of crystal and silver. Imbedded as markings on its head and carapace were various murky gems: agates, carnelians and discoloured pearls. This splendid, sickly fly would rest upon her swarthy flesh as if about to dine. From her throat would be suspended a chain of heavy gold, a series of linked scarabs, Egyptianate and massive, reaching to a point just short of centre between her small, rouged breasts. One of her soft arms would be bare, but the other would have on it a gold and amethyst bracelet forming two intertwined serpents, and on her left ankle would be a solid bangle of gold, set with a single large ruby, matched by a similar ring on her fourth toe. She had a variety of small rings on her thumbs and fingers, and the hardness of the gold accentuated the delicacy and fragility of her youth.

As an old friend of Frau Schmetterling I had been allowed to enjoy that child on a number of occasions but I believe my chief delight in her came not from her body, which was delicious, but from a particular quality of mind she possessed: she seemed half-mad. Just as with Alexandra, for whom I have of course far more responsibility, the child had been consumed by a subtle urgency, an almost inhuman sexuality, which had in it a peculiar and perhaps unwholesome intelligence. It was as if she had come into the world with her intellect and her appetites fully-formed, with a pagan greed for a conscious and specific form of sensual experience which never waned and was yet never completely satisfied; a mind which was unsleepingly aware of itself, its surroundings, of those souls who came into its sphere. She had feasted upon me during the course of a season and I had been powerless for every second I had spent in her company; as drained and as miserable when I departed from her as I was enriched and inspired when with her. She had possessed virtually no reality for me. I had never attempted to converse with her. I had come and gone in silence, almost in secret. The business had taken on the atmosphere of a shameful liaison. By the end of that season I had become exhausted and my morale was in ruins. Yet that same insect-child who had so sapped my vitality was now an ordinary young woman walking with her husband at Tivoli on a Sunday afternoon. Had she been in any way responsible, then, for my condition? Or had I been entirely a victim of my own dreams? So I wonder as I move my body in and out of Thérèse, forcing myself not to become afraid of the girl who sits a few feet away from me drinking her absinthe and watching me with eyes which neither reflect nor absorb the light: blank eyes, lost entirely in a universe of private fantasy. Yet will she always be like this? Was she like it before? Momentarily the terror grows in me. I began as her seducer and now I feel that I am her pawn, performing sexually for her entertainment. How does she see it? The same? She says she wished only to please me. I have beaten her. I have raised bruises and welts on her body, with rods, with shoes, with straps; I have played the cruel master and she the slave; I have practised all kinds of humiliations upon her with her consent. She has been at times wholly in my power. And yet I feel that I am now in hers, willing to renounce all ordinary happiness, ordinary pleasure, spontaneous lust, in order to please her, while she continues to pretend herself my victim. It is a child's game. I know it is a child's game. I tell myself that I should know better, yet the child in me, the child I thought vanished but whom I had merely silenced, is yelling for satisfaction again. Thérèse thrusts back at me with skilled strength; my orgasm when it comes is thin and quickly dissipates. Alexandra kneels beside us on the bed, still fully clothed. She strokes my rump with hesitant fingers. Perhaps it is her inexperience which binds me to her, why I am so willing to help her discover novelty after novelty so that she will forever be encountering something which is fresh to her. Will I continue to love her when all sexual experience is familiar to her? And what are her motives in this? What does she really want from me, save companionship in her adventure? She says that she loves me, but she is too young for the words to have any substance. She is fascinated by my reputation, which like most reputations of the sort is greatly exaggerated: I have probably been rejected by as many women

57

as I have conquered and for every one who has believed me an inspired lover I have had others whom I have failed to satisfy. The needs of the body are actually as subtle as the needs of the personality. She is kissing Thérèse even as she strokes me. The feel of her dress on my skin is delightful. She touches Thérèse's nipples, again with that same sweet hesitation. She lies across my back, slowly moving her groin against me. Thérèse strokes her wrist. Their perfume almost drugs me. I am passive between them as their passion increases. Alexandra lets Thérèse begin to unbutton her dress. Eventually both naked bodies press on mine and gradually grow more confident with each other. A breast brushes my shoulder; a knee leans on my thigh. Lying face down in the bed I find it almost impossible to tell which little body is which. The sensation is wonderful as their ardour grows; the moans and grunts become sighs and gasps; they touch, they stroke, they scratch, wonderfully oblivious of me as anything more than a body. I slip my hand down to my cock and begin to masturbate as their movements grow more urgent. Papadakis says: 'You haven't enough light in here.' He pulls back the curtains. There is a glimpse of distant blue, the sea. I can hear it quite clearly today and it does not irritate me. The sun seems mild and warm. 'What's today?' I ask him. 'The first of May,' he says. 'You might be able to go outside soon.' I become suspicious of him, protective of my manuscript. I put it under the pillow when I sleep. He must not see it, at least until it is finished. 'It reminds me of Nicosia this morning,' he says. Then he scowls. 'That bastard of a father.' He will often sink into these private references. 'And I felt such a fool in the hat.' I become impatient with him again. 'You are disturbing me,' I say. 'I am not interested in your childhood. Bring me some tea in half-an-hour.' I am making more of an effort to be polite to him. Perhaps I have misjudged him. He seems to be showing some respect for me at the moment. But I cannot afford to allow him too much of my time now or he could go on about his frustrations and his achievements all day. He claims to have academic degrees, but becomes vague when asked where they were obtained. He also boasts, sometimes, of the famous painters and writers he has known and it is true that he once acted as a go-between for some artists I knew in London. That was how he eventually came to work for me. I do not deny his usefulness, but it is a bad idea to let him begin talking. I know he resents it when I silence him. I know that he sees my work as some sort of rival, although he originally claimed that he wished to support me in my efforts. That was before I became ill. He is abstracted today, still staring out of the window, whistling some popular tune under his breath. It sounds like *I'm Forever Blowing Bubbles*. 'Let me finish this,' I say, 'and I will earn enough money to send you home to Nicosia.' He is surprised. 'Why should I want to go there? I was thinking of Venice.' I tell him to play some Chopin on the phonograph in the next room. 'And don't let the record wind down as you usually do.' I remember when he was more agreeable, when he thought my title meant something and that I had more money.

Deciding to leave Alexandra and Thérèse in each other's company for a while, since this will benefit me, I believe, in the long term, I dress myself and go downstairs into the public salon. There are a few gentlemen here, chatting in quiet voices, and one or two of Frau Schmetterling's girls, looking like any young ladies one might meet at a provincial ball. Frau Schmetterling, as usual, has retired to her kitchen. The whores are acting as hostesses. I ask for a glass of champagne and take a seat near the far window, casually watching a card game between two upright middle-aged gentlemen and two women whom I know as Inez and Clara. Inez claims to be Spanish (though she speaks German without an accent) and dresses accordingly. Clara wears a costume suggesting that she is an English countrywoman. Her speciality is with the crop and the tawse. The men are probably rich professional people. Both have grey beards and one wears a monocle while the other has pince-nez. All four are absorbed in their bridge at present. I make an effort to read the evening newspaper, but in spirit I am still upstairs with Alexandra and Thérèse. I have decided that I will dine here. Frau Schmetterling always provides an excellent light supper for those who require it. My earlier concern has vanished for the time being. I enjoy a cigar. The salon is furnished comfortably, in restrained good taste, reminiscent of the better class of Parisian hotel. Next to it is a billiard room and I am about to rise to go into it when the double doors of the salon open and the Princess Poliakoff comes in on the arm of a nervous young man whom I assume to be her latest gigolo. I get to my feet and bow. She recognises me and seems relieved to see me. I kiss her hand. She is as usual wearing a mannish black costume with a ruffle of lace at her breast. Her thin face is bright with severe paint and by the size of her pupils I would say she is drugged. She draws her young man forward. 'Ricky, this is my eldest son, Dimitri. We are on tour, to finish his education.' I shake hands with Dimitri. He has a pleasant, awkward smile. 'We shall be leaving for Trieste tomorrow,' she says. 'I am so glad you are here. You are just the man Dimitri should talk to.' I am amused. 'Why so, my dear Princess?' I ask. 'It is obvious, surely! You are a man of the world.' She speaks sardonically and yet it is a compliment. 'I am at your service, m'sieu,' I say to her son, and bow again. We are speaking French. The Princess Poliakoff is a notorious Lesbian. She has for some time had the reputation of frequenting the Rat Mort and La Souris in Montmartre where she gathered about her a group of female admirers, chiefly actresses and opera singers, who would vie subtly with one another to be her choice of the evening. I am glad to see her, for she is a familiar face, but I have no great liking for her. Her beauty is of that neurasthenic, slender kind; her skin seems almost transparent and the rouge only heightens its pallor. She has a long, thin nose and large, wide lips, high cheek bones, exceptionally large, languid hands, and she wears nothing but black or, in winter months sometimes, a tawny wolfskin cap, cloak and gloves. She is rumoured to have had affairs with half the famous female stage-performers and painters in Paris and I heard that when she appeared in public with Louise Abbema at L'Opera, embracing and kissing, her father upon receiving the news at his Russian estate shot himself and has never properly recovered from the head wound which left him with only one ear and one eye. She is now about forty. She still retains that look of boredom which to many makes her so fascinating and apparently remote. It was her boredom, she claims, which led her to experiment with almost every vice and it was vice, she says, which led her ineffably back to boredom. To which, she usually adds, she is now completely reconciled. 'You must explain the secret of your success with women, Ricky,' she says. 'There is no secret, Dimitri,' I tell her son. 'All one needs is a relish for sexual pleasure and a certain amount of time to dedicate to its pursuit. After a year or two one becomes known as a rake and women's curiosity does the rest.' Princess Poliakoff laughs. 'You are such a terrible cynic, Ricky. What would your eminent brother think of you?' I shrug. 'The von Beks have one black sheep in every other generation,' I say. 'It is a tradition. My brother is content because he believes that family customs should be firmly maintained. I have an agreeable nature and the assigned role happens to suit me very well.' Princess Poliakoff lights a small cheroot for herself. 'And what are you doing here now? I had heard that you have taken up with schoolgirls. Or was it schoolboys?' I am a little alarmed at this. It means that very soon my liaison with Alexandra will be discovered. 'Negroes,' I tell her, hoping to divert her from the truth. 'What?' she says, 'Really?' She can be extremely gullible. 'They are wonderful,' I tell her. 'I should have thought that in Paris . . . ' She sighs. 'It is their size. I am absolutely terrified, dear Ricky, of large organs.' The girl comes with a tray of champagne. I hand them each a glass. Her son is smiling like a puppet at a fair. 'They are not always monstrous,' I say. 'And this schoolboy?' she continues relentlessly. 'He is black, then?' 'As your hat,' I say in English. 'He is the son of a king in Africa. Being educated here.' She chuckles, willingly believing me. 'You must pass him on to me when you are finished with him.' Princess Poliakoff has always characterised me as a hard-hearted roué who uses people as she does. She makes no allowances for my Achilles heel, my sentimentality, and I see no reason in admitting to her that I am not what she would wish me to be. 'It's a bargain,' I say. I look at the ormulu clock over the fireplace. 'I shall see you later, I hope, at dinner. I must get back to my little negro.' Again her hand is kissed, her son's shaken. He is blushing deeply. I wink at him and return up the stairs, deciding that we shall have to dine in our room. Knowing what a gossip Princess Poliakoff is I hope that her talk of me will create a useful smokescreen. I am somewhat surprised at how cunning I have become since I began my affair with Alexandra. I pass the two bridge-playing gentlemen as they emerge from the toilet. 'This raising of an army hasn't perturbed him much,' one says. 'But I gather he found the desertion of about half the garrison something of a shock. They say he's at his hunting lodge now, with those mechanical models of his. The business will be bloodless if it comes off at all. Holzhammer isn't a bad sort. And he'll keep taxes down.' The significance of the conversation escapes me. I reach the blue door and knock before I enter. Thérèse and Alexandra lie in each others' arms, smiling and giggling. Both look thoroughly dissolute, with their hair wet and scratch-marks on their bodies. 'And how have you enjoyed yourselves?' I chuckle, glad that they are happy and that Alexandra is no longer in her original mood.

Papadakis brings me a cup of tea. 'And will you eat something now?' he asks. 'Perhaps some Camembert,' I tell him. 'And something blue and soft. Something tasty. What have we?' He strokes at his beard with his finger and thumb. 'There's a little Cambozola. You used to enjoy that.' I nod at him. 'Excellent. And a glass of red wine.' He purses his lips. 'Wine? It will kill you!' I put down my pen. 'I am better now. Can't you see that? Some red wine.' He shakes his head. He is becoming surly again. 'Not according to the doctor. But I will bring it if you want it.' He leaves. Alexandra, Thérèse and I dine off smoked salmon and cold duck in our room. The two girls manufacture secrets and I pretend to be intrigued, to please them. Later we shall make love again, playing games with considerable zest and good humour. Then, at about three in the morning, Alexandra and I will order a cab and leave the brothel, promising to see Thérèse the next evening.

Papadakis takes the limousine to town. He likes, I know, to pretend that it is his because it gives him stature with the local peasants. Papadakis says he understands peasants and how they think. He hates them, he says. But his information about them is useful to me and gives me a greater knowledge of his attitudes. He is supposed to get me some patent medicine containing a stimulant but he will quite likely forget; most of the time he thinks only of himself, living in a dream of an unsatisfactory past and an unattainable future. Sometimes across his face comes the enthusiastic expression of a boy, a memory of his former charm. Pyat, the famous confidence trickster, had a similar appearance when I met him at Cassis with Stavisky in the mid-twenties. I have told him it is his duty to care for me when I am ill. He will sometimes reply it is the doctor's job. He was hired, after all, to be my secretary. The fact was I took pity on him. I offered him his last chance and he accepted it. Now he wriggles to be free, but there is nowhere for him to go. And he brings me my soup and fish and he changes my linen when the old woman is too drunk to do it. The pain has come back in my groin. Is Alexandra a mirror? Is the ugliness I believe I detect in her simply a reflection of my own? Since I was sixteen women have told me that I must change. I have always said to them that I am too old to change. If they do not like me as I am then they have the right to find someone they prefer. But I think I am changing for Alexandra and that is perhaps why I am occasionally frightened. I tell everyone that I am in love with feminine beauty in all its aspects. The fact is I become bored in the company of women who have no sexual presence, no matter how intelligent they may be. I think I dislike such women because their condition indicates their own fear of themselves and consequently of the world around them. I have known many women who express the same impatience with non-sexual men. Sexuality is the key to personality. She undresses. She removes the rose silk frock, the delicate chemise; she rolls down her stockings and puts

63

them carefully on the back of the chair. She has a habit of slipping her garters over her wrist while she removes the rest of her underwear, then, holding them in her right hand, she will go into the bathroom and set them on the ledge in front of the mirror. If they are a pair she particularly cares for she will give them a little parting kiss. I say it is too late to bathe, we should go to sleep at once, but she insists. While she is in the bath I fall asleep. I awake briefly at dawn. My blood has quickened. I begin to anticipate what we shall do together later. I turn, thinking she is still bathing, but she is fast asleep with her back to me, the sheets pulled tightly about her as if she fears something. Can she fear me? Will she come to resent me? Asleep, with her face in repose, she sometimes resembles a baby. At other times, when she is snoring and her mouth is open she reminds me of a dead rodent. I wonder if that is really all she is when she is not responding to me: a tiny unimportant predator. But when she wakes her eyes destroy my prejudice. Did her eyes always possess that strange, heated glaze? I remember how she had seemed so innocent when we first met. The prospect of making love to a virgin had driven all caution away within a few minutes. Then, I think, the expression had been there, but hidden. She had only glanced at me directly once and her eyes had told me of her desire for me. Is she a natural predator? She says she loves me, but that is meaningless. She loves what she thinks I must be, what she thinks I possess, and she lusts after my cock. She is doubtless surprised, also, that she can achieve control over others through her sexuality. Unless she is an unusual female she will continue to use her sex as her only certain means to power. She will have no notion of any other way to get what she will want for herself. Even if other ways are described to her she will not quite understand what is said, for her chief experience will have been of sexual control coupled, perhaps, with certain practical services given to the one who desires her. Her will to power, which she has in common with everyone, if satisfied only through sex could ultimately leave her empty of feeling and therefore could destroy any ordinary capacity to know desire,

64

causing her to pass from lover to lover in a perpetual cycle of lust to dissatisfaction. As I fall back to sleep I wonder if I have created a whore. More likely, I think with grim amusement, a monster which will turn on me and take my soul. I do not believe I possess the character of a natural whore-master. I am not strong enough to control her. And this is the knowledge which sometimes excites me and brings flagging senses back to peak again. These are the thoughts of my infrequent solitude. When she is awake I scarcely think at all but remain perpetually fascinated, perpetually on guard, like the tamer with his tigress. We breakfast late in the sitting room. She pours coffee for us both. The light is pale, slanting into our windows from misty skies. The air is cooler today. She sits in her maroon dressing gown, wonderfully composed, seeming thoroughly rested. She makes no reference to the previous night's adventure. Indeed, she seems healthier, younger, more cheerful, than she has seemed for some while. I compliment her on her good humour and her freshness as I light a cigarette. 'I have never felt more alive in all my days!' she says. 'My body is waking up. It never stops now. It wakes and wakes and wakes.' Her smile is spontaneous and beautiful. She says: 'Are you looking forward to this evening?' I am surprised. 'Yes.' I expected her to have doubts. She sits back in her chair in a posture of contentment. She looks towards the window. 'Isn't it wonderful outside?' I smoke my cigarette and stare carefully at her. Her courage, I believe, is the courage of ignorance. But whatever its nature it transmits itself to me. 'You enjoyed Thérèse?' I ask.

'Well enough,' she says. 'I have had better. Younger and without any experience. I think I should like a different girl after this evening. There are things Thérèse told me. Girls with special skills, apparently.' I nod: 'Oh, yes.' She takes my hand and kisses it. 'Could any woman possess a finer teacher? I want to experience everything you have experienced. I want us to be together when we discover new things.' I love the softness of her lips on my wrist, the way her slender body curves in the gown. 'There could be experiences you will not enjoy,' I tell her. 'Of course,' she says, 'but then I will know what they are.' I laugh. 'You are too fond of the novels of Huysmanns and de Goncourt. The critics are right about them. They have a pernicious influence!' I am, in my fashion, expressing my hesitation. This is the moment when I could call a halt to the adventure. But of course my curiosity overwhelms me. I acquiesce. She becomes suddenly active and begins to clothe herself. We take a drive in the afternoon, she in her cream frock trimmed with broderie anglaise and a hat with a thick veil, I in my tweeds. I shade my face with a wide-brimmed hat. After a little while I begin to notice that the tempo of Mirenburg is subtly different. There are many more soldiers in the streets today. Carriages hurry past us on their way to the station. An unusual number of people are leaving the city. I tell our driver to stop in Falfnersallee and send him to buy a paper from one of the kiosks. He says: 'It is the war, your honour. The Civil War. Hadn't you heard?' Alexandra looks with some impatience at the newspaper as if at a passing rival. Count Holzhammer has half the country on his side, including a good proportion of the Army. He has issued a proclamation demanding the abdication of Prince Badehoff-Krasny and the dissolution of Parliament. He argues that the new Armaments Bill will ruin Wäldenstein. He claims the Prince has deliberately set himself against the will of the majority of the people and that he is in the power of a handful of alien industrialists. Count Holzhammer is financed with Austrian money, of course, and his ranks are swelled by Bulgarian cavalry and artillery loaned by Austria but calling themselves Volunteers. The newspaper wonders if the Germans will now send aid to the Prince. So far there has been no response from Berlin. Count Holzhammer has his headquarters in an armoured train. His forces have won a battle at Brondstein. The loyalists have regrouped near Mirenburg. Count Holzhammer awaits a response to his demands. His train is some seventy miles down the line, at Slitzcern. The paper believes the Prince will refuse the Count's demands. Mirenburg has never been taken by siege, says the editorial, in all its long history. During the

Thirty Years War she successfully withstood five separate attacks. She remains impregnable. Count Holzhammer must know this and is therefore almost certainly bluffing. There is a likelihood that the Prince will order Parliament to scrap the Armaments Bill and make one or two concessions to the great landowners who are giving Holzhammer their backing. I shrug and hand the paper to Alexandra. The whole business has a comic opera aspect to it and I cannot take it seriously. It is a storm in a tea-cup, I tell her. A full-scale Civil War is in nobody's interest; the matter is bound to be settled by negotiation. I express some admiration for Count Holzhammer's audacity and remark on the cunning of the Austrians, who doubtless hope their support of Holzhammer will increase their influence over Wäldenstein. But Alexandra is concerned about the effects of the business on her own plans. 'It could mean my parents will return,' she says. 'Or will send for me.' I give the problem swift consideration and arrive at a solution. 'Then go home now. Tell your housekeeper you are leaving Mirenburg with friends who fear for your safety. Give her an address in Brussels – anything will do – then send an appropriate telegram to Rome. In that way we can benefit from this situation.' She is impressed by my cunning and agrees to do as I say. The carriage leaves me at my usual corner opposite the Radota Bridge. The water is like silver in the early afternoon light. I sit at one of the outside tables and order anis and a sandwich while I wait for Alexandra to do as I have instructed. Troops come and go across the bridge. They seem in fine form. The officers wave batons and swords, pointing this way and that. They have a decisive, self-important manner which I find amusing. They are so wonderfully pompous, like eunuchs who have overnight been blessed with testicles. Alexandra seems to take no time at all, even though she returns with two or three new trunks. 'I am going with her full approval,' she says with a smile. 'She thinks it is for the best!' We drive to the hotel. The manager, an anxious beaver, approaches me, seeing the new luggage being taken up by the porters. He would be obliged if I could tell him if I intend to leave the hotel in the morning. I shake my head. 'I have every intention of staying for some time.' He is relieved. Apparently most of his residents will have departed by tomorrow. 'They are running special trains to Danzig,' he explains. He has the distracted look of a man who fears ruin. 'Surely they are being overcautious,' I say. 'Even if the Count takes control it will scarcely effect your guests. They are all foreigners. This squabble will be resolved in a few days and everything will be back to normal.' His estimation, he agrees, is much the same as mine. 'But there is a panic. Half our business people are leaving for Berlin and Paris. The Stock Market is chaotic. Exchange rates are fluctuating. Such things bother them, you know. Many visitors are returning to their firms. And Count Holzhammer is very direct about his hatred of industrialists, particularly the Jews and the Germans. They have a right to be nervous, I think.' I suggest they will all come creeping back within a week. 'What can they do to Mirenburg? Who would threaten her beauty with cannon-shells? It is impossible.' The manager laughs. He seems relieved by my reassurance. I order a pot of tea and some pastries to be sent to our rooms. We take the lift to the third floor.

We dress ourselves carefully. Alexandra wears her flowing red evening gown and has over it a full cape of dark brown velvet. The streets are almost deserted as we make our way in a cab to Rosenstrasse. Here and there are groups of silent soldiers, standing guard over nothing. Groups of urchins run about pretending to shoot at one another. There are unexpected echoes to make the twilight eery. The brothel, when we arrive, seems like a haven of normality. We are received by Trudi but do not see Frau Schmetterling. Thérèse awaits us behind the blue door and we again enjoy, with increasing assurance and relish, our pleasures of the previous night. As we rest, Thérèse is more talkative. She speaks enthusiastically of Frau Schmetterling and the establishment. She expresses her affections, her jealousies, her dislike of certain other girls. Alexandra has assumed the role of her confidante, greedy for every bit of information. We smoke a little opium. Thérèse repeats a great deal of what I have already told Alexandra, about the special rooms, the preferences of some clients (who according to the brothel's protocol she cannot name) and the predilections of the girls, the attitudes they have to their work, their clients, themselves. Growing bored with this I take Alexandra almost by force, deliberately humiliating her in front of Thérèse, then I make Thérèse kneel and accept my cock, wet with Alexandra's juices, in her mouth while Alexandra licks my anus. I come in a convulsion of release that has little actual pleasure in it, forcing Thérèse to swallow my semen. Alexandra stops her activities but I order her to continue, telling Thérèse to fetch one of her ivory dildoes from the drawer. Then I hand the dildo to Alexandra. Together they take turns buggering me while I sob in pain and helpless terror until I am so weak they can turn me any way they please, teasing me, making me shudder. Thérèse lies with her vagina rubbing against my face while her lips nip at my cock, bringing it to life again. Alexandra joins her, fondling my balls and then squeezing them hard to inflict greater agony. They are taking their revenge on me. Slowly they bring me to the point of orgasm and then, with deliberate cruelty, they begin to kiss one another, ignoring me completely. I put my hand to my cock. Alexandra sees my movement from the corner of her eye and forces my hand back while she pushes herself against Thérèse's thigh. I do not possess the strength to take either of them and yet my frustration continues to build. Again I am turned over. Again the dildo is rammed into my anus and left there. Thérèse rests her head on my buttocks while Alexandra sits over her, leaning her hands on my back and scratching at my flesh, letting Thérèse lick her clitoris until she achieves an orgasm which makes her scream and rip at my skin. My body begins to vibrate and it is as if the shock of Alexandra's orgasm has transmitted itself to Thérèse and myself. We are all shaking, almost as if we experience petit mal. I turn and tug weakly at Thérèse's hair, drawing her up towards me. Still shaking I enter her and we tremble together, making virtually no movement, letting our bodies shake us to orgasm. This time

Thérèse comes first, her vulva contracting and distending rapidly and I am yelling, feeling Alexandra's hand slapping again and again at my bottom, at Thérèse's thighs, as she laughs in high-pitched harmony with our noises. I become suddenly blank. I have passed out for a few seconds. When I awake Thérèse and Alexandra are lying one on each side of me, cuddled in my arms like two tranquil puppies.

'Tell us a story,' says Alexandra. She is by no means the first woman to make this demand of me. I can think of nothing but sexuality so I begin to tell them of the beggar girl I met in Naples three years ago. It remains one of my strangest experiences. I had been walking alone by the sea just before nightfall when one deep shade of blue merges with the other; over the water I had been able to detect the lights of Capri and Ischia and had come to this area of the front in the hope of meeting an attractive whore since my mistress of the moment had elected to spend an evening with her husband. The air was filled with the music of hurdy-gurdies and accordions coming from the little cafés where the working classes enjoyed themselves at supper. The few whores I encountered were not pretty – Neopolitan women of that sort are generally too plump and lewd for my taste – and I began to long for Clichy or Montmartre. Pimps approached me and were waved away with my stick. The air, I remember, was very humid. I was conscious of the sweat on my back, wondering if it would begin to show through the linen of my jacket. The music kept me cheerful enough and I was preparing to go home unsatisfied when a black-haired little thing with ringlets falling over her oval face appeared before me, deliberately blocking my path. She was slender, in ragged pinafore and petticoats and probably no more than fourteen. Her expression was singularly attractive, that mixture of innocence and defiance. Her boyish stance and figure were very much to my preference and although I could scarcely understand a single word of her voluble patois I humoured her, smiling. This seemed to make her lose her temper. She gesticulated, this little Carmen of the waterfront, rubbing her fingers together in that universal sign

70

for money and pointing over her shoulder with her thumb. 'Do you wish me to go home with you?' I enquired in my polite Roman Italian. This question was unexpected and caused her to frown. Realising I was a foreigner she spoke more clearly. 'I need money,' she said. 'You are rich. I want a few lire, that's all. Are you French?' I told her I was German and this seemed to disappoint her. 'You do not have the look of a German.' She began to turn away but I stopped her, putting my hand on her shoulder. The feel of her tensing muscles under my grasp increased my desire for her. She was lovely. 'Why do you want money?' I asked her. 'It is for my father,' she replied. 'Is he ill?' I said, willing to show sympathy. She became angrier. 'Of course he is ill. He has been ill for years. He fought with Garibaldi. He was one of the conquerors of Naples and was wounded by the Austrians. He has lived on the charity of others ever since. He has educated me. He has supported me. And now he is too ill even to beg.' I was not entirely convinced by her story, even if I did not doubt her sincerity. 'So you beg for him now?' She had rounded on me. 'I ask for Christian help, that is all.'

I smiled at this. It was a phrase often heard in Naples. 'I am willing to give it,' I told her. 'But what will you or your father give me? You see I am not a believer in charity. Giving it or receiving it reduces human dignity. Look at you now. You are angry because you are forced to ask a stranger for help. You resent me and would resent me if I gave or if I refused. This in itself, I will admit, makes you an unusual beggar-girl. However, if your father has something to sell, I'll be pleased to consider a bargain.'

She frowned. 'We have nothing.' I shook my head. 'On the contrary. You possess one of the most wonderful treasures in the world.' She pouted, but I had engaged her attention. 'You sound like a priest,' she said. 'I assure you,' I told her, 'that I am no priest. I have no interest at all in your soul. It is yours and should remain yours. The treasure to which I refer has yet to be discovered by you. It has to be brought out into the light and then it has to be polished before you will believe how

71

beautiful and valuable it is.' I caressed her dirty neck and she did not draw away. Her curiosity held her. I believe she guessed my meaning but wished her suspicion to be confirmed. If I confirmed it at once I would probably lose her. It was up to me to maintain her interest a little longer. 'If you take me to your father I will explain what I mean,' I said. Again she was surprised. 'My father? He is a good man. Few are as saintly. He has taught me virtue, signor.' I offered her my arm, bowing to her. 'I am sure that he has. What father would not? You are a lovely young woman. It is easy to see you are of a different class to most. Was your mother a refined woman?' The girl nodded. 'She was. She owned land. She gave up everything to support Garibaldi and my father. She was a Sicilian. From a very old family.'

'Just as I thought,' I said. 'Well, let me escort you to your home.' She consented, of course, because she had little to fear. She took me into a warren of alleys where children, dogs, women and old people seemed in perpetual conflict, and down the steps of a cellar from which came the faint smell of urine. She pushed open the door. Everything was damp and the mould gave off such a pervasive stench that it almost took on the character of perfume; it excited me. She lit a little oil-lamp, nothing but a floating wick, which made flickering shadows and revealed the sleeping face of a man who in health must have been a giant. I was surprised by the face. It had far more character than I might have expected. I could see that my attempt to buy his daughter from him would not be as easy as I had thought. He opened clear blue eyes and looked at me as if he had seen an old friend. An expression of irony crossed his face. 'Signor,' he said. 'I am glad to see you.' He spoke with easy familiarity and it was plain this was not his normal tone with strangers, for his daughter looked from one to the other and said: 'Are you acquainted?' Her father lay amongst rags. It was impossible to tell what was his body and what its coverings. He shook his head. 'Not really,' he said. 'But I hoped it would be this way. You are a gentleman, signor?' There was considerable meaning to the question. 'I hope that I am,' I said. 'And you are wealthy?' I inclined my head. 'I am modestly well-to-do. But, of course, I am carrying virtually nothing on my person.' He nodded. 'I can see that you are also no fool.' He knew exactly my reason for being there. 'Well, have you come to offer my Gina the chance to appear on the stage? Or is it to be service in a fine house? Or do you wish to take her away to educate her, signor?' Gina was still too surprised by all this to speak. She went to the far side of the cellar and sat down on a mattress, her elbows on her knees, her face in her hands, watching us. I smiled at him. 'None of those things,' I said. 'I think it would be insulting to you if I pretended to any but the real feelings which brought me here. I have indicated as much to your daughter. You know what I wish to buy. But I will promise you this. If you sell, I will leave you both with something of increased value, and your daughter will still be yours. I will not take her away.' Gina heard this. 'I would not go!' she said. 'She would not,' said her father, 'unless I insisted upon it. I have some power left, do you see?' I acknowledged this. 'You have considerable power, signor.' I felt almost humbled by his dignity. 'And I am willing to negotiate, as I believe, now, you are.'

He sighed. 'I think so. I think so. You seem a man of the world. You have no disease?' I shook my head. 'None.' He sucked in his lower lip then once more offered me that direct, blue stare. 'The price will be high and there will be conditions.' And so we began negotiations for the virginity of his daughter while she listened without resentment, having absolute trust in her father, who proved to be one of the most honest and realistic men it had ever been my pleasure to meet. A price was agreed and it was, as he said, high, but he understood the rarity and value of what he sold and was relieved that Gina was not to give herself away out of infatuation, which could have ruined her and consequently left him without support. His other condition was harder to agree to. She had to be enjoyed here, in the cellar, and he must be present to ensure, as he put it, that no harm came to her. 'Moreover, signor,' he admitted, 'I am denied most pleasures so it would hearten me to be able

73

to live through what you both experience.' My desire for the girl was so positive that I found myself at last giving in to what he asked. It was agreed I should return the next morning with the money and I said I would arrange for fresh bedding. I did not intend to take possession of my purchase in such utter filth. He told me he could make the cellar into a fairy palace if I chose since everything else I brought would add to his comfort and become an asset. And the price was for a twenty-four hour period. If I wished to stay longer, I must renegotiate the bargain. I accepted this, also. We both asked Gina if she was prepared to enter into this contract and she said she owed everything to her father and she would do whatever he thought best. The old man cared for her very deeply, I could tell, and by this means he was able to maintain his protection and ensure that both of them benefitted from his daughter's defloration without unduly disquieting consequences. I returned the next day with some new lamps, furnishings, in fact a whole van-load of comforts, which were efficiently installed by the two carters I had employed.

Her father's body, seen in good light, was swollen and bloated, although his face and hands were not at all fleshy. He allowed rags to be removed and cushions, carpets and mattresses to be brought in. With the aid of the carters he was transferred from the old to the new without difficulty and sat amongst his luxuries like a Buddha. Both he and his daughter had washed themselves and were wearing clean rags. I had brought her several simple dresses which she thanked me for and hung on a hook in an alcove, making no attempt to wear them. The beggar directed the carters to replace the pile of straw with the mattress in the opposite corner while Gina spread one of the new sheets on it, together with the long bolster I had also brought with me. The smell of mould remained, but since this was pleasant to me I was not disturbed by it. My lust was building with every improvement to the appearance of the cellar and at one point the beggar reached out to pat my leg, murmuring: 'Patience.' A peculiar conspiracy had grown amongst the three of us. The carters

sensed it and were disturbed. I was anxious they should leave
and paid them off rapidly. They made a bewildered departure,
the door was closed, and we were alone. 'You may begin as
soon as you like,' said Gina's father. She poured him some of
the milk I had brought. He accepted it gracefully. 'And my
cheese, I think,' he told her. 'The cheese I could not eat last
night.' She fetched it for him and put it in his other hand. She
had begun to blush. He recognised her confusion and took her
little face in his finger and thumb. 'This gentleman can be
trusted,' he said. 'You could not wish for a better initiation,
my love. It will be exquisite, I am sure.' He waved her towards
me. I now stood beside the mattress, coatless, ready to embrace
her. She brought her slight, delicate body up to mine. I kissed
her head, stroking her neck, slowly beginning to undress her. I
was unusually gentle. There are some women, no matter how
physically strong they are in actuality, who one is always
convinced will break if handled too roughly. They are often the
fiercest lovers, but it can be an effort to forget that sense of
their fragility and give oneself up completely to one's passion.
And so I took her and she was as delicious as I had expected.
She, under my caresses, completely forgot the presence of her
father and at times I was hardly aware of it. She had her back
to him, but frequently I could observe him. To my great
satisfaction I was able to bring her to orgasm by means of my
mouth and hands before I had completely entered her. It is not
always possible to do this at such an early stage with a virgin.
But she had natural generosity and lust and I have always
found that the more generous the spirit of the woman, the more
easily she can attain the fullest sexual delight. My chief
memory of this encounter, however, is of her father. I can
still see the tolerant wisdom in the eyes of that unnaturally
bloated veteran republican as he sat amongst his cushions, a
piece of mouldy cheese in one strong fist, a wooden bowl of
milk in the other, almost gracefully regal in his relaxed and
unselfconscious posture, drawing my attention away from the
blank, ecstatic face of the girl, even as my body performed its
functions and satisfied its lust. He watched without curiosity,

75

without pleasure, almost without interest. He was benign. It was as if God Himself blessed our passion.

As I came he raised his head and sniffed, smiling. The scent of our fluids was an ovation. He took a sip of milk and sniffed again, nodding, approving, perhaps recalling a memory of love. I fell to her side, still regarding him. He saluted me with his piece of cheese and spoke a few sultry words in his own dialect. His daughter, as if noticing him for the first time, turned her head towards me and beamed. Our mutual joy was so intense we all three found ourselves laughing aloud, the sound completely drowning the noise of perpetual contention from those Neopolitan alleys. With Gina's father's consent I returned to their cellar every day for something over a week, paying for every visit. My enjoyment of the girl was not at all marred by the presence of the old man; we made love for his benefit as well as our own. When the time came for me to leave Naples I gave him an address through which he might contact me if Gina became pregnant. 'She is our daughter and our mistress,' he said to me as we shook hands. 'She now knows what it is possible to have from a man. And she knows that she need not feel guilty in seeking that out. Thus I ensure myself of her company while quieting my own fears for her future. On the money you have paid us I will be able to support us for at least a year. Thank you, signor. We'll remember you with gratitude and affection. And we shall pray for you.' Gina kissed me gravely, like a wife saying farewell to a husband leaving for work. I have not seen or heard from either of them since. Thérèse says: 'It is good for a young person to be instructed by an older one, whether it be a man or woman. But the parting can be a great tragedy. Your Gina cried for you, I think, when you had gone.' I am not sure. 'She had her father, don't forget,' I say. I leave them to sleep and dress myself to go downstairs as I did yesterday. Rudolph Stefanik, the Czech aviator, is in the salon. He has dark untidy hair and a look of distracted boredom. His evening clothes seem to restrain his massive body which threatens to burst through them. His beard bristles as he speaks. At least half the men and women in the salon have gathered around him to listen to his balloon adventures, but it is plain he is as impatient with them as he is with his own anecdotes. He looks from girl to girl. He has come to Frau Schmetterling's for a purpose and does not really care to be diverted from it. I hear him say: 'So they caught their daughter sucking at my cock in the gondola. I had no choice but to fling her out and cut the tethering lines. Another two seconds and they would have set fire to the canopy.' And I hear an old Mirenburger bore interrupt with what he supposes is wit: 'You have flown the world in the service of Venus. But what now? Will you fly in the service of Mars? Will you help the Prince against Count Holzhammer?' Rudolph Stefanik looks over his questioner's head. 'One makes love in silk, and makes war in iron. My balloon is silk and hemp and wicker.'

'What a beautiful combination.' Clara, the Englishwoman, puts long nails on the dark cloth of his arm. She is tall and thin. Her figure and her face have those fine brittle bones one associates with red setters. I have decided that she has no character. Few whores have; or rather they assume so many characters it is impossible to tell if one is real and the others false. In this they are like all mediocre actresses. A great whore, like a great stage performer, has the brains and the sense of survival always to present one face to the world when off-duty. Clara looks to me for approval. I am prepared to smile. It costs me her attention, for she immediately detaches herself from Stefanik. Her perfume seems acrid. 'Do you know the Count?' she asks. 'I have not had the pleasure.' I am dragged towards him and introduced. It appears to me that we exchange nothing but sympathetic and knowing looks, and bows. 'You arrived recently, I gather,' say I. 'Yesterday, I think,' he says. 'Poor timing,' say I. 'So it would seem,' he says.

'And you will leave in your balloon?'

He shakes his head. The truth is that he cannot afford to fall, as a Czech nationalist, into Austrian hands. 'Not with those trigger-happy Bulgarians all over the place. They'll shoot at me. There isn't a soldier in the world who doesn't automatically shoot at any balloon. I have stored it and shall leave it stored until this stupidity is over. It cannot be more than a week.'

'Less,' say I. 'Nobody has anything to gain.'

'Oh, let us hope so.' It is little demure Renée. 'My father was at Metz. He told me how wretched the citizens had become when at last the army entered the city.'

'Count Holzhammer is not a brute,' says Clara.

'He is a gentleman. He and the Prince must soon come to a civilised agreement,' says the plump banker Schummel, all insouciant confidence and avuncular good humour. 'My dear von Bek. How is your illustrious brother?' We chat about Wolfgang for a few minutes, about Bismarck, but already I become impatient to return to Alex and Thérèse. The salon contains that blend of cigar-smoke and rosewater I find delicious, a blend of characteristically masculine and feminine scents. The perfection of the candelabrum, cold fire and crystal, the depth of the Persian carpet and the elegance of the company have revived in me that euphoria I was losing. Schummel stands with his back to the rose-marble fireplace. His balding white head is reflected in the mirror, together with the large central chandelier. Renée holds her folded fan at her side and listens while he speaks about his recent visit to Algiers where he stayed at the Grand Hotel St George, Mustapha-Superieur. The manager, a Swiss named Oesch-Muller, is such a splendid, helpful fellow. Do I know him? I agree with his opinion of the manager, though I can hardly remember him. I prefer Kirsch's Hotel, near the English Club. Renée seems very attractive tonight. She wears pale blue and gold. Her auburn hair is allowed to fall on one side in three thick ringlets to her naked shoulder. She, too, has memories of Algiers, where her mother worked as a housekeeper for a German trader. Schummel is delighted. 'Aha, admit it! You were a white slave in a harem. But you escaped!'

'True,' says Renée. 'Life in a brothel is so much more comfortable!'

'Well, at least you have the choice of how to spend your later years,' says Schummel. I feel almost jealous as he offers her his arm and moves away. I decide I will have a word with Frau Schmetterling and perhaps book Renée for another night. 'And you have so many friends,' he adds, 'you never need get bored as you would with one master.'

I glance at myself in the mirror. I am handsome. My moustache is perfect, my figure exquisite and my evening clothes are a wonderful fit. I have deep, dark eyes and glossy hair. My bearing is elegant without being in any way arrogant. It is no surprise to me Alex should find me so attractive. I look at my mouth. The lips are red and have a kind of refined sensuality. I am a catch for any woman. Does Alex have hopes of marrying me, I wonder. I cannot think how it would be possible, at present. It would be foolish of me to consider it. She is too young. And I do not believe she really loves me. As I return to the group around Count Stefanik I have a sudden frisson of fear. I refuse to admit I love her. Yet there is already pain, even at the thought of her desertion.

The talk is still of the war and Count Stefanik grows visibly restless. I have the notion that soon his buttons will begin to pop off his waistcoat. 'Four of the new Krupp cannon could destroy Mirenburg in a day,' says Stefanik, almost with vindictive relish towards those who are keeping him away from his pleasures. We look about for a military man who will confirm or deny this. There are none present. Frau Schmetterling discourages even generals from Rosenstrasse. She says they spoil the atmosphere, that their talk is coarse and too much about death. But Herr Langenscheidt, the Deputy, believes he can speak for the Army. After all, his son is a captain – a loyalist, thank God – and Herr Langenscheidt supplies the livestock and provisions to the garrison. 'Holzhammer has no German artillery,' he says. 'He has inferior Austrian and French guns.'

'Nonetheless,' says Clara, attaching herself again to me and scratching delicately at my wrist with her thumbnail, 'it should not stop you ascending, Count.'

Stefanik is dismissive.

'A white flag would do it,' says Langenscheidt, his little body all a-quiver. 'Wave a white flag!' Schummel argues that for Count Stefanik to rise above the walls of Mirenburg brandishing a white flag might mislead Holzhammer into believing the entire city had surrendered and that would not be sporting. Indeed, it could be exceptionally embarrasing to everyone.

The aviator sighs. 'My balloon stays where it is.' He signals to Lotte and Hyacinta, both beautiful natural blondes, and with the briefest of acknowledgements to the rest of the company, departs upstairs with them. I take a glass of red Graves from the buffet which tonight has been placed near the window. As always the windows are thickly curtained in red velvet glowing like a fresh rose. I smell patchouli, and woodsmoke from the fire, the cheeses and cold fowl on the table, and I am now completely relaxed, no longer so eager to return to my two girls. Clara comes to eat another peach. 'It's my third. Aren't I greedy? They're all the way from Africa, I believe.' I wonder why she is pursuing me. I have no desire, tonight, to enjoy her special talents. She fixes me with a compulsive eye. Or perhaps it is Alex she desires, having heard about her from Thérèse. 'I so enjoy Count Stefanik,' she says, 'don't you? He is absolutely committed to the idea of powered flight. He calls it "heavier than air"? What does that mean?'

'Such machines are notional, and probably not possible. It means to fly like a bird, which is heavier than air, not like a dirigible, which contains lighter than air gas.'

'What?' she exclaims with a laugh designed to please and flatter me. 'Are we all to be angels?'

'Some of us are already so blessed,' I say with reluctant and unconvincing gallantry, looking up eagerly as the doors open and a woman enters. It is Princess Poliakoff, but now she no longer has her son with her. I cannot leave, for she has seen me and will be suspicious if I repeat my ploy of the previous evening. I smile at her and go to greet her.

I do not recognise her thin female companion. 'Sent on,' she says of the boy, 'to Vienna. I couldn't risk an encounter with

Holzhammer. He holds such awfully long grudges. Do you know Rickhardt von Bek, Diana? Lady Cromach.' We are introduced. Lady Diana Cromach is a writer, a correspondent for several English and French journals. A Lesbian, she lives in Paris. 'What brings you to Mirenburg, Lady Cromach?' I enquire in English. 'I am a professional vulture,' she says. 'The whiff of blood and gunpowder, you know. The war.' Everyone seems to be babbling tonight. The salon is fuller than usual. Someone has placed a record on the cabinet phonograph in the corner. It plays a sentimental German song. All at once the place has the atmosphere of a provincial wedding-breakfast. Lady Cromach wears her dark curls close to her head, a circlet of pearls. She has an oval face, a rounded chin, grey-green eyes, a strong noᵤe and a slightly down-turned but full mouth, very flexible for an Englishwoman. Her family estates are in Ireland. She is almost as tall as me and has an excellent, if slight, figure in an ivory gown trimmed with very light brown lace. Her voice is soft. Every statement seems full of implicit irony, no matter how banal it sounds on the surface. Has she learned to modify an otherwise mundane personality by cultivating this mannerism or is she really as clever as the Princess now insists? 'Have you read her articles for the *Graphic* or *La Vie Francaise*? So perceptive! She is a seeress. You are a Cassandra, my dear.' The Princess is plainly intoxicated with her friend. In her black costume she contrasts so emphatically that I smile and tell them I feel I am addressing a pair of chess queens. This pleases the Princess who laughs coarsely. 'But we play a game without kings, dear Ricky.' At this, Lady Cromach smiles and looks down at her fan. I find the Englishwoman, with her boyish shoulders and gestures, extremely attractive and give her more of my attention than I believe she desires. I am at my most charming, but she is not charmed, though she seems pleased to acknowledge the effort I am making and so is, I believe, flattered at least. Princess Poliakoff notices and almost growls at me. 'Where is your little nigger tonight, Ricky?'

'Resting,' I reply. Lady Cromach displays more curiosity

than before and it is my turn to smile a little. Doubtless she has heard an elaborate story from the Princess but only now believes it. Such apparently unconscious confirmations give substance to the most outrageous lies. I feel satisfied on a number of levels and my spirits lift considerably. I have excited Lady Cromach's imagination; I have become interesting to her. I offer them both my cigarette case but Lady Cromach does not smoke and Princess Poliakoff prefers her little cheroots. She is quick to introduce her Diana to a safer acquaintance and once again I find I am with Clara, whom I now believe is either a little drunk or has made use of the box of cocaine for which she is well-known. She has never shown such interest in me before and I cannot understand why she is attracted to me tonight. She has an eye for vulnerability. Can I seem vulnerable to her, when I am so full of confidence? The phonograph is playing a Strauss waltz. 'It is like a Friday or a Saturday,' remarks Clara. 'Not like a Wednesday at all.' She is pleased, but I am beginning to feel slightly irritated and claustrophobic. All the same Clara's pursuit has its effect. I have no intention, however, of returning to Alexandra with the marks of a birch on my behind; not yet. 'You are looking so beautiful tonight, Ricky,' says Clara. 'You have only to ask Frau Schmetterling and I could join you a little later.' I laugh. 'You are after my – ' I hesitate. She makes a movement of triumphant withdrawal and our eyes meet even as she straightens her back. 'We shall have to see,' I say. 'But I think it could be arranged.' We all seem to be playing the same game tonight. And Clara grins, biting her lower lip, and winks. She is off into the press. I am alone. My first impulse is to leave quietly but before I know it I have crossed the carpet to where Princess Poliakoff and Lady Cromach, arm in arm, are amusing themselves at the expense of a red-faced dodderer who has mistaken them for whores. 'I do hope we shall meet again,' I tell them. I kiss their hands. Princess Poliakoff is a little cold, but I am under the impression that Lady Cromach has almost imperceptibly squeezed my fingers. To the strains of the waltz I make a lighthearted departure and spring up the stairs to our room. I find with disappointment that my little girls are asleep. Alexandra has her mouth open and is snoring. She looks, as she often does, like a replete rat, and I turn my attention first to her youthful flesh, then to Thérèse who, in sleep, seems slightly puzzled, just a trifle worried by something, and yet her lips are innocently curved in a smile. Alexandra opens alarmed, accusatory eyes, then composes her features in a way I have only seen on a much older woman. 'I wish I could join you down there,' she says. 'You've enjoyed yourself, haven't you?' Her voice is low and loving. 'I was missing you.' I lean down to embrace her. Thérèse grunts and stirs but does not wake up. 'I think we should go,' I say. 'Are you satisfied.'

'With Thérèse?' She frowns. 'Oh, yes. We'll come again tomorrow, shall we? For a different lady?' I am indulgent. 'You don't think we should rest, be by ourselves, at least until Friday or Saturday?' She is displeased. 'But it is getting so exciting. Are you bored already?' I shake my head. 'Not bored. Merely patient.'

She puts her feet to the floor and looks at herself in the mirror. 'What's wrong?' I reassure her and, of course, within moments am promising her that we shall return tomorrow, that I will speak to Frau Schmetterling before we leave. I would do anything to preserve this dream and will avoid, if I can, any hint of conflict between us. 'You are a wonderful, wonderful friend.' Naked, she raises herself to put her arms around my neck. 'I adore you. I love you so much, Ricky.' I kiss her violently on the mouth and then pull away from her, attempting gaiety. 'Get dressed. We must slip into the night.' Sadness and distress have invaded me so swiftly that I am angry, as if faced with a physical enemy. Much as I control myself she notices. When she is ready for the street she says quietly. 'Have I upset you?' I deny it, of course. 'Not at all. I met an old buffoon downstairs who insisted on boring me about the war. He all but ruined my evening.' She becomes tactful. 'Perhaps you're tired of our adventure? Perhaps we should rest tomorrow, after all.' But I am by now fierce in my insistence that we continue. 'You're certain you want to?' she says. 'Of course,' I reply. The anger fades. She appears to be mollified. I, in turn, become astonished at how easily she can be reassured. But she is a child. It is experience which encourages us to pursue our suspicions; that and the memory of past pain. She has not known pain. Only boredom. In a woman of my own age I should sense an echo, some form of sympathy. But with Alexandra there is no sympathy. And I continue to conspire in her ignorance because it is the child I love. If she were to become a woman I should lose interest in her in a matter of weeks at the most. We persist in a conspiracy in which I alone am guilty, for I know what I am denying her. I refuse my own reason. I refuse to consider any sense of consequence. She is what I want. I will not have her change. And yet I have no real power in the matter. I can only pray the moments will last as long as possible for it will be Alexandra, in the end, who will make the decision either to stop dreaming or, more likely, substitute one dream for another. I look carefully at Papadakis's sallow, bearded face. At the deep hollows under his morbid eyes whose melancholy is emphasised by the spectacles he affects. Even the grey streaks in his beard have an unhealthy look, as if a saprophytic plant invades it. He turns away from my stare to pick at something with a quiet, fussy movement. I have made him self-conscious. I enjoy my moment. 'You should take more exercise,' I say. He grunts and shifts towards the shadows: a need to hide. His shoulders seem to become more stooped than usual. I am driving him into the darkness where he feels safest. 'Have you been looking for the evidence again?' I ask. 'I have told you, the photographs are not in the house.' He pushes back the heavy green curtain which covers the door of my bedroom. He disappears behind it. I pause to refill my pen. Alexandra is petulant. Her full lips turn downward and she pulls a hand through wet hair. Her skin seems to have lost its lustre this afternoon. Her shoulders and her breasts in particular have a lifeless look: a wax statue. 'You are eating too much custard,' I call after Papadakis. 'Too much bread and jam!' Alexandra pulls herself together, evidently displeased with her own mood.

I hand her a glass of champagne. She accepts it; she is placatory
– 'Could we find some opium? My nerves. Or some cocaine?' I
shrug. 'Are you afraid? Do you want to go home?' I am still
sluggish and am not properly awake. She shakes her head. 'Of
course not. But with all this news, not knowing who is doing
what or where my parents are and so on – Well, it's not
surprising I'm a little agitated. Could you get some opium?'
She begins to dry her hair, staring hard at her face in the
mirror of the dressing table. 'I'm sure it's possible,' I tell her.
'But is it wise?'

She pouts, glares at me in that gesture I have come to
recognise as her substitute for direct anger. 'Is any of this
wise?' And then turns as if to say What have you made of me? I
am in no mood for accusations. 'Are you suggesting – ?' But
of course she has suggested nothing in words. 'You are only
what you were before we met. I am merely the instrument of
your desire. I have told you that from the beginning. You can
return to your parents' home if you wish and we'll say goodbye
as friends.' I know that she will not go. I have countered her
attempt at manipulation. 'I love you, Alexandra,' I say. She
begins to cry. 'You have overtaxed yourself. Lie down for half-
an-hour. Tonight I'll see if there is any opium to be had. When
you've rested we'll go shopping. Some new clothes.' She cheers
immediately. She has almost no sense of the future. She lives
only for immediate, meaningless victories. She chooses not to
rest but to get dressed so we shall not find the shops closed. I
put on my dark brown suit with the buff waistcoat and kid
boots and gloves, the cream cravat, a pearl pin. I am pleased
with the effect. Today I think I look younger than she, but her
paintbox and her powder soon adjusts the balance. She wears
pale green silk with darker green lace ruffles, a matching hat
with pheasant feathers. Her boots and gloves are also of the
dark green. I pick up my stick, she her reticule, and we are off
on our expedition. Carriages are lined up outside the hotel,
eager for business. I am uncomfortable with the situation, for
we, almost the only guests left, are more conspicious than
usual. I wonder about changing hotels, but once we are in the

carriage and she has lowered her veil I dismiss my anxieties. On the way to the fashionable arcades of Falfnersallee we note the increased number of soldiers. Some of the shops have their shutters up. Here and there workers are moving sandbags against walls. I smile. 'They are taking this all very seriously, eh?' She smiles mindlessly at me for she is already thinking of the dress she will buy. The ladies of Falfnersallee are delighted to see us. We have all their attention as we move from shop to shop. She orders dresses, underclothes, a tea-gown, an umbrella, a Japanese kimono, all of which I must approve and pay for. Trade is slow at present, I am told. For my own satisfaction I take her to a jeweller's and there buy a Lalique brooch for her, green and white wisteria which looks perfect on her dress. She kisses it, kisses me and she is my happy schoolgirl again. We return via the quays and stop the carriage to watch two swans bobbing on the choppy waters. The misty light of the evening softens their outlines and they seem to merge with the silver river and vanish. The poplars in the dusk of Falfnersallee are black as Indian ink on a grey wash and rooks are calling from them like bored boys on a Sunday; noisy but unenthusiastic. Otherwise the great avenue is eery, virtually deserted. 'Has everyone abandoned the city?' I say. 'Have we the whole of Mirenburg to ourselves?' We embrace. In our rooms, with the gas lit, we inspect her parcels, her new hats, her brooch, a gold chain, a silver bracelet, her shoes. She spreads them all over the bed. She has the air of a soldier, triumphant from a looting expedition. She bites her lip and grins. She might have stolen all this. Unexpectedly I realise I could be preparing her for someone else, someone for whom she will make every sacrifice she will not make for me. It is not that I frighten her, though she says I do, it is that I do not frighten her enough, for real, committed love must always have a little fear in it or it would hardly be so precious. It is I who am afraid. I hate myself for my mysterious cowardice. I cannot identify its source. I continue to smile like a fool. I am more intelligent, more powerful, more experienced, even more humane than she: yet I am helpless. I grin like a clown as she parades her booty. My cheque-book is almost exhausted. I must go to my bank and get a new one tomorrow. I can always telegraph for more funds if necessary. I have not yet over-stepped the mark with my family, I am certain, although of course they would not support me if they received any word of this escapade. I begin to doubt the wisdom of asking for Clara, as I did last night. There is still time to telephone to Frau Schmetterling. Alone, I would enjoy Clara's attentions, would happily give myself up to her, but now I am afraid Alexandra will think less of me. Even as I smile at her I become deter-mined to make a show of strength tonight.

Just before we enter Rosenstrasse I pause in the darkness, certain I can hear distant gunfire. 'They must be fighting quite close,' I say. She shakes her head, impatient with me, eager to reach the house. 'It's just the river. Loading a boat or something.' It is definitely gunfire. We mount the steps. There is a pretty French song coming from the salon. As usual, we go straight to the room to which Trudi directs us. It is a little larger than the other two, with rather less furniture in it: some potted palms and two vases of gladioli which I know Clara favours. 'Beautiful colours,' says Alexandra. Her maroon linen rustles. 'Not one stem is the same.' Although she has accepted my rules for the evening her hand shakes as she reaches for a flower. I take off my jacket and throw myself into the big armchair. I feel exhausted, but I am controlling myself well. She is far too self-involved at present to notice any subleties of mood in me. 'I prefer this room,' she says. 'The other one was vulgar.' I light a cigarette. 'I enjoy vulgarity. And surely these are the premises for discarding good taste occasionally.' Someone taps on the door. 'Our mistress has arrived. Open it for her.' With a deliberate gesture of submission she obeys. Clara stands there, all in grey, with a silver choker about her throat. To this is pinned a small, blood-red rose. 'Thank you Alexandra. You are as lovely as I was told.' She kisses my child on the forehead and closes the door herself. 'Well, another crowded evening downstairs. So hot!' She opens her fan and waves it once or twice under her face.

There is a suggestion of mockery in the composed smile she offers me. 'Sit down, Alexandra.' She indicates a straight-backed chair. Alexandra hesitates. Clara frowns. Alexandra sits. She is beginning to join in the spirit of this game. 'First we shall have some cocaine,' says Clara. 'Do you know how to take cocaine, Alexandra?' The child shakes her head. 'I will show you how to prepare it for sniffing. For my part, I prefer the syringe.' She touches her own cheek, laughing at herself. 'Like Sherlock Holmes.' From a drawer she takes a square box covered in black velvet. 'Do you know the stories, Alexandra?' She expects no reply and receives none. Alexandra is fascinated. Clara opens the box and takes a bottle of clear liquid from it. Beside this, on the marble of the chest's top, she lays a silver syringe. 'That is for me. But for you two, the crystals.' Out comes a tiny cut-throat razor with a mother-of-pearl handle, a small green-glass jar with a black screw-top, a hand-mirror in a silver frame. Clara works like a surgeon with these instruments. Every placement is precise. Without turning she says: 'I think you can remove your clothes now, Alexandra.' I avoid looking at either of them until Alexandra has actually begun to undress. Clara's rituals are often different and this one, of course, is completely unfamiliar. 'You may keep the necklace and bracelets,' says Clara. 'Fold your clothes neatly. I hate untidiness. Then come over here.' With deep concentration she shows Alexandra how much cocaine to take from the jar on the little spoon, how to chop it this way and that with the razor until it is as fine as it can be, measuring it into four lines of near-identical length and width on the glass of the mirror. 'You will prepare the next one,' she says. She fills her syringe and takes a little piece of cotton-wool which she has saturated in disinfectant, laying the syringe's needle on it. 'Now both of you may undress me,' she says. 'You may behave as you like during this part of the evening.' Thérèse had worn only a chemise and drawers, but Clara is all buckles and pins and combs. We set upon her, Alexandra and I, like hungry peasants at a chicken, picking and pulling, until our mouths can fasten on breasts, stomach, thighs. And all the while Clara is a statue, hardly moving, maintaining dignity and equilibrium at every tug and pressure, as if she challenges us to move her. Then Alex is kneeling and licking at her sex. 'That is enough,' says Clara. 'Get undressed Ricky.' I do as she commands. Now we are all naked save that Clara keeps her necklet with the rose and Alexandra retains her jewellery. Clara dabs at her upper arm with more cotton-wool, then very slowly applies the syringe. When she has finished she takes two thin silver tubes from her box. 'One measure in each nostril,' she tells us. 'You first, Ricky.' I lean over the mirror and sniff up first one line, then, changing hands, the second. Alexandra imitates me and is surprised, I can tell, that she feels no immediate sensation. Clara gives a little gasp and looks towards her bottle with the affection one normally reserves for a loved one or an especially fine wine. My head is suddenly all delicious tingling sensitivity, a feeling which spreads through every nerve of my body and seems to excite blood and flesh to new, exquisite life. 'Oh!' Alexandra is receiving the same effect. I envy her this first experience, as I am sure does Clara. 'Oh! Oh, Clara!' She looks with gratitude towards the whore who continues to smile that same knowing smile. Then Clara orders me to my chair, Alexandra to the bed. With cold concentration she begins to explore the girl's body, scratching here, stabbing with a nail there, discovering her most sensitive parts. She takes a hatpin from the table and deliberately slides it down Alexandra's left-side, drawing spots of blood, so Alexandra moans and gives vent to a strange, thin wail. She tries to move, to embrace Clara, but Clara will not allow it. She repeats the operation on the girl's right side, from shoulder to waist, over the buttock, down the thigh, the calf, to the foot. She leans to lick the blood, rolling it on her tongue like a connoisseur. I now lie beside Alexandra on the bed and receive two fiery lines to match hers. Then Clara begins to scratch, to slap, to whip with a thin cane until we are both writhing for her, moaning for her and I am certain I shall die if all this delicious agony is prolonged another second. Alexandra's voice is hoarse with those thin sounds she has almost continuously made. Clara is grunting. She turns us on our backs and repeats the process until almost every inch of our flesh is tender with bruises and tiny cuts. Then Alexandra lies with her face pressed to my genitals while Clara produces a china dildo shaped like a penis and, using a minimum of cream, thrusts it into Alexandra's small behind. There is now naked pleasure on Clara's face. With cruel delight she rams the dildo in and out while I hold Alex's head against my groin, glorying in the hot gasping breath on my cock. Alex's nails dig deep into my thighs. The movements of the struggling skull excite me and I begin to roll in unison with Clara's relentless thrusts. I find Alex's lips and try to enter them, but Clara pushes the girl aside and, leaving the dildo where it is, squats astride me to move herself to a banshee's orgasm. She yells. Alex is astonished, but I know Clara of old and begin to shout with her, reproducing all but the act of spending before, with hardly any hesitation, I turn Alexandra onto her front, remove the dildo and replace it with my cock, buggering and buggering while Clara slaps at my arse like a jockey on the winning stretch. My orgasm is monumental, horrifying, draining. Clara takes my place and the dildo is used again, this time in Alex's cunt, brutally, until with arms spread wide, with legs spread wide, she begins to shake like an epileptic, her hoarse screams rising to a shuddering crescendo until it seems to me she is going to vomit. Then it is over. A full five minutes later Alexandra begins to weep. Her sobs are deep-throated and, like her orgasm, move her entire body. Clara leans back on her pillows and smokes a cigarette with an expression of complete satisfaction. I am still unable to move. My vision is blurred, perhaps through the effects of cocaine. I can smell nothing but sex. My skin is still flaming; my groin aches. There is no question of visiting the salon tonight. Lulled by Alexandra's sobs, I fall asleep. When I awake my body feels white hot and my mind is overwhelmed by such appalling desolation I can think only of death. When I eventually turn my head it is to see Alexandra's bruised and bleeding body bending over the chest as she prepares more cocaine. I am ready to weep with hatred and jealously at her ability to recover so rapidly. I retreat into sleep. I am soon awaked by the soft touch of Alexandra's hand; it is a tender gesture, a gesture of love. My mood changes to one of easy happiness almost at once. 'There is more cocaine for us,' she murmurs. 'Come, my darling. See if you can sit up.' Clara wears a white lace negligée. 'You men have no stamina,' she says affectionately. 'The drug will revive you, Ricky. What a beautiful couple you are.' She has the air of a woman proud of her prize-winning dogs. 'I have some ointment for you to put on.' I lift my head to sniff up the cocaine and almost immediately feel improvement. Alexandra begins to rub the ointment into my skin from top to bottom. When she has finished I tend to her. A certain perspective returns. Clara is in no hurry to leave and just now I have no great desire to be alone with Alexandra. We smoke cigarettes and discuss the charms of other lovers we have known. Clara is rather more willing to gossip than Thérèse. We drink some good claret and eat tiny pieces of cheese. Clara wants to know about Lady Cromach, but I can only repeat what I have heard. 'She seems to like you,' she says. 'Who is this?' asks Alexandra, not really jealous. 'They have a room here,' says Clara. 'She and the Princess. But they do not seem interested, as yet, in any of the girls.'

'Oh, I would love so much to go down there,' says Alexandra. 'Wouldn't it be possible, Ricky?'

'Too dangerous. And I doubt if Princess Poliakoff would be deceived, even if we smeared some burnt cork on your face and lent you a pair of my trousers.' I move in the bed. The touch of the soft linen on my body, the effect of the cocaine, are superb. We are all three so happy that my former fears, my caution, my common-sense seem banal to me. 'But what can anyone say?' she asks. 'Oh, there are ways of saying things. But I'll put my mind to the problem. Let's get dressed while we can.' Slowly I lower my feet to the carpet and stand on trembling legs. Clara brings my clothes to me. We laugh as the material makes us wince. 'We've overdone it. Tomorrow we must definitely rest. I thought I was going to die tonight.'

'Me, too,' says my Alex. 'But what a beautiful death. You have taught me so much, Clara. Thank you.' She is far more enthusiastic about Clara than she was about Thérèse. I cannot fathom her tastes or her motives. There is a knock. Frau Schmetterling is apologetic. 'I'm glad I haven't interrupted you. I thought you'd be leaving. I wanted to speak to you, Ricky.' Alexandra is alarmed, like a schoolgirl caught smoking. 'Good evening, my dear.' I have never known Frau Schmetterling to visit one of the rooms before. She is stately as ever, in black and white, but seems agitated. 'Would you excuse me while I have a word with your gentleman? Ricky?' We move out into the passage. 'This is not the best time,' she says, 'but I have decided to go to bed early. It has been too busy for a weekday. We were not really prepared. Poor Mister can hardly stand up. Ulric has threatened to leave. It is the War. The threat of death is a great encourager of lust. I thought I'd invite you to stay here, in one of the private suites, if you would feel better. I am keeping it aside for you. Until the business with Holzhammer is over. I have heard rumours. Well, as you'd expect. No truce has been reached and Holzhammer . . . He means to win, I gather, at any price. The city could suffer. You know how fond I am of you. Your hotel is so near the centre. Here, we are more secluded. Well?' Her dark, maternal eyes are earnest.

I am moved by her concern. 'You have always been so kind,' I say, touching her arm. 'I'm comfortable enough at the Liverpool, at least for the moment. There is also the young lady to consider.'

'If you could promise me there would be no scandal I'd willingly extend the invitation. The Prince intends to defend – Oh, Ricky – Simply reassure me.' She seems doubtful, reluctant to have Alexandra as a guest. Her little fat face is full of worry.

'There would be no scandal, I promise.' But I am lying, of course. If Alexandra's parents were to find out where their daughter was it would be the end of Frau Schmetterling's business in Mirenburg. For that reason I am firm in declining her offer. 'What danger can there be to civilians, even if Holzhammer marches in tomorrow? Mirenburg is not Paris. There is no Commune here!'

'The Prince means to resist,' she says again.

'Then Germany will come to help him and Holzhammer will be trounced once and for all.'

'The guns . . . ' she murmurs. 'They say . . . '

'Holzhammer will not bombard Mirenburg. He would arouse the hatred of the civilised world.'

Frau Schmetterling is unconvinced.

'I'm a little exhausted,' I tell her gently. 'I desire very much, madame, to get to bed.'

'Of course.' She squeezes my hand. 'But you must remember, Ricky, that I am your friend.' She waddles away down the passage, then pauses. 'I care for your well-being, my dear.' She waves her plump arms as if to dismiss her own sentiments. She lets out a matronly chuckle. 'Good night, Ricky.'

Our carriage is loud in the expectant streets; Alexandra wants to know the substance of my conversation with the madam. I tell her. 'But it would be so convenient,' she says. 'Why didn't you accept?' My instincts are against it. I can hardly explain my feelings to myself and I am already tiring. My nerves are bad, my body no longer sings. I desperately want the comfort of the Liverpool's sheets. Alexandra is still euphoric. She kisses and hugs me. I am her master, she says, her beautiful man, the most wonderful lover in the world. Horses race by with soldiers on their backs. I see lamps moving, hear the occasional voice and I wonder how much of the tension I sense is external, how much comes from within. I am thinking of Princess Poliakoff. Several years before, in Venice, I attended one of her parties at which, she told me, I was to be the guest of honour. She had brought in some peasants from her country estate: young men and women whom, I believe, worked for her. 'Here,' she had said, 'are your pupils. They know all about you and are willing to be educated by you.' Those strange, fresh faces, so wholesome and natural in tone and colour, yet so fundamentally degenerate, looked towards me eagerly as if I were Satan Himself, a Magister of Corruption to whom they could offer their souls as my apprentices. The responsibility was completely beyond me. I told Princess Poliakoff such games bored me. I fled the house. I am aware of my own limitations and, to some degree at least, my own motives. I live as I do because I have no need to work and no great talent for art; therefore my explorations are usually in the realm of human experience, specifically sexual experience, though I understand the dangers of self-involvement in this as in any other activity. Those peasants had been creatures for whom sexuality had become an escape rather than an adventure. They had made no choice at all; they were dependent upon the Princess for their bread. They had no faith in themselves, no belief in their rights as individuals to strengthen and maintain their own wills and to accept any consequences of their own actions. And in this they are dangerous. In this, I would go so far to say, they were evil. And I believe Princess Poliakoff evil, I think. Yet, surely, I am now doing something which I refused to do then, in Venice. Have I no morality left to me, after all? Alexandra clings to me, kisses me with soft, little girl kisses. It is all I can do at this moment not to shudder.

We tug off our clothes as soon as we are in our bedroom. She laughs and kisses my wounds. She looks at herself in the mirror at her bruises and welts, as if she surveys a new gown. 'Oh, Clara is marvellous. Such presence! Don't you think so, Ricky?'

I am already in bed. 'Would you wish to be like Clara?' I ask.

'A whore? Of course not. But to have such power!'

I shake my head. 'She has no power in reality. She pretends it, to serve her clients. She is paid to act that part. The fact that she enjoys it is probably why she is paid so well. But she – '

Alexandra crawls in beside me. 'Ssh, Ricky. You are too serious. Can you see me as a Clara?'

I take her tenderly to me. She is almost immediately asleep, her face in the pillows. It is as if she lies just below the surface of freedom; head down in an unsecured coffin from which, if she merely turns her body once, she can immediately escape. I dim the lamp but do not extinguish it. The sky outside becomes grey. I intend to sleep at least until the evening. I dream of a dark femme fatale whom I cannot identify, mother and priestess, wicked and tender; she laughs at me and pulls thorny roses from her body; her laughter is gutteral and there is a thin, overbred dog at her side which whines, cringes and bares its teeth at me, barking whenever I try to approach her. Panting, I awaken. Dawn is yellow ivory barred with dusty gold. My body aches, my muscles are tense. I have no energy; my skull seems clamped. There are noises from outside. Momentarily I mistake them for the sounds of surf and wind. I hear a distinctive whistling, a boom. I hear voices from the open window. Taking up my dressing gown I walk on stiff legs to the balcony and stand there, supporting myself on the iron railing. The light is painful. There is smoke rising everywhere, as if from large fires. I look across the square where figures are running this way and that. Another terrible whistling, and before my eyes I see a Gothic spire crack and fall. My predictions were meaningless, comforting, without foundation; little tunes hummed to keep dark realities at bay, for Holzhammer is bombarding Mirenburg! I turn into the room. Alexandra continues to sleep. She has pushed away the covers. There is a smile on her face. I check the impulse to wake her and stumble back to bed to light a cigarette and lie looking up at the bed curtains, listening to the sounds of destruction. Then I am drawn again to the balcony. For most of the morning I remain there, still incredulous, as the enemy shells smash a Romanesque column or erode the delicate masonry of a modern apartment building. It is probable that I am not yet free of the cocaine because I begin to think the bombardment is bringing a new kind of beauty to the city, for the moment at least, perhaps also a dignity it has not previously possessed. Just as a woman in middle or late years will achieve grace and poise through vicissitude and pain making her more attractive than ever she could have been in the prime of her youth and looks, so Mirenburg seems now. I do not grieve for her. It seems relief must soon come in the form of a truce. It is not possible that, in all humanity, the besiegers could place upon their consciences the responsibility for the annihilation of so much nobility and optimism, those centuries of civilisation. And sure enough, at exactly mid-day, the guns become silent. Prince Badehoff-Krasny will not let his city be destroyed. The autumn light is washed with grey; clouds rise from the ruins like baffled souls. I return to bed and sleep, my own wounds forgotten. Old Papadakis brings more boiled fish. I am surprised because I can smell alcohol on his breath. 'You were so proud of all your abstinences,' I say. 'You sought them out as if they were positive virtues; as if they gave you merit. You were so full of yourself. But you know what it is, too, don't you, to be ruined by a woman?' He sighs and puts the tray over my knees, below my writing case. 'Eat if you want to. Haven't you finished your story yet?' We are both exiles. We have no other bond. 'Are you afraid of it?' I ask. 'Look how much I've written!' His dark eyes stare into a corner of the room. I remember when, relaxed, he used to seem like an eager boy. 'Self-denial is not the same as self-discipline,' I tell him. 'You remain an infant. But you have lost your charm. She found out what you were, didn't she? Widow-hunter!' I believe I am making him angry. For the first time he looks me full in the eyes, as an equal. 'All those dead painters! Vulture! Bring me a bottle of decent claret. Or have you drunk it all yourself? Why do you feel you should be rewarded? You have spent your life responding to others and you thought it would always pay. And now you have only me and you cannot bear to respond, can you? I am your nemesis.'

'You are mad,' he says, and leaves. I continue to laugh. I disdain his pieces of fish. I continue to write. I am writing now. The ink is the colour of the Mediterranean, flowing from my silver Waterman. What have the Italians become? What does their Duce mean to me? And Germany is destroyed. What dreadful perversity led to this? Was it all prefigured? How could we have known better? Can God be so small-minded that he disapproves of a Lesbian salon? But it is not that which He set out to destroy. Oh, the pain of movement. Alexandra is whispering in my ear. 'Ricky, I'm hungry.' One dream washes into another. I smile at her. 'I love you. I am your brother, your father, your husband.' She kisses my cheek. 'Yes. I'm hungry, Ricky. Do you feel rested? I feel wonderful.'

I begin to sit up. 'Have you looked outside?' It is nearly dark. 'No,' she says. 'Why should I?' I tell her to go to the balcony and tell me what she sees. She thinks it is a game. Frowning and smiling she obeys. 'What's happened? Oh, God! They have pulled down – '

'They have shot down,' I say. 'Holzhammer's seige is beginning in earnest.' First she is frightened, and then she begins to show delight. 'But Ricky, it means I'm completely free. People must have been killed, eh?'

I draw in a deep breath. I have never known any creature so unselfconsciously greedy. 'What a wonderful animal you are. Don't you want to try to get to Vienna? Or Paris?'

'And leave Rosenstrasse? Is there anywhere else like it?'

'Nothing quite like it.'

'Then we'll see what happens.'

That night we visit the brothel and before the new girl (an unremarkable creature called Claudia who submits to Alexandra's rather clumsy imitations of Clara) arrives, Frau Schmetterling pays us a call. 'Remember my offer,' she says. 'They are not interested in this corner of town.'

On our way home we are stopped by soldiers. I tell them who I am. Alexandra invents a name. The soldiers refuse to laugh at my jokes and insist on escorting us back to the hotel. The next morning I receive a visit from a policeman with orders for me to accompany him to his headquarters. He is perfectly polite. It is an examination to which all foreign nationals must submit. I tell Alexandra to wait for me in our rooms and if I do not return by evening to inform Frau Schmetterling. At Nurnbergplatz, however, I find an apologetic police captain who claims to have met my father and to be an admirer of the new Kaiser. 'We have to be cautious

97

of spies and saboteurs. But, of course, you are German.' I ask if it will be possible to have a safe-conduct from the city. He promises to do his best, but is not very helpful. 'My superiors,' he says. 'They cannot risk anyone reporting to the enemy. Have you been told about the curfew?' No private citizens are allowed to be on the streets after nightfall without special permission. This threatens my routine. I hardly know what is happening. While we are talking, more shells begin to land within the city walls and now I am aware that the defenders are firing back. The policeman is despondent. 'We are being attacked with our own guns. Holzhammer seized the train from Berlin. Those are Krupp cannon. Even more powerful than the ones you used against Paris. But I should not tell you this, sir. It is hard to become secretive, eh? We are not very experienced at such things in Mirenburg.' I return, despondent, to The Liverpool. Alexandra is half-dressed, busy with her pots and brushes. 'Oh, thank goodness,' she says, without a great deal of interest. 'I thought they had arrested you.' She returns to her mirror. I find her amusing today, perhaps because I am relieved to be free. 'The guns stopped at twelve,' she says. 'I thought so. Some ultimatum of Holzhammer's. I believe, though the newspapers are vague. They are being censored.' I put them down on the bed and remove my jacket. 'Are you sure you want to go to Rosen-strasse tonight? There's a curfew. We must leave before dusk and return after dawn. We could eat at the hotel and have an early night.'

'But it's Friday,' she says. 'Clara promised to bring that friend. You needn't do anything. Just watch. I know you're tired. Don't you want some more cocaine?'

I am incapable of complaint. 'Then we must be ready to leave by six. Did you have lunch?'

'I wasn't hungry. You could order something now.'

I go into the sitting room and ring the bell. I tell the waiter to bring some cold ham and a selection of cheeses and patés, some bread, a bottle of hock. I retrieve the papers from the bed and return to the sitting room. The idea that I am trapped in this city makes me uneasy. I hope that my bank will not be affected. I have forgotten to get a new book of cheques. The papers say there is every expectation that the food-rationing system will preserve supplies of basic commodities for the duration of the War. A well-informed source has assured a correspondent that Germany is bound to send troops soon. There is no reference to Holzhammer's capture of the Krupp cannon. A sortie by Bulgarians has been successfully driven back at the Cesny Gate, to the south. Various regiments are deployed about the first line of defences beyond the walls. All the loyalist soldiers are in good spirits. Morale amongst Holzhammer's 'rag-tag' of mercenaries, misguided peasants and treacherous rebels, is said to be already very low and the world has received the news of the cannonade with horror. Comparisons are made to the Siege of Paris, to Metz and elsewhere, but in all cases those cities were, we are told, far less well-prepared. 'Her name is Lotte,' says Alexandra, her cosmetics in place. She smiles at me and comes to nibble on a piece of cheese. 'The one Clara says had to leave Paris in a hurry. Why was that?'

I decide to take a bath. As I undress I tell Alexandra what I know of Lotte. She used to specialise in a bizarre tableau known as The Temptation, Crucifixion and Resurrection of the Female Christ, in which she would resist any temptations invented by her customers, be tried, punished and then tied to a large wooden cross, whereupon she would be revived by the attentions of the clients. This tableau had been famous in Berlin and Lotte had been the most sought after 'specialist' in Germany. She had transferred herself to Paris and continued with her presentation there until pressure from the Church, which owned her house, caused her to seek the protection of Frau Schmetterling who accepted her on condition that the tableau no longer be performed. Frau Schmetterling, although Jewish in origin, is a pious woman. The last time I had talked to Lotte she told me she planned to return to Berlin eventually and start up in business again; but she would not skimp. You had to spend money to earn money. She prided herself on the elaborate details of her show. She was saving every pfennig in order to make a rapid return from 'the wilderness'. She was an actress, she had told me, at heart. Alexandra listens. 'She sounds an interesting woman. You know Clara has invited us to her own room tonight. She seems to like you very much. And me.'

It is perfectly true that Clara is attracted to both of us and this puzzles me; to some extent it alarms me, also. Refreshed, I dress in my evening clothes. Alexandra is wearing a pink dress trimmed with red. She looks unusually beautiful. Our cab takes us through streets full of gun-carriages and supply-wagons; workmen labour amongst the half-destroyed shells of houses and shops, shifting beams and rubble. Alexandra hardly notices as she chatters to me, until we have turned into Sängerstrasse and she gasps. 'Oh, my God! The Mirov Palace!' The seventeenth-century building has received a direct hit which has caved in part of the roof and left a huge gap in its upper floors, and yet the trees surrounding it remain as tranquil as ever, the ornamental gardens as orderly. I expect her to be frightened, but she is not. I suspect she has still failed to understand the reality of what is happening. She is half-grinning as she stares around, wide-eyed, at the destruction. 'Oh, my God!' And I realise that for her it is merely another dream come to life. Perhaps that explains her peculiar attitudes: she perceives all this experience as merely a more intense form of dreaming. Something in her still expects to wake up and find everything ordinary again. That is why she is so heedless of consequence. Yet surely I am dreaming, too. A scarlet motor-car goes past. In it, looking rather self-conscious, are four high-ranking officers in tall helmets and a great deal of gold braid. Alexandra giggles. 'Each one could be Franz-Josef himself! Are they in the right army, do you think?'

I insist that she wear her heavy veil as we pay off the carriage and enter the peace of Rosenstrasse. Starlings are swarming overhead in the hazy October sky and the beeches are beginning to shed their leaves. 'The air smells so good,' she says, hugging my arm. 'I am very happy, Ricky.' She compliments me for her state of mind. At the door, Trudi takes my hat, stick and gloves, my top-coat, but Alex remains dressed until we reach Clara's quarters, two large rooms near the top of the house, overlooking the lawn and fruit-trees of the garden. I have never visited Clara's private rooms before. The hangings, cushions and upholstery are predominantly dark blue, black and gold, and the perfume seems to come chiefly from the large, yellow lilies which fill vases on either side of a mahogany desk. There are books in this room, and a small piano, showing that Clara has, after all, some taste for culture, for the pieces on the music-stand are by Mozart and Schubert and the books are either German translations of Fielding, Scott and Thackeray, or works by Goethe and Schiller. Clara claims to be English, but she has nothing in English on her shelves. There is a modern novel or two by von Roberts, some French novels of the cheaper sort, as well as Zola's *Nana* (which all the whores of my acquaintance read with jeering fascination, more interested in his originals and how they correspond with the fictitious characters than the story or the moral), a number of histories and biographies, some books of travel. Clara comes in from the bedroom. She is wearing a black and white riding costume. 'I am so pleased you could come,' she says. She kisses first Alexandra and then me. 'Lotte will be with us in a little while.' I remark on her good taste. 'I'm easily bored,' she says. 'Only substantial music and books seem to please me these days.' I indicate the bookcase. 'Yet you have nothing in English . . . ' She smiles. 'I prefer German and French. After all, it is years since I was in London.' She resists my interest in her story, cocking her head and smiling into my face. She is so pale. I would think her consumptive if I did not know otherwise. As she chats about her favourite novels and composers she begins to undress a passive Alexandra. She leads my girl into the bedroom and I follow, leafing through a volume of Le Sage and remarking on the quality of the engravings. Alexandra is spread on the dark yellow bed, face down. Clara tells me that the book had been a gift from a novelist who had travelled all the way from Brussels to be with her. She applies cream to Alexandra's anus and crosses

101

casually to a chest of drawers to take out her china dildo. 'Do you care for Le Sage?'

'I had the usual enthusiasm for him once,' I say. 'Like Molière, he can seem like a revelation when one is young.' She smiles in accord, parting Alexandra's cheeks and pushing the dildo in hard. Alexandra groans. 'Cocaine,' she says. 'Not yet,' says Clara. 'You can have some later. This is my little pleasure, before Lotte arrives. And I think Ricky needs arousing tonight. You look tired, Ricky.' I let her know I had not planned to join in much. 'To tell you the truth the only use I have for a bed is to sleep in one. But I might feel better later.' Clara removes the dildo, wipes it and replaces it neatly in its drawer. This exercise, then, has been for me. Alexandra does not move but I can tell from the set of her shoulders that she is petulant, though not as yet prepared to demand anything of Clara. 'Stay there, ma cherie,' says Clara. We both go back into the other room. Clara hands me a book. It is by Flaubert, his *Salammbo*. I admit that it has always defeated me. Clara is pleased. 'I am glad to hear it. My friend from Brussels recommended it. I have started it so many times and have perhaps managed a hundred pages at best. I am not much interested in the exotic aspects of history. So many of these modern painters leave me cold. Moreau, for instance.' I cannot agree with her. 'My moods change. Sometimes I like the smell of incense and the feel of heavy gold. It can be soothing to the senses. You are more of an epicurean than I, Clara.' I give her back the Flaubert and she replaces it precisely. 'Are Princess Poliakoff and Lady Diana still in residence?' She nods. 'They have hardly left their rooms, either. I think it must be the beginning of an affair, or one which was interrupted. I don't know. Certainly the Princess is infatuated. As for Lady Cromach, I am not sure. She seems anxious to please the Princess but not from what I would call any driving enthusiasm. She is perhaps too intelligent. Are you attracted to her?' I shake my head. 'Not attracted, but I think she is interesting. She is a type of Lesbian I have not really encountered before. Very self-assured, eh? Yet . . . Oh, let's say less

102

narcissistic than the general run of those one associates with
Princess Poliakoff.' Clara sits down on a Liberty chair and
lights a cigarette. 'I know what you mean. That woman goes
about her business and takes exactly what she wants from
people. Yet she has none of Poliakoff's greediness. Would you
like me to send for Lotte yet?' I shake my head. 'I've been
ravenous all day. I can't stop eating. Let me leave you here
with Alexandra. She loves you and might like to be alone with
you for a while. I'll go down to the salon for half-an-hour or
so.' Clara seems concerned. 'If you would like some of the drug
now . . . ?' I shake my head. 'Perhaps later. Really, I am quite
content. Tell Alexandra some of your stories. Or let her sleep.
I'll come back shortly.' As I descend the staircase I realise that
I am curious about the progress of the War and am hoping that
I shall learn something more than what has been reported.
Newspapers are particularly untrustworthy at this time. The
salon is half-empty. There are many more women here than
men. Some of the girls have not even bothered to give
themselves the special 'poise' which Madame demands.
They are still relaxed. The casual way in which their legs are
positioned hints not at any particular carelessness of
temperament; they unconsciously assume the habitual
attitudes of their calling, as a soldier will stand at ease even in
civilian dress, or an off-duty coal-heaver will rest one side of his
body in favour of the other. But they are beginning to become
'ladies'. Caroline Vacarescu is here, agitated, speaking
urgently to an old dandy in a French-cut coat who spreads his
hands and shakes his head. 'But why arrest him? What has he
done?' She sees me and appeals to me. 'Ricky. Tell Herr
Schmesser that the Count is a man of honour.' I raise my
eyebrows. 'Mueller?' Herr Schmesser shrugs. 'He was caught
red-handed with the documents destined for Holzhammer. My
dear lady, if you had been with him, you too would now be
under arrest. Think yourself lucky.'

'They will shoot him, Ricky,' she says. I am sympathetic.
She is about to lose a powerful protector and is in no position to
find another quickly. I cannot pity Mueller. Indeed I feel only

satisfaction he has at last been caught. 'Caroline,' I say. 'If I can help you, I shall. I am not entirely certain at present how much money I have. But I shall do everything in my power to save you from embarrassment.' I have always liked her. 'Mueller is to be shot,' she says, as if we have not absorbed the enormity and then, realising we are unmoved, rushes from the room, presumably to seek help elsewhere. Herr Schmesser looks at me. 'If she goes out after curfew, she, too, will be arrested. But not,' he adds with a small smile, 'shot. You know of Mueller's activities?'

'I can assume he was spying.'

'And you can be sure that Fraulein Vacarescu was helping him. Together with Budenya-Graetz, who discovered an opportunity to reinstate himself, of course, and is probably already in Vienna with every detail of our defences. It is a disgusting business. The treachery, my dear sir! I cannot tell you how much there has been. My faith in human nature has been ruined in the space of a few days. And this bombardment! Can Holzhammer justify it? His own countrymen. His own city!' He sighs and lifts a glass of champagne to his lips. 'I am very sad.' I pat him on the arm. 'You will cheer up here. After all, there are no disappointments at Frau Schmetterling's, eh?' He nods seriously: 'I hope you are right.' I make a good meal of the buffet. The evening begins. The salon fills. The girls become elegant and alert to the conversation of their guests. The phonograph plays a waltz and everything is as normal. At length, I return to Clara's. Alexandra has by now had some cocaine. Lotte, a plump dimpled blonde, all thighs and bust, is using the dildo on herself while they watch her. I take off most of my clothes and, wearing a dressing gown supplied by Clara, sink down into a chair and become part of the audience. Alexandra will later play the part which Clara played earlier, but somehow without Clara's delicate assurance, and I will continue to watch until I am aroused enough to couple naturally and cheerfully with Clara for a few minutes before falling soundly asleep until morning. At about ten o'clock, after a good breakfast in Clara's rooms, we return through the

104

chilly October sunshine to the Liverpool. The shells are directed more towards the East of the city this morning and our journey seems safe enough until the cab turns the corner into the square and we see that the building next to The Liverpool has sustained a good deal of superficial damage. I look towards our apartment. Servants are nailing boards across shattered windows. We hurry upstairs. There is glass everywhere in the room. The manager is there. He is deeply apologetic and tells us that we can move to 'safer' rooms at the back of the hotel. Without a word to him or to Alexandra I go downstairs and telephone Frau Schmetterling. She has one of the few private telephones in Mirenburg. 'I would like to take you up on your offer,' I tell her, 'if it is still possible.'

'Of course,' she says. 'I'll have the rooms prepared at once. When will you arrive.'

'Probably in an hour or two.'

She hesitates. Her voice becomes faint as the line fades. 'You are bringing your friend?'

'I am afraid that I have no choice.'

'I will see you at lunch-time,' she says.

While Alexandra sees to the packing, I make enquiries after Caroline Vacarescu. She has not returned to the hotel, says the manager. I pay my bill with one of his blank cheques. He continues to apologise so much I feel sorry for him and am able to smile cheerfully enough. 'Please don't worry. I will be back here, I am sure, within a couple of weeks.' I do not inform him of my destination. Alexandra and I are about to disappear. If we should be discovered, when the War is over I can always make her father an offer. I can marry her and save the scandal. But for some reason I do not tell Alexandra of my plan as, with boxes and trunks in three cabs, we flee the ruined Liverpool to the sanctuary of Rosenstrasse.

Chapter Three

The Siege

The atmosphere at Rosenstrasse had become increasingly convivial during that first week of bombardment and, even though the shelling has stopped and the Siege proper has begun (the city now has an air of desperate calm) this mood remains with us. It is Friday, October 29th 1897. Seven of us who are permanent residents have taken to eating together, rather like passengers on a small ship or guests at a provincial boarding house. Frau Schmetterling presides: our landlady, our captain. Alexandra continues to be my secret and grows resentful of her exile from the public rooms. She is beginning to exhaust me. Clara has developed a habit of keeping her company, largely I suspect to relieve me. 'The child is bored. I'll take her for a stroll,' she says, or, 'I've invented a new game for our little girl.' At night Alexandra and I sleep together as usual, reserving our evenings for 'adventures'. We go out rarely. Mirenburg has become depressing. I cannot stand to see the boarded windows and doors, the sandbags, the rubble. We have now enjoyed, singly or in combination, almost all Frau Schmetterling's whores. The only other residents who hardly ever make an appearance at the table together are Princess Poliakoff and Lady Cromach. The Englishwoman is frequently out, presumably gathering material for her articles. I lunch while Alexandra goes with Clara to Falfnersallee 'to look for bargains'. I enjoy a good bortsch and a veal cutlet. 'Mister' and Trudi wait on us. Frau Schmetterling is kind to both of them. Occasionally 'Mister' will be asked to join us, but usually he smiles and refuses, preferring the company of Chagani, the brooding ex-acrobat, who sometimes assists him. His gentleness can be disconcerting, even sinister. His drunkard's face, so youthful and open, and at the same time so cruelly ruptured, expresses a peculiar eagerness. The ruined veins, the rough, red flesh, the set of his soft mouth and the watery innocence of his eyes give immediate notice of his despair, his determination to remain in some way unprotected against the terrors of the world and so, surely by an effort of will alone, retain the untroubled perceptions of boyhood. Elvira, Frau Schmetterling's daughter, sometimes dines with us. When she and 'Mister' are together she seems the more mature; a self-possessed, tiny version of her mother. 'Mister's' expression becomes softer, more attractive, in her company. Madame's chow dogs, black and unpredictable, complete the menage, panting around our feet as if they are waiting for one of us to drop dead. The Dutch banker, Leopold van Geest, sallow and animated, wearing a sort of invalid's blanket-jacket, cuts enthusiastically at his meat. He has decided that it will be at least a month before Berlin sends help. 'The Prince should have made a Treaty with one or another of the Powers. Then Holzhammer could not have acted at all. Badehoff-Krasny was too confident. He thought he stood on a platform balanced over the torrent. But it was a tightrope, yes? He leaned back to relax and – Pouf!' He gestures dramatically with his fork. 'Now the Germans will let him drown a little before fishing him out. They want the best terms, after all.' He shrugs. He has a wife and thirteen children in the Hague and is in no hurry to return home.

'The whole city could be destroyed within a month,' says Rakanaspya in that husky voice of his. The anarchist has been placed under a sort of house-arrest by the police. Frau Schmetterling had agreed to his staying 'so long as he behaves himself,' she said. 'We want no morbid subjects discussed

108

here'. He wipes his lips and beard with his napkin. 'All those poor people dead while kings and princes play at diplomacy!' Frau Schmetterling catches his eye and utters a small cough. He sighs. Caroline Vacarescu, beside him, is sympathetic. She, too, is on sufferance, having been released from custody four days ago. She is dressed magnificently as usual. She has no intention, she assures us, of lowering her standards. Her face is heavily made-up. Mueller was tried by military tribunal last week and executed for espionage. The papers have been emphatic: his fate was an example to others. Some of us are a little uneasy in her defiant, knowing presence. Count Belozerski, the eminent Russian novelist and the most recent arrival, leans his handsome face over the table and murmurs in French: 'I have never seen so many dead soldiers.' He was turned back from the walls while trying to leave Mirenburg. He alone has witnessed the reality outside and is allowed to say more than anyone on the subject. Frau Schmetterling indulges him because she admires, she says, his mind. But she is also impressed by his connections and his beauty. His pale blond hair, together with his slightly Oriental cast of features, give him a striking and dominating appearance. He is tall and slender and his military stance is tempered by a natural grace which serves to soften the first impression of a distant and somewhat menacing figure. Count Belozerski is proud, he says, of his Tartar forebears. He sometimes refers romantically to his 'Siberian blood'. He is in all important respects a gentlemanly European. 'Of the best type,' says Frau Schmetterling. Caroline Vacarescu also dotes on him, but Belozerski has confided to me that he is determined to have nothing to do with her. 'Her selfishness,' he told me last night, 'is mitigated only by her recklessness. Of course both qualities are alarming to a man like myself. One should be in love with such women in one's youth. To take up with the likes of Caroline Vacarescu in middle-life is to risk too much. My cousin was, for a short while, involved with her. She almost ruined him. She is the most extravagant creature I have ever known and I prefer to admire her from a distance.' I, of course, feel friendly towards her, but that could be because I have nothing that she would want. It is my belief Count Belozerski is attracted to her. He is a little inclined to overstate his case. He adds: 'One is dealing, as a novelist, all day with ambiguities, with problems of human character. One does not need any more ambiguities in one's life.' Perhaps he is right. I am not a novelist. I tell him I thrive on ambiguity. For me a woman must always have it or she is not attractive to me. He laughs. 'But then for you life is a novel, eh? Thank God not everyone is the same, or I should have no readers.'

'The hospitals cannot cope with the wounded.' Egon Wilke sits immediately to the left of Frau Schmetterling, across from Belozerski. He is a stocky fellow, with the body and bearing of an artisan. His hands are huge and his large head has brown hair, cropped close to the skull. He wears a sort of dark pea-jacket and a white cravat. He is an old friend of Frau Schmetterling's, apparently from the days when she ran a house of an altogether different character in Odessa, where criminals had gathered. These acquaintances from her past are usually discouraged from visiting Rosenstrasse, but Wilke, who has been introduced to the company as a jewel merchant, is the exception. Frau Schmetterling is evidently very fond of him. He saved her, it is rumoured, from ruin (perhaps prison) in the old days and lent her the money to start the Rosenstrasse house. He always stays with her when visiting Mirenburg and, like me, is treated as a favoured client. He behaves impeccably, never bringing his business to her house, though he is almost certainly still a successful thief. He chews his food thoughtfully, takes a sip of wine and continues: 'They are requisitioning convents, private houses, even restaurants, I have heard. These Mirenburger soldiers, poor devils, aren't used to fighting.'

Frau Schmetterling says firmly: 'We know how hellish it is at the defences, and I am sure we sympathise, but this is scarcely appropriate conversation for luncheon.' Wilke looks almost surprised, then smiles to himself and continues to eat. There is not much else to talk about. We have no real information.

Holzhammer has made a grandiose declaration in which he has praised his own sense of humanity and love of beauty in stopping the bombardment 'to give Prince Badehoff-Krasny time to reconsider his foolish and unpatriotic decision which is causing misery to so many'. He claims that most of Wäldenstein is now his. The newspapers on the other hand are continuing to report failing morale and shortage of supplies amongst the rebels. The peasants and landowners have all deserted Holzhammer, they say, and he is entirely reliant on his 'Bulgarian butchers', his Austrian cannon. Prince Badehoff-Krasny took his State Carriage into the streets during the bombardment and rode the length of Mirenburg, from the Cesny Gate to the Mirov Gate, waving to cheering crowds. Deputations of citizens have signed oaths of undying loyalty to the Crown and the Mayor has sworn to take a sword, if necessary, and personally drive Holzhammer from the battlements, should he try to enter the city. Holzhammer has probably decided to attempt to starve Mirenburg into submission, saving his troops and his ammunition for a final attack. The blockade is total. The river is guarded on both sides and water-gates have been installed under the bridges on the outskirts so that no citizen can leave by that route or bring supplies in; while a huge barricade has been thrown up around the city, making it impossible for anyone to come or go either by road or rail. Belozerski has reported seeing corpses left to rot in trenches, or half-buried by their comrades as they fell back towards the walls. Field-guns, too, have been abandoned. He observed one trench which was 'a single, fluttering mass of carrion crows'. Private citizens are no longer allowed on the walls. We are under martial law. Yesterday, at lunch, Belozerski said: 'God knows what appalling treachery led to this situation. It was a massacre out there.' And then he became embarrassed, since Caroline Vacarescu could probably have answered his rhetorical question, at least in part. She had continued to eat as if she had not heard him. We are all as tactful as possible, even Rakanaspya who sometimes fumes like one of his own anarchist bombs but never explodes. It is only in

111

private, in the company of one or another of our fellow guests, that we express strong opinions. Last night I sat with Clara in her sitting-room while Alexandra giggled in bed with Aimée, who comes from my native Saxony. Clara is in a better position than many to hear what is actually going on. Her regular clients seem to make up half the Mirenburg Civil Service and she sometimes has a General come to see her. She is discreet, in the main, but she believes that the situation might be worse than most of us imagine. 'A military train is believed to have arrived from Vienna. If the Austrians give Holzhammer direct aid then Germany must either begin another war, which she does not presently want, or turn a blind eye to what is going on here. I think she will turn a blind eye.' I found this difficult to believe: 'With so many of her citizens still here?' Clara had looked at me knowingly. 'How many, Ricky? And how many German soldiers would die in a war with Austria-Hungary?' Then Alexandra had called to me and I had gone in to smile. She had tied one of Clara's dildoes onto her in some way and was inexpertly fucking Aimée who was helpless with laughter. 'Help me, Ricky, darling!' There is an ache in my back today. Papadakis says I am not resting enough. He says I should set these memoirs aside. 'You will kill yourself.' I tell him that it does not matter. 'Can't you see I am living again? Can't you see that?' He wets his red lips. 'You are mad. The doctor told me to expect something like this. Let me bring him up.' I set my pen on the pages, across the words. I am patient. 'I am more purely rational,' I tell him, 'than I have been for two years. And I should point out that there is hardly any pain. It is quite evident that much of what I was suffering was psycho-somatic. Haven't you noticed how much better my morale is? You would rather I was ill, eh? You have no power over me now that I am recovering!' He will not respond to this. He sits beside the window, staring down towards the sea. His back is to me. I refuse to let him irritate me. Leopold van Geest and I stroll in Frau Schmetterling's garden. Most of the flowers are gone. It is a mystery where she continues to find fresh ones to fill her house. Beyond the walls are the roofs and turrets of the

112

deserted monastery. 'In here,' says van Geest, 'one is permitted the illusion of power. But we know that Frau Schmetterling is the only one who really wields power and that she derives it from her ladies. From the cunt.' He shakes his head and pulls the blanket-jacket more closely to him. 'Yet we have power in the outside world to create a society which needs and permits brothels. Why cannot we exploit that power directly? Why do we feel the need to come here and be masters when we cannot feel that we are masters in our own homes, over our own women – at least, not sexually. Not really. You can sense the difference.'

'I have very little experience of the domestic life.'

Van Geest nods as if I have made a profound observation. He is moody this afternoon. 'Your instincts are good, von Bek. Marriages are based on romantic lies and decent women demand that we maintain those lies at all costs, lest the reality of their situation be brought home to them. Here the whores are paid to lie to us. At home we pay for our domestic security with lies of our own.' He looks up at the sky. 'Do you think it will snow?'

'It's a little early for that.'

He turns to go back inside. 'Well, I shall probably be home for Christmas,' he says.

Clara comes to join me. 'Our Alice has bought herself a thousand new petticoats!' She kisses me on the cheek. Somehow we have taken to calling Alexandra 'Alice', while I use 'Rose' as a nickname for Clara. She, in turn, calls me 'Your Lordship' in English. Alexandra does not know our nicknames. 'She is upstairs, now, trying them on.' Van Geest lifts his cap and enters the house. 'What were you talking about?' She is all rustling velvet in her long winter coat. 'Marriage, I believe,' I say. 'I'm not altogether sure. Van Geest seemed to want to get something off his chest.' Clara is amused by this. 'That's our job. Whores are trained to listen. What was he saying?'

'That domestic bliss is founded on a lie.'

The argument is familiar to her. 'Working here, one begins

113

to disbelieve in any great difference between people. The girls in this house have more varied personalities than most clients, and that's saying very little, I should think. You cannot pursue individuality here. There's more realism and virtue, perhaps, in celebrating commonality. There are certain lies, surely, we would all rather believe.' She links her arm in mine. We are almost like husband and wife.

We go to peer in at Frau Schmetterling's little hothouse, at the orchids and the fleshy lilies, and at her aviary where a pair of pink cockatoos, an African Grey parrot and a macaw fidget. 'Frau Schmetterling has no interest in birds,' says Clara. She puts her lips together and makes kissing sounds at the gloomy creatures. 'These were given to her at the same time, I believe, as the peacocks. The peacocks died. She's sentimental enough to want to keep her parrots properly, but they get no attention from her. 'Mister' looks after them. Some of us have asked to keep them in our rooms, but she says it would be vulgar.' I am becoming impatient to see Alexandra, even though I know she will be demanding something of me the moment I walk in to our room. 'Shall you be going to the celebration this evening?' asks Clara. I had forgotten. Frau Schmetterling had mentioned it at lunch. 'To honour the end of the bombardment,' she had said. 'It will cheer us all up.'

'I'll look in for half-an-hour or so,' I say. 'And you?' Clara nods. 'Oh, yes. I think it will be amusing.' Since Alexandra will sulk if I go I have almost made up my mind not to bother. 'They are difficult, these children,' says Clara. 'More trouble than they're worth, sometimes.' I feel a moment's resentment of what I take to be her criticism, but she squeezes my arm and the mood vanishes. I enjoy Clara's company more and more and continue to be impressed by her tolerant intelligence. 'By the way,' she says casually, 'did you hear that they had attempted to burn down the synagogue. The Jews are being held to blame, as usual.' I laugh at this. 'Where would we be without them?' But Clara is not pleased with my response. 'I came through the Quarter on the way home. It's miserable. No market, of course, to speak of. Such a terrible sense of fear, Ricky.'

'You must guard against getting too sentimental, Rose my darling, at times like these. It's not like you.' I kiss her cheek. She shakes her head and does her best to dismiss her mood. It occurs to me for a second that perhaps she is worried about her own fate. After all, Frau Schmetterling is Jewish, at least by birth. I return to the rooms. Alexandra is wearing a new negligée of chocolate-brown trimmed with cream lace and her little body, now marked with the fading reminders of a dozen violent nights, is pale in the afternoon light which enters through embroidered nets at the windows. Couch, floor and chairs are piled with new chemises and drawers, with white ostrich feathers, with an ermine-trimmed stole, like froth on a river, and she tugs at her curls, peering with ill temper into an oval mirror which hangs on the wall over a lacquered Chinese sideboard. 'Another raid on Falfnersallee,' I say with a smile. She pulls down an eyelid, looking for blood. 'They're almost giving things away, Ricky.' She has bought a selection of new cosmetics, which she has scattered over the sideboard, and begins to try them out, asking me for my opinion of this lip-rouge and that powder. 'You'll destroy your skin,' I say dispassionately. 'You have youth and health, natural beauty . . . ' She makes a face. 'You are certainly no lover of what is natural, my dear.' I bridle. 'Nonsense. But play at grown-up ladies, if that's what pleases you. Did you buy a paper?' She is distant. 'I forgot.' I am irritated. 'It's not a great deal to ask.' I pick at feathers and linen, becoming even more angry when I think I shall have to ask Frau Schmetterling for more cash. I have given her a blank cheque, to cover our expenses. 'You should have told Clara to remember,' says Alexandra. 'She's always reliable. Anyway, what do you want a paper for? You told me there's nothing in it now but lies.' The negligée has fallen back to reveal her ribs. 'You're not eating properly,' I say. 'You're getting too thin.' She sets down a little pot with a rap. 'Men want everything. A lady has to be thin in society and plump in bed. Yet you complain about the way I lace my stays!'

115

'I'm concerned for your health. I feel some responsibility.'

'You should not. It is none of your business.'

I want to put an end to this. I embrace her, fondling her shoulders and breasts, but she pulls away. 'You treat me like a child! You spend all your time with other people. Are you fucking the whores while I'm out?'

'You know I'm not. You enjoy Clara's company. You told me so. You're always off on expeditions.'

'In a veil. Like a Turkish concubine! You don't love me. You're bored with me. You refuse to let me be myself. I'm not your daughter. I wanted to get away from that. You sound worse than my father sometimes.'

'Then you should not behave like a little girl.' Such banal exchanges are terrible. I hate listening to the words on my own lips. I have said nothing of this kind since I was eighteen. 'All the interesting people are downstairs,' she says. 'You talk about them. I never see them. Princess Poliakoff, Count Belozerski, Rudolph Stefanik. You and Clara joke about them. I am left out of everything. Why do you want me? You could have a dozen whores and never notice I was missing.'

'I love you,' I say. 'That's the difference.'

She snorts. 'You don't know me.'

'I'm beginning to think there is not very much to know. Perhaps you are entirely my invention.'

'You bastard!' It is the first time she has sworn at me. She repeats the oath, as if to herself. 'You bastard.' She begins to weep. I go to comfort her. She pulls away again. 'What have you made me!'

'Nothing which you were not already, or did not wish to be. I told you at the start: I am the instrument of your pleasure. I put myself at your disposal. And when I have warned you of excess you haven't listened to me. Now you're over-tired and self-pitying. And you're blaming me.'

Her weeping becomes more intense. 'I don't know any better. How can I know any better? I want so much to go to the party tonight. But you're afraid I'll embarrass you. And when I try to look grown-up you complain. You confuse me. You lie to me.'

'How dare you pretend to be so naive,' I say. 'You have no right to demand honesty of me and argue with such patent ingenuity when you know full well what you mean and what you want. It is malice and resentment which motivates you and your methods amount to blackmail. I will not be insulted by you in this way. I will not be silent while you insult yourself. What is it that you want?'

But she refuses to be direct. The rhetoric continues between sobs. 'You have destroyed any will I might have had. Any self-respect. You spend your time with Clara. You laugh at me behind my back.

'Clara is your friend. You told me that you love her.'

'She criticises constantly.'

'Not to me.'

'I know what she's saying. You're a fool if you don't realise what she's up to.'

I light myself a cigarette. 'You are attempting to manufacture a crisis,' I say, 'and I will not be drawn. Tell me what you want.'

'I want respect!'

'Eventually,' I continue, 'it is very likely that you will wear me down sufficiently so that out of weariness or exasperation I will make you an offer and thus save you the responsibility of making your own decision. Or I will become remorseful and give you that which your conscience cannot demand. Well, I will have none of it. When you have made up your mind to speak to me directly I shall be pleased to continue this conversation.' I sound ridiculously pompous in my own ears. She wants me to take her to the party. I am almost ready to do so, even though I know it would be unwise. But I want her to ask. Somehow I am carrying too much of the burden. I am at the door when she wails: 'I want to go to the party!'

'You know it would be too dangerous for us,' I say.

'I don't know. I only know what you tell me. Are you frightened of their opinion?'

I am frightened, of course. I am frightened of the dream

117

ending, of reality intruding. I leave the room. She has wounded me and I am full of self-pity. I am furious with her. I had thought things had reached a decent balance. But she is not content with promises of Paris and I can scarcely blame her, since there is no means of knowing when the siege will be over. But she has changed. I can sense that she has changed. What alterations have occurred in her strange, fantastic brain. I am as much at a loss for a satisfactory explanation as if I had attempted to analyse the perceptions and motives of a household pet. Like a pet she is able to take on the colour of any master; to respond to whatever desires that master displays. Yet she is not doing that now. Does that mean she is ready to find a new master? I feel I am somehow making a mistake; as if I have failed to understand the rules of the game. Perhaps I should not have been so direct with her. Perhaps I should have disguised my desires and remained more of a mystery to her. Or will I lose her anyway? To someone else who will represent liberty and escape to her? It seems increasingly important that we should leave Mirenburg. I will go to Police headquarters in the morning and try again to get passports for us. I have miscalculated. I blame the drugs, the atmosphere of the whore-house. Sensuality has given way to a sort of erotomania. It could destroy everything. I must make an effort to impress her with my own common-sense. I must not weaken. Alice! I want what you were. My little girl! Have you no notion of all the emotions you have aroused in me? The tenderness, the willing-ness to sacrifice everything for you? You cannot know what I have given up already, what I am still prepared to give up. You are myself. And we are Mirenburg. I find that I am outside Clara's room. I knock. She tells me to enter. She has Natalia, her dark friend, with her. They are drinking tea. 'I am so sorry to disturb you.' I make to go, but both wave me in. 'Is the child sleeping?' asks Clara. 'No,' I say, 'she decided to have a tantrum, so I've left her to cool down.' Clara and Natalia both seem to approve of this decision. I fall into Clara's couch, immediately relieved. 'What am I to do with her?'

'You wouldn't welcome my answer,' says Clara.

'True. You think I should have told her to go back to her parents.'

'It isn't my business to say.' Clara offers me her own tea-cup. I accept it. 'I intend to marry her,' I say, 'when we get to Paris. As a wife, she will have more power, more self-respect. She'll begin to grow up in no time.'

Natalia and Clara exchange a look which is meaningless to me. 'My father wants me to marry again. Her father will be only too happy to let her marry me once he finds out what has happened. I'm worrying about nothing. She wants to come to the celebration tonight. I'll bring her.'

'That should relieve her boredom,' says Clara. 'I've heard Princess Poliakoff and Lady Cromach have decided to attend. And there are other guests. Some politicians. Some intellectuals. It will be a fine night. You might meet Dolly's fiancé, too.' Dolly is the most sweet-natured girl in the house and much in demand with older clients. She is by no means beautiful, with her long nose, large teeth and her frizz of dark hair, but she is good-hearted and genuinely interested in the doings of her gentlemen, spending hours chatting with them. One of these, a pleasant man by all accounts, the owner of a large furrier's business in Ladungsgasse, is determined to marry her as soon as she wishes to retire. It is a standing joke between them. They often discuss the bridal gown she will have, the church they favour, the places they will visit on their honeymoon. Dolly has taken to wearing her gentleman's engagement ring: an emerald. She will accept presents from nobody else and on Wednesdays and Sundays when he calls will always make sure she is available only to him. Natalia and Clara continue with their conversation. They are discussing a woman I have not met. The mother had been supporting her drug-addicted daughter, I gather, for some years, paying for her opium and morphine, but her daughter had become homeless and needed work. Against her normal caution, and because the daughter was known to her, Frau Schmetterling had agreed she could work at Rosenstrasse for a few weeks until she saved the fare to go to relatives in Prague. 'Frau

119

Schmetterling is so innocent in some ways,' says Natalia. 'She was surprised at the demand when it became known that a mother and daughter were working in the same house. She could not believe so many of her customers would insist on having the two women in the same bed at the same time! She was very glad when what's-her-name went on to Prague.' Clara takes her empty tea-cup from me. 'She's a funny little woman. Quite prudish sometimes, eh? What do you think, Ricky? You've known her longer than any of us really.'

'She's the mother I never had,' I say lightly. 'I love her. She worries about me so much!'

'Oh, I think we all do,' says Clara. She seems to be making some sort of joke, so I smile.

'I hear that General von Landoff will be here tonight,' says Natalia. 'Madame has decided to treat with the military for once. She's making a big concession, eh?'

'A prudent one at this time,' I suggest. 'She would rather have one general invading Rosenstrasse than a regiment of privates. War can make politicians of us all.'

'We are expert politicians here,' insists Clara with a smile, 'every one of us. If Frau Schmetterling had been in charge, there would have been no War to begin with!'

Natalia is weighing a piece of her lace collar in her small palm. 'It's pretty material,' she says, 'isn't it? That very fine cotton which sometimes I prefer to silk. Silk is too much like skin. There is no contrast. Shall I go on telling you what the Mayor asked me to do?'

'I'd love to hear,' I say, settling back in Clara's cushions. 'You old eunuch,' says Clara affectionately. 'I sometimes think you'd rather gossip than fuck!' Natalia begins a rather ordinary tale about the Mayor's make-believe, his penchant for imitating farmyard animals. I learn more, too, about Caroline Vacarescu. Clara says she deliberately pursues and conquers the wives of famous men. 'It used to be her speciality. Her seductions became an inextricable mixture of business and pleasure. Her mistresses were often grateful for the opportunities for dalliance without much risk of scandal and they

120

were party to secrets which proved useful to Caroline in her other activities. They say she's probably a millionairess. The truth is she's probably spent everything. Caroline Vacarescu's extravagances have taken on the nature of an art; her raw materials are other people's money (or, at a pinch, credit) and her canvas is the fashionable world. Her clothes are the most expensive, her houses the most richly furnished and her presents to her protectors (who, of course, supplied her with the means to make the purchases in the first place) are generous. But this affair with Mueller was more serious, I think. His death has affected her quite badly. She's desperate to get back to Buda-Pesht. She's asking everybody. If anyone can do it, Caroline can.' I take my leave of the ladies and return to my Alice to announce she can go to the ball tonight. She hugs me and kisses me as if I am a favourite uncle. We fall into bed together and once again the dream comes alive.

Papadakis seems to be ill. Perhaps he weakens as I grow stronger. 'As soon as this is finished I shall be getting up,' I tell him. 'And we'll travel. We'll go to Venice first and then Vienna, or perhaps Paris. What do you think?' He is a mangy old spaniel. He looks at me and wheezes. 'You must be careful,' I say. 'You aren't getting any younger. What was the name of that woman who worked for you in London? The one I slept with?' He frowns. 'Sonia, wasn't it?' I say. 'She was Jewish, I think. She used to sit in that little basement flat of hers in Bloomsbury and curse you. Then we'd go to the British Museum in the twilight, just before it closed. I can smell the leaves around our ankles. She made you seem far more interesting than you turned out to be. She was obsessed by Egypt, I remember. By the Book of the Dead. What's happened to your daughter? You haven't had a letter in a year. Two years. She has forgotten her Papa.' Papadakis has brought an uncorked bottle of Niersteiner and a glass. He puts it on the table beside the bed. 'Tell me when you need more,' he says. 'What? Is it poisoned? Or do you hope I'll drink myself into silence? Your daughter. Isn't she divorced yet, from that foolish Frenchman? Or are you a grandfather, do you think? Are you a grandfather? There is still time to accept the responsibilities of a parent. I am not going to be on your hands much longer.' He pours some of the wine into the glass. 'Think what you like,' he says. 'Do what you like. Say what you like. It's good wine. There are a few bottles left. Let me know when you want some more.' I sip the hock. It is perfect. I am in charge of myself again. 'Buy flowers when you're next in town,' I tell him. 'As many as possible. Deep reds and blues. Good, heavy scent. Whatever you can find. Spend what you need to spend. I'll have flowers instead of food. I am celebrating the death of an old friend and my own return to life. Did you ever really visit that doctor I recommended? That follower of Freud's?' He shakes his head: 'I have no time for psychoanalysis or any other fashionable remedies. My faith remains in Science. The rest is just quackery, no matter how it's dressed up.' He amuses me. '*Oh, what we owe to Vienna*!' I sing. I descend with Alexandra on my arm. I am dressed in perfect black and white, she in scarlet and gold, with diamonds, pearls, rubies, with black-rimmed eyes and gaudy cheeks, her age unguessable, her identity engulfed. She walks with back straight, her head lifted with arrogant cocaine. We reach the foyer and pause. From the salon comes Strauss and a swell of voices, smoke and the scents of fresh-cooked meat. Alice trembles with pleasure and I am my happiest. We have concocted our masquerade: She is to be the Countess Alice of Elsinore tonight, from Denmark, although her home is now in Florence. She is twenty-three and my cousin. The lie is not meant to convince, merely to confuse the curious. 'No one will recognise me,' she says. 'Friends of my father or my brother know me only as a little girl in sailor-blouses.' I am feeling so euphoric that I believe I might even welcome a scene in which her father, for instance, was present. We are through the doors now and into the plush and velvet, the crystal and marble, of the salon. The place is alive with potential danger: journalists and several of the great scandal-mongers of Mirenburg, including Herbert Block the song-writer and Voorman the painter. Voorman is the only real problem, but he has no memory of her as the same creature he pretended to court at The Amoral Jew. He kisses her hand as he is introduced and she listens with some merriment as he suggests, again, that she is the goddess he has always imagined he will one day paint. A young Deputy, Baron Karsovin, her distant cousin, suggests as he wrinkles his pink brow beneath an already balding head, that they must have met before, 'perhaps in Venice', but he is anxious to return to his discussion of the Prince of Wales, Mrs Keppel and French foreign policy. And an old gentleman, wearing all his orders on his coat, says he believes he knew Alice's mother. 'Indeed he did,' she whispers. 'He was her lover four or five years ago and used to bribe me with chocolates from Schmidt's. He bribed Father with secrets of the Bourse and paid for our new house as a result!' The General is already here, back to the fireplace and looking so brave he might be facing a firing squad. I almost expect someone to blindfold him. He is very tall and thin, with blue veins in his long neck and white whiskers a little yellow about the lips and chin. His hair is quite long. He wears outdated evening-dress, standing with his hands behind him under his frock-coat and talking to Frau Schmetterling (in unusual off-the-shoulder royal blue and silver with a small bustle) and Caroline Vacarescu whose reputation, I suspect, he knows, for he is wary as well as reassuring, though she has succeeded in flattering him. Alice and I are introduced.

'Is there no chance of getting up a group of those who wish to leave?' asks Caroline, all sweet perfume and vulnerable, whispering russet flounces. 'If only we could reach the mountains, say. Under a white flag. There must be some sort of communication between the two sides. Some understanding that the civilized world would be scandalised when it found out how decent people were being treated.'

'But my dear lady, there is absolutely no danger to you here,' says the General. 'Holzhammer has used up all his ammunition. And the bombardment, you must have noticed, was concentrated entirely on the centre of the city. You are far safer in Mirenburg. There are bandits abroad in the country areas. Deserters. Disaffected peasants. You can imagine.'

'Are we to understand that no permits will be issued at all?' I say.

'No chance whatsoever, at present.' The General speaks as if he imparts the best news in the world. 'Holzhammer can scarcely hold out another week with all the desertions. Then – a quick counter-attack, with or without Berlin's support – then it will be over. We are biding our time. It is a question of choosing the moment.'

'So our losses have not been as great as they say?' says Caroline almost waspishly.

'Our losses, dear lady, have been minimal. Austria is going to regret her involvement in what is, after all, little more than a domestic squabble.' Caroline darts me a look, as if she hopes for an ally, but I am helpless. With a little nasal sigh, like a lioness who has made too short a charge and has seen her prey escape, she stalks off in search of other game. Clara greets us. She has discarded her usual tailor-mades and is wearing a gold dress, her hair in a Pompadour. She looks at least five years younger and is arm in arm with a rather drunk Rakanaspya who wears a dove-grey suit a little too large for him, evidently borrowed. He speaks so elliptically to the General, in such thick French, that nobody understands him. 'You have nothing to fear,' says von Landoff, and nods, as if to a simpleton. 'Another week or less and you may go home.' Rakanaspya, with one eye on Frau Schmetterling, lapses into the security of Russian, plainly saying all he wishes to say in that language and so releasing his feelings without giving much offence to his hostess. Clara says: 'Good evening to you both. You look stunning. A perfect match,' and she bears against Rakanaspya with her shoulder to steer him off towards the middle of the room where Block enjoys the flattery of the ladies and Stefanik drones moodily on the subject of flight. Princess Poliakoff makes her entrance. She is in black tulle and pearls, true to form, while her lover is a swan in fold upon fold of Doucet lace, approaching as if she has just landed on water and is coasting towards the shore. Her short curly hair has a torque

124

around it bearing two pale mauve ostrich feathers which match her fan. She seems to wear no make-up but is delicately English in her healthy colouring. Alice wants to know who she is and when I tell her she whispers: 'Let's talk to them. They seem far more interesting.' Occasionally, by a less-than-careful movement she betrays her youth. We make our way to the Lesbian couple. Everyone is introduced. 'We have seen nothing of you,' I say. 'You snub us indiscriminately!'

'I haven't been well,' says the Princess. 'And Diana has been a saint. Also, of course, she has to look for material.' Lady Cromach takes a testy interest in her fan, then offers me one of her soft, sardonic stares and says in that insinuating voice: 'And how is your health, Herr von Bek?'

'Excellent, as usual, Lady Cromach. Thank you. Are your articles about the War already entertaining the readers of the *Gaulois* and the *News*?'

'The telegraph is down. And the carrier pigeons are unreliable. I have no idea. For a while I thought I was bribing a little man in the military despatch office, but he was dismissed a few days ago. I fear my work will be retrospective when it appears, and nobody is overly interested in the fate of Mirenburg. Are they?' She seems to want to know. 'I content myself with doing atmosphere-pieces for the monthlies. I keep busy. What a charming brooch, my dear.' She peers towards Alice's breasts. 'You say that you are a guest here, too?' Princess Poliakoff looks distracted and jealous. She puts one of those elongated fingers to her mouth, then withdraws it carefully to her side. 'How's the minstrel, Ricky?'

'Singing as sweetly as ever,' I say. 'And teaching me to play the banjo.' I'm surprised she still believes me. She pulls her companion away from us. 'You have a lovely cousin,' says Lady Cromach; she winks at me behind the Princess's back. I find her extremely attractive. I believe she is thoroughly intrigued by me. Alice fumes. 'What an awful witch!'

'Lady Diana?'

'Of course not.' She is on my arm again. We move towards the buffet. 'It's much more ordinary than I expected. I'd imagined it – well – Oriental. Decadent. It's almost like one of Mother's Evenings.'

'Except that most of the women are whores and all the men are lechers.' I hand her some cold salmon.

'Then it's exactly like one of Mother's Evenings.' She laughs. I have not for a long time known her so carelessly cheerful. I love her. It is such a relief to feel that things are normal again. 'You look very handsome tonight,' she says. 'As you always used to look. I'm glad you seem happy, Ricky.'

'I'm happy that you're happy. It is so easy, my little one, to make you happy.' I am full of tenderness for her.

'I'm happy because you've taken me seriously and are treating me – I don't know – as an equal. I'm far older than my age. People have often said so.'

You will always be my own sweet little girl, Alice. My lascivious child, my dreaming daughter-wife. I want the soft, sudden flesh, the sweet dunes, the little caves. The music of your shouts and your pleasure. I bite your neck, your throat, your shoulder. I will do whatever you want. I will say and become whatever you want, to keep you as I want you to be. This turn in her conversation begins to depress me. I ask her whom she would like to meet next. 'That's Van Geest, the banker, with Thérèse. And that, of course, is Count Belozerski. Our Lesbians are talking to Wilke, the jewel-thief. Would you like to meet him. He's usually very grave and of course doesn't talk much about his work.' The salon is growing noisier, a trifle more boisterous. The General moves away from the fireplace beaming like a baby with Natalia on one arm and Aimée on the other, to sample the buffet. He is here, after all, to forget the War. There is champagne everywhere. The corks are a cannonade which mocks recent events. We banish Holzhammer and the doors are rolled back before we can approach the Russian novelist; the little ballroom is revealed where, on a curtained dais amongst potted palms, sits an all-woman orchestra. 'How terrible,' says the Princess as she sweeps past with her friend, 'that we should look to Vienna for our gaiety when she is presently causing us so much pain.' And she and her lover boldly begin the dancing, to the applause of the others, who gradually begin to join them on the floor: by Clara and a scowling Stefanik, watching his feet and hers, Frau Schmetterling and the courteous Belozerski, by Alice and myself. 'Ta ta ta, ta ta tum,' shouts General von Landoff, spinning with Natalia. It is as if we are suddenly all much drunker. The real world is whirling silk and painted flesh, wine and perfume and flowers. Soon I am standing back and laughing as Clara dances with Poliakoff and Alice with Lady Diana. Skirts are lifted, ties are loosened, petticoats bounce in the warmth of the chandeliers. The orchestra is made up chiefly of middle-aged women, a little shabbily dressed, and respectable, but there are three young girls, all dark-complexioned and possibly sisters. It is the cellist who attracts my attention. She is as plump as the others but considerably prettier and playing with evident passion, her legs spread to accommodate her instrument, and her whole body swaying as she plies her bow, her eyes as rapt as a woman's in the throes of love-making. Belozerski is talking to Natalia. 'I had decided to visit the estate of a favourite old relative in the Ukraine,' he says. 'I'd spent most of my boyhood summers there but this was the first time I'd gone in winter. Earlier that year I received a pardon from St Petersburg so was no longer an exile, but by then had established a home in Paris and felt no great wish to uproot myself. However, this visit was as much to confirm my pardon as to satisfy curiosity about cousins and aunts and uncles, whom I had not seen in fifteen years. Most of the journey from the railway station was by troika, for it was snowing. I had forgotten how wide the steppe was. The snow was like a white ocean and trees stuck out over the horizon like the masts of wrecks. My wife, who is French, chose to remain behind so I was alone save for the old peasant who drove the troika. We were about half-way to the estate when memory suddenly came back. I have never experienced the like. It was a dream: I seemed to drown in recollections which were as vivid as the original events. I relived those summers, even as the sleigh moved rapidly over the snow, so by the time I arrived I was actually shocked to notice it was winter. The poignancy of that experience, my dear Natalia, is indescribable. It left me rather depressed. I mourned for lost opportunities and deeply regretted the ill-considered romanticism which had led me to take up the cause of nationalism. Yet I know my life has been worthwhile and far more interesting in Paris than if I had remained in the Kiev gubernia where I was born.' He smiles wistfully. She smiles back in some astonishment, then turns to pour him another glass of champagne. Captain Mackenzie nods to me, on his way to speak to Count Stefanik. The Scotsman's eye contains a kind of alert sweetness at odds with his battered and drug-ruined features. Alice and I join him. A scar causes his lip to curl in a sort of grin and his soft German, pronounced with a distinctive Scottish accent, is often impossible to understand. When one of us attempts English, however, it becomes plain that he is even less comprehensible in that language. He speaks enthusiastically with Rudolph Stefanik on the subject of balloons. He has seen them used for scouting, he says, and he has heard they had also been employed in the bombardment of Paris thirty years ago, although the Prussians had of course denied they had ever done anything so inhuman. He laughs. 'Is Holzhammer denying the destruction of Mirenburg, I wonder? They are planning to dam up the river, apparently, and set it in a new course, so that we shall have no fresh water. Have you heard anything about that, von Bek?' I have not. 'I receive virtually no real news, captain. All we get here are fantastic rumours and a little gossip. We are a desert island. But you must be privy to a hundred revelations a night!'

'I make it my business to hear nothing.' He is almost prim. 'It is necessary, I believe, to the rules of my particular trade. Confessors and the proprietors of opium-dens.' He laughs. 'We have something in common with lawyers, too.'

'And doctors,' says Alice.

Captain Mackenzie nods slowly. 'And doctors, aye.'

Rudolph Stefanik moves his body in his clothes as if he is about to burst them and reveal a pair of wings. 'It would make good sense,' he says. 'If they were to dam the river. This whole campaign has been unprofessional. It causes needless suffering, both to troops and to civilians. The Austrians, of course, can be hopeless. I understood Holzhammer was trained in Prussia.'

'Most of the Mirenburg officers received their schooling there,' I tell him. 'But they have had no practical experience. And the conditions are unusual, you will admit. Do you believe that Holzhammer has had as many desertions as they say?'

'I was approached to find out. They wanted me to inflate the balloon and take her up on a fixed mooring. I refused. One shot would destroy my vessel – and me, for that matter. They are now talking of manufacturing their own airships. I said I would willingly give them advice.' Stefanik smiles suddenly down on Alice. 'As soon as this affair is settled I shall be only too pleased to take a pretty passenger into the sky and show her the world an angel sees.' Her eyes are bright as they meet his. 'Oh, I am not innocent enough, Count, to be able to see what an angel sees.'

'But you are able to tempt as the devil tempted;' I tell him, leading her away. He laughs. Voorman and Rakanaspya are deep in drunken conversation. Voorman is entertained by Rakanaspya's seriousness. 'The lure of this putrid sweetness!' he exclaims. 'How can you resist it?'

'It is the lure of disease, of dissolution, of death – the yearning to absolve oneself of all political and moral responsibility,' says the Russian earnestly. 'It is often attractive to those who have had the strictest of upbringings, who display the greatest guilt about themselves and how they should conduct their behaviour in society. They are, indeed, guilty. Guilty of stealing from the poor. Guilty of creating wars and famines. They are responsible for murder and they come here to find a kind of death, a release, a punishment . . . ' He is a little incoherent. 'They are the fathers of corruption!' he concludes unsteadily.

Voorman giggles and turns to one of the floral displays. 'Lilies, lilies, lilies! I shall be a father to the lilies. I shall tend

129

them as my own children. And when they die I shall bury them with proper ceremony and raise a stone to them and put more lilies upon it so that the scent of the living shall mingle with the smell of the dead. I know where my responsibilities lie. It is to the lilies!'

Rakanaspya appeals to us, but we are laughing too heartily at Voorman. The Russian puts his back against a pillar and pretends to listen to the orchestra as it plays a sort of gypsy dance. The General joins us, with Frau Schmetterling on his arm. His face is red; not wishing to show he is in any way exhausted he controls his breathing. Frau Schmetterling is pleased; she seems to have extracted some sort of promise from him. 'I will put young Captain Mencken in charge of the matter.' He hands her a glass of champagne. He bows to Caroline Vacarescu, who continues to court him. Caroline is talking first to Clara and then, as the two women approach closer, to Alice and myself. She is quite drunk. 'It was the chemistry between us,' she says, 'I could not help myself. I cannot explain. And yet it was failing. I know he felt this loss. The intensity was gone and without it one becomes very easily bored.' She seems to be referring to Mueller. Clara listens patiently. 'We tried to recapture passion which overpowers all constraint, all conscience, but it became hollow. Yet we were linked to each other, by virtue of what we had done to one another and to friends and strangers.' Caroline looks at me suddenly, as if to test my response. 'We were partners in crime. All I could do was watch as he seduced the others who would eventually all become linked to us. That was how we worked, how we affirmed the validity of our habits of life, and justified them. Was that so wrong? Is one reality any better than another?'

Rakanaspya is the only person with an answer. 'One is sane,' he says, 'the other reality you describe is not. Such powerful Romanticism eventually destroys its proponents. It is always the case. And the process of destruction is neither Romantic nor bearable. It is merely sordid. Save yourself, if you can, while you have the chance. Never link your star to a man such as Mueller again.'

She becomes uncharacteristically sentimental. 'You can never understand what someone like Mueller has. He radiated authority. He snapped his fingers at convention. He made fools of them all.'

'And now he is dead,' says Clara softly, trying to distract Caroline.

Voorman watches cynically as they move back through the salon. 'I heard Fraulein Vacarescu is only at liberty now because Mueller was caught through information she supplied. Perhaps she found her own way of freeing herself from that "chemistry".'

'Somewhat radically.' I do not believe him. Caroline seemed genuinely distressed by Mueller's fate. I catch sight of a man I have often seen here in the evenings and whom I continue to confuse with the current Mayor. He is in fact the ex-Mayor of Mirenburg. He reels about the dance-floor in a kind of vulgar parody of the polka. Herr Kralek's tie is lost. He has spilled food down his shirt-front. Dolly, alone, will dance with him. Almost every night he comes to visit the girls, to drink plum brandy and eat cream-cakes until dawn, when he returns to his wife, to make love to her, we have heard, until he is inevitably sick. His huge red neck ripples. His face is a featureless mass of purple. He usually displays resentment and self-pity in all his tiniest gestures: demands respectful attention and receives instead the amiable kindness of the girls, which he mistakes for fear. He describes himself as an honest burgher – or rather he describes his opinions as those of an honest burgher: 'Your honest burgher believes the Jews should all be expelled from the city proper,' he will say. 'Your honest burgher isn't happy with the idea of increased taxation.' I remember one naive visitor asking him why, since he was so evidently the voice of the respectable citizens of Mirenburg, they had signed a petition to have him removed from office. He replied seriously that most of the signatures had been forgeries, the petition had been a plot of Zionist elements afraid of his position of power. 'Where I could no longer exercise my ever-

131

watchful eye.' He stumbles now and falls to the floor. Dolly attempts to help him up. Dolly's fiancé is not here. Voorman tells Alice about another guest, a small, middle-aged journalist on the far side of the room. 'He awoke in the hospital, still convinced he was at Frau Schmetterling's, and immediately ordered one of the sisters to remove her underwear. She had obeyed with alacrity. It was four days before it dawned on him he had somehow been transferred from the brothel. The sister had no wish for him to leave. Being responsible to her superior to report his condition, she continued to insist on his poor rate of recovery. She kept him for another week until one of her colleagues demanded a share of the patient and was refused. The sister was reported and dismissed on the spot. She accompanied him back to the brothel where she stayed for a while as medical advisor to the girls.' Alice is disbelieving. Voorman insists he is telling the absolute truth. The General confides to Frau Schmetterling, also on a medical matter: 'My physician had the nerve to suggest mercury treatment, which means he thinks I have syphilis. But until the fool comes out with it directly and tells me I have the disease I shall carry on as I have always carried on. The responsibility is his, not mine.'

'You have put the question to him?' asks Frau Schmetterling.

'In as many words.'

'But not directly?'

'Has he been direct with me, madam?'

The air is growing warm. It is difficult to breath. We move closer to the door. Wilke, perhaps the most dignified person here, with a look of self-possessed humility, is talking to Clara about Amsterdam, which they both know. He seems untroubled by the noise and laughter which surrounds him. His large hands move in a circle as he describes a certain district of the city and asks her, with his usual gravity, how long it is since she was there. 'Doesn't he look a marvellous brute,' murmurs Alice as we go by. 'Such a man, compared to the rest of these!' I pretend to be insulted. 'Perhaps I should introduce you?' She gives me a look of mock-irritation: 'Oh, don't be silly. Someone like that has no real interest in women.

132

He is either friends with them, or takes them quickly and leaves, or is faithful to his wife, if he has one. That's obvious to me, even at my age!' How many of these observations has she received from her mother?

I am again unsure why Alice should find me attractive. Is it a certain weakness which makes me more easily controlled, or less inclined to go my own way when it suits me? I have no idea. I look around at the crowded salon. How could I have thought that this was normality? We are all crazed. We are all in Hell. I stare at every face. There are only two women here I have not fucked. One of them is Frau Schmetterling herself. The other is Lady Cromach. She and Princess Poliakoff also stand near the door. Lady Cromach chews on an olive. 'Frau Schmetterling tells me that you write, Herr von Bek. Do you work for the Berlin journals?' I shake my head. 'I am a dilettante, Lady Cromach. I do not know enough about life to be able to write with any authority, and I am, moreover, horribly lazy.'

'Is that why you prefer to stay in a place like this when you travel?'

Princess Poliakoff snorts, saying something coarse to Alice who begins to giggle. I continue to speak to the English woman. 'There are few houses as elegant as this and few which have such excellent ladies. I'm sure you know that most whores have a dislike of men and a crude sort of self-involvement which makes them very dull. How can one possibly be aroused very often or very satisfactorily by a dull woman?'

'I find men much duller than most women,' she says.

'I am inclined to agree with you. And the dullest of all men are German, eh?'

'They have their points. What they lack in imagination they make up for in cleanliness. I nearly married one, when I was a girl. And at least they are not as boring as Frenchmen, who seem to believe their attractiveness is in direct proportion to their vanity. I blame their mothers. And Germany is so modern! Though, as you suggest, a little on the tame side. When were you last in Berlin?'

133

'Several years ago. My family is content for me to travel.'

'An embarrassment of niggers, eh?'

'Quite so.'

Princess Poliakoff, her hands on Alice, tells my girl a story she heard about the de Polignac circle (she had a brief affair with de Polignac which ended with neither woman speaking to the other for over a year) and some female composer in love with the Singer, as she says, not the Salon. She continues on this theme of gossip by suggesting that there are now so many homosexuals of both kinds in Paris the city will be 'quite depopulated in another quarter-of-a-century'. She speaks to Alice as if she, the Princess, has perfectly conventional sexual preferances. Homosexuals are referred to as 'they'. I find her wit without much substance and let her continue to entertain Alice, who is thirsty for scandal.

I chat to Lady Cromach until we are joined by Clara. The women are friendly. This is a relief to me, though I do not know why. The five of us drift towards the dais to listen to the orchestra playing reasonable Chopin. The more athletic dancers have subsided. 'It seemed to me earlier, this evening,' Clara links her arm in mine, 'that we were all dead; that Mirenburg was destroyed and that we were ghosts dancing in the ruins. You're looking tired, Ricky. Would you care to borrow my little box. It might revive you.' I thank her, but refuse. 'I am trying to restore my sense of perspective, Rose, dear.' She finds this funny. 'You have improved your relations with the child.'

'We have found a balance, I think. I was restraining her too much. And please don't call her that, Clara. She is more grown-up than she seems.' Clara draws in her lips for a second. I wonder how I have angered her. 'I apologise,' she says. 'However, my offer remains, if you need a restorative.' She begins to talk to Lady Cromach. She is particularly fascinated by the Derby and whether the Prince of Wales's horses are always allowed to win. These girls. Their soft bodies brush against me; they smell so wonderful. They have all been mine, most of them in the space of a few days. And they have been

Alice's. I hesitate in my rapture. My mood alters radically. We are in danger of losing what is individual to us. Alice has the over-animated, slightly guarded look she reserves for people who make her nervous. Princess Poliakoff holds her arm, hugs her shoulders, whispers in her ear and Alice laughs. Lady Cromach and Clara move to one side to continue their conversation. But I am in no mood to rescue Alice yet, so I take Natalia onto the dance-floor for a mazurka. We dance well together. It is strange, however, how trapped I feel here sometimes; I felt more secure in Rosenstrasse when I was not a resident. Natalia laughs and lifts in my arms like a happy gibbon.

When I return to my ladies I discover that Diana Cromach has rescued Alice. They are talking seriously. Alice nods a great deal and smiles at the older woman. Lady Cromach is deliberately setting out to charm her. I relish the notion of an amorous liaison between them. Alice catches my eye. We exchange signals. If it happens I shall not mind at all: it is the best route through to Lady Cromach, who excites my imagination and my lust. I pause beside them for a few moments; then, making my own decision, I leave them to it. I chat to Block, who complains it will be 'months before I can visit Vienna again'. At about two o'clock in the morning I am approached by a furious Princess Poliakoff who wants to know if I have seen Diana Cromach and 'that disgusting little cousin of yours'.

They have escaped the salon. I feel a thrill of curious pleasure, deny all knowledge, and pretend to be utterly disconcerted.

I spend the night in Clara's bed, fucking with a lusty carelessness I have not experienced for a year. It is so easy to summon the recollection of that delicious ambience, knowing my Alice and her beautiful English writer were enjoying each other to the full; that Princess Poliakoff fumed alone, while I relaxed in the arms of a tolerant Rose. I fall back on my pillows to smoke a cigarette, to relive the wonderful happiness I knew. How can I possibly relish it so much when I completely failed to anticipate the disaster to follow? Perhaps that night was a kind of apotheosis; my last true moment of happiness. The gladioli which Papadakis brought are already beginning to discolour at the edges; the leaves have streaks of brownish yellow in them, yet they are still beautiful in their pinks and delicate oranges, their blues and mauves and their deep scarlet. The carnations give off the richest scent. I lie here, resting from heady sensations. I have some pain, mostly in my groin but also, strangely, in my nipples, and my back hurts; but this is nothing more than old age. I had once hoped medical science would progress so swiftly I might expect to outlive the twentieth century, which I perceive as an insane intermediary period between one rational age and another; the Great War is over, but they fight in Spain. And Russia must soon begin another conflict; it is almost her certain destiny. One would need money for such medicine, even if it existed, and my capital shrinks; I have even less than Papadakis fears. My will, when I die, shall reveal a pittance and the name of the chief beneficiary will be unknown to anyone. I doubt that she still lives. Mirenburg has succeeded, for the moment, in restoring her balance. Clara and I take an early-morning stroll. I am anxious to demonstrate my approval of Alice and Lady Cromach and have no intention of seeking them out, at least until lunch-time. I can be certain Princess Poliakoff will make some kind of scene and it would be best for me if I were not involved. 'Let the vixen fight it out amongst themselves,' I think. In heavy coats (mine is borrowed) Clara and I stand beside the river. A thin pillar of steam comes from somewhere on the other side. A factory in the Moravia sounds its siren; cans clank as a milkman's wagon turns the corner, its wheels squeaking, the hooves of its horse plodding softly on the cobbles: the mingled smell of milk and a horse recently out of the stable brings a reminder of childhood safety. Then the milkman, crouched like a white hare on the high seat, gives voice: 'Fresh milk!' and his bell begins to clang. We stop him and buy a cup, which we share. It is warm and soothing. 'There must still be cows somewhere,' says Rose. Neither of us

136

has any desire to return to the brothel. 'Where now, your Lordship?' We go towards the ornamental lake in the Botanical Gardens. Our breath creates clouds around our heads, like ectoplasm. The Gardens are as neatly kept as they ever were, with no evidence of damage, although for some reason soldiers guard the great hothouses. They salute us as we pass. We walk along the gravelled main avenue, between marble statues of nameless heroes, until we reach the lake, which is flanked by willows, poplars and cypresses. There is a brownish scum on the surface. Water-birds make trails in it as they swim listlessly about, occasionally diving into the purer water beneath. Clara sniffs. 'It's becoming stagnant,' she remarks. 'It looks so foul and smells so good to me. Why should it remind me of being a little girl?' We stroll through the artificial peace. On the other side of the Gardens we enter Baudessinstrasse. Rather than mount the Mladota Steps we take winding Uhrmacherstrasse, with its shops and bourgeois houses; the street progresses slowly up the hill, following the curve of old roads which led to Castle and Cathedral when Mirenburg was young. There is a clapping noise. I mistake it at first for horses; then down the street towards us at a rapid trot come soldiers with shouldered rifles. The troop surrounds a collection of civilians wearing either a defeated or a defiant air. Not a few are hatless, as if they have been seized from their beds or captured while attempting flight. 'Who are your prisoners?' I call to the troubled young captain leading the party. 'Looters and profiteers,' he says curtly. The majority look ordinary enough to me: chiefly working-class and lower middle-class people from many walks of life. 'They are taking this very seriously,' says Clara. She indicates one of the recently-issued notices pinned to a tree. It threatens punishments and offers rewards and is signed by General von Landoff, 'Military Governor of Mirenburg for the Duration of Hostilities'. Up beyond the Hussite Square we come upon ruins. 'Oh,' says Rose, 'that's where my milliner used to live. I hope she's not hurt.' Scaffolding is already erected around some of the wounded buildings and workmen attempt to make good the damage done by Holzhammer's cannon. 'Do you want to find out?' I ask her. We visit some local shops, learning that Frau Schwartz has already left the city, to stay with relatives in Tarndoff. We emerge from a little toy-shop in time to see an army band go by, all bugles and fifes, pompous in blue and red, in gold and silver braid. The soldiers are closely followed by about forty young men in badly-fitting uniforms wobbling on bicycles. I have read about them. They are the newly-formed 'bicycle volunteers'. The cycling-clubs of Mirenburg have joined up *en masse*. Things begin to take on a comfortably comic aspect. I for one am rather happy that all motor vehicles have been requisitioned for military use. The streets are far quieter than usual. In the coffee-houses the students display a new patriotism and drink to the death of Franz-Josef, speak of an alliance with the 'Empire of the Slavs' and go off to apply for commissions in the army. Exiles enjoy a greater sense of freedom since the Austrian secret policemen have been arrested. Schemes for defence, counter-attack and means of involving the Great Powers in the Wäldenstein Question are noisily discussed at length. The Bourse continues to pretend it is trading. Shops have re-opened everywhere. Barricades have been removed, shutters thrown back. Fancy foods have been bought by the ton from grocers whose shelves are virtually empty; nothing can be replaced. Warehouses have been stripped. Boats on the river rock in silent moorings; there is stillness in the market-places and people bargain, when they bargain, in secretive voices. The railway stations are deserted. Empty trains stand at empty platforms and a few hopeful creatures read notices of cancellations or rap hopelessly on the shutters of ticket-offices. Pigeons and starlings are noisy in the great, hollow roofs; the dusty locomotives are covered with bird-droppings. Railway workers lean against the trains, smoking and chatting, adjusting useless watches. Mirenburg's turrets and gables have turned pale in the winter light; she is shocked and vague, like a cripple not yet come to terms with the loss of a limb. The Kasimirsky Palace is heavily-guarded. Voices of soldiers are loud in the air. Guns are wheeled up.

Walls are continuously fortified. People stand in small crowds near the Central Post Office, hoping to learn that the telegraph has been restored. Everywhere officers move groups from place to place, dissipate gatherings, oversee requisitioned carts of food and raw materials, or stop individuals and inspect their new identity cards. Alice is now officially a Danish national. I have already explained to her how useful this will be in disguising our trail to Paris. At times of crisis it is easier to change one's name and background than it is to stroll uninterrupted in a park. Detachments of cavalry move slowly through Little Bohemia to discourage anti-Semitic gangs who have already tried to burn the Great Synagogue. Mirenburg is no Warsaw or Odessa and it would be a smirch on her honour if she tolerated such uncivilised behaviour. This official protection, of course, enables citizens sympathetic to Holzhammer to claim that Prince Badehoff-Krasny supports the interests of the financiers and foreign bankers. 'There will be no scapegoats,' General von Landoff has promised. 'Only those guilty of profiting from the general misery will be punished.' The army issues orders on every aspect of daily life, from hygiene to the price of fish. 'The poor have never been so protected,' observes Clara. 'Is this Socialism?' We pass the Liverpool. It has been repaired. It might never have been damaged. 'By next spring,' I say, 'Mirenburg will be gayer and lovelier than ever. Look how wonderfully Paris recovered. The Prussians and the Communards between them should be praised. We'll scarcely remember any of this.' I was not born, of course, in '71, but I visited the city in '86, when I was fourteen, and was impressed by its beauty, though I prefer the denser texture of Mirenburg.

Clara insists we visit the Art Museum 'to look at the Fragonards.' But half the museum is closed and the pictures are being crated. We glimpse a few Impressionists before we are asked to leave. I am infected, however, by Clara's enthusiasm. She is familiar with so many of the names. I have never known a whore like her. Few women have a genuine relish for Art. 'You could teach me so much,' I say. 'You are the best governess in the world.' Appreciating the *double-entendre* she laughs heartily as we descend the steps. 'Let's have lunch out.' I am perfectly willing to agree. Half the dishes listed on the Restaurant Prunier's menu are 'unavailable'. Soups and sauces seem thinner than usual. We make the best of it, congratulating ourselves on our good fortune in being fed by Frau Schmetterling and her cook. 'You seem confident today,' Clara declares as we leave the restaurant. 'Even happy. Like a little boy on holiday from school. Aren't you worried about your Alice? Don't you anticipate some sort of awful scene?' I shake my head. 'I have designs on Lady Cromach myself. Alice will be only too willing to share her new pleasure with me. She owes me that.'

'And Lady Cromach? What will she say?'

'Lady Cromach finds me attractive. I suspect Alice is her passport to me.'

Clara shakes her head. 'You people are such predators! I am amazed by you. It must be a habit of mind, and perhaps of money. Do you inherit it, I wonder?'

'I am in love, Clara. There are different expressions of love. You can accept that, can't you? What a whore will do for her pimp, I will do for Alice and Alice for me. It is the noblest kind of self-sacrifice, and brings pleasure to so many!'

'I'm not sure,' she says, 'that your kind of love is within even my experience.' She pats my arm to show she is not condemning me. 'We had better get back.'

As we arrive on the steps of Rosenstrasse there is an old woman there, already ringing the bell. Clara knows her as Frau Czardak. She is withered to the colour of pemmican, yet her long double-jointed fingers are supple and flexible, for they turn cards all day. She is in great demand with the girls who, with so little emotional security in their lives, look to superstition to offer them an interpretation and analysis of the world. The abstract and the metaphysical are frequently preferred by prisoners of almost any kind, since it is usually the fear of ordinary reality which leads them to their condition in the first place. 'And how soon will the Germans come to our relief,

Frau Czardak?' asks Clara. 'Have you seen it in the cards?'

'In the wax. In the wax,' says the old woman cryptically as she proceeds ahead of us. She is greeted by Trudi who directs her to Frau Schmetterling's kitchen. Through the open doors of the salon we see porters still clearing up. Maids sweep and dust. Great baskets of used glasses are carried down. 'Mister' supervises it all with the grim eye of a well-trained guard-dog. He might even snap at my heels if I try to interfere with the ritual. He looks impassively at an approaching porter. The man drags a reluctant maid, apparently his wife, who has up to that point been dusting. 'She refuses to visit the dentist. Look!' The porter forces her jaws apart to reveal her blackened, broken teeth, while she glares up at him. 'Does any man – any human being – have to live with that? She disgusts me. She has the habits of a wild-beast.' Clara and I pause to enjoy this scene. He sees us and appeals to us. 'In bed, when I require my rights, she bites me – with those horrible fangs! She could poison me. I could die. So what's wrong with wanting to leave her if she won't improve herself? Am I to remain chained to a sub-human because in my youth I thought her habits cureable? I support her, don't I? I find her good jobs, too, like this one. But I don't have to live in the same house with her!' He turns back to 'Mister' who blinks once. 'Do I?' At this his wife snarls at him and wrenches herself away. He throws up his hands and looks to us again for sympathy. 'You're laughing at me. You don't care! But this is my life! This is my whole life. I don't believe I shall have another. I am desperate. I am married to a beast and therefore I receive no respect. It is not funny. It is a tragedy.' His wife hisses at him and tries to bite his arm. Unable to contain our laughter we move on towards the stairs to find Frau Schmetterling confronting us. 'Ricky, you must do something. Your girl and Lady Diana.' She drops her voice. 'They've locked themselves in your room. Princess Poliakoff has threatened everything from murder to the Law, and now she's in her room, storming about and breaking things. She had Renée with her last night. The poor child's black and blue. I've had to make it plain to Princess Poliakoff what I think.

You may stay, Ricky, but if your friend causes trouble, she must go. In any other circumstances you would all be out, immediately.' She looks frantic. 'I hate trouble. The ambience is so important. I expect people to behave like ladies and gentlemen. You've always been so good, Ricky. But this child!' She pauses, blocking our path up the stairs. 'Will you do something?'

'Princess Poliakoff is an hysterical trouble-maker, dear madame, as you yourself must know.'

'You're the man. You must sort it out.' She is firm. 'And before this evening, too,' she adds as we pass.

'What am I to do?' I say to Clara. 'Challenge Princess Poliakoff to a duel?'

'If you're to challenge anyone, it should be Lady Cromach,' Clara is weary of this.

I smile. 'Unfortunately, it is not Lady Cromach who apes the male. What a difficult situation, my darling Rose.'

'And one which your darling Rose will have nothing to do with,' she says. 'I am entirely on Frau Schmetterling's side. It is up to you to settle matters quickly and quietly. At times like these, Ricky, the atmosphere of the house is even more important. Your intrigues and squabbles could drive customers away.'

'I'll talk to Princess Poliakoff,' I promise. And I walk directly to the Lesbian's room at the end of the second landing.

Although it is cold, Princess Poliakoff has opened a window. The room is finished in a sort of Louis XIV style, very much at odds with her own taste. She stands shivering by the gilded fireplace wearing a full set of masculine evening dress. The hat is on the mantelpiece near her hand which rests there, holding a cigarette. Her hair has been pinned and flattened. There is an expression of suppressed agony on her aquiline face. She is genuinely distressed. I have never been impressed by her in this way before. She looks older than her forty or so years. She refuses to appeal to me. 'What a strange pair of cuckolds we make, Ricky.' Since I have acquiesed in this adventure, albeit silently, I cannot feel genuine sympathy –

that sympathy of echoed self-pity. 'It's very unexpected,' I say. Then, because it will suit me, I try to pretend anger. 'I thought you had your eye on her, but I never guessed . . . ' I cross to the window and look down into Rosenstrasse. It is already growing dark. An old woman with a dog on a lead walks slowly towards the archway on the opposite side of the street. 'Men never notice,' she says. Women will always say that. What they actually observe is that men frequently do not comment. I am relieved, at least, that she has failed to blame me for the business. I take advantage of her need to see me as a fellow sufferer. 'What are we to do about them?' she wants to know. I suggest that perhaps they will see reason. It can all be cleared up in a few minutes if we are careful to reduce the tension. She is horribly distressed. 'I love Diana deeply. But as for reason, I sometimes think the very word is meaningless to her.' This suggests she has already tried to persuade her lover to have nothing to do with Alice. 'She is a cruel and heartless woman. It's up to you – up to you, Ricky – to remove that little wanton from this house.' I tell her I have given the idea consideration, but there is nowhere to go. 'There is Stefanik's balloon,' she says. 'He's already offered to help Diana escape. You could use it instead.'

'It's an offer he makes to every woman he desires. It's neither a possibility nor a danger.'

'You didn't have a nigger at all, did you?' She knocks the hat, spasmodically, with her hand. 'Why were you lying to me?'

'Oh,' I shrug, 'for privacy.'

'Because you thought I'd try to take her away from you? There's an irony.' She fits another cigarette into her holder. Her hands continue to shake.

I frown, pretending to consider the problem.

'Well?' she says.

'I'll see if they'll speak to me. But you must be patient. I'll come back as soon as I can.'

'Please,' she says. 'This is unbearable. I'm suicidal.'

I leave her and go up to our rooms, knocking softly on the

door. 'It's me, Alex. Could you let me in? I'd like to change my clothes.' I keep my voice as light as I can. She – or more likely Lady Cromach – will be suspecting a ploy. Anything I say will seem like an excuse to them. Their curiosity or their tension or their high spirits are all that will decide them. There is some movement from within. Eventually Alexandra opens the door and I enter. She is wearing her Japanese kimono. She kisses me quickly and grins to involve me, to placate me. 'Have you been all right?' She smells of some new perfume. The door to the bedroom is closed. 'Yes, thanks,' I say. 'And you?'

'Wonderful.' She pushes at her messy hair. 'I'd have told you, only we couldn't ruin our chances. We had to act quickly. That witch has been hammering on the door for half the night and most of the morning. What a harpy, eh? Have you seen her?'

'She's calmed down.' I go directly to the bedroom and open the door. Lady Cromach is in bed. She looks offended, then flushes like a travelling salesmen caught with the farmer's daughter. 'Good afternoon, Lady Cromach. I'm sorry to disturb you. I thought, since lunch-time has come and gone . . . '.

She recovers herself. I can almost see her controlling her colour. She drops her head a little and looks up at me, half-smiling. 'Of course. We have been thoughtless.'

'Understandable, in the circumstances.' From the wardrobe I pick out a shirt and underclothes.

'You have been sailing under false colours.' She is not accusatory. 'How unkindly you misled the Princess. You know she loves proof of the most extravagantly unlikely gossip. Is she all right, do you know?'

I seat myself heavily on the bed and stare into her glowing face. 'She says she is suicidal. That she loves you. She seems very distracted.' The bed reeks of their love-making. I feel almost faint.

'She won't kill herself.' Lady Cromach settles back in my pillows. 'She'd be more likely to kill one of us. The Princess can't bear to be thwarted.'

144

'Neither can I.'

She puts a hand on mine. 'But you have not been. Have you?' The sheet falls away from her shoulders. She is lovely, like a young boy. 'Alice tells me you are a stranger to sexual jealousy.'

'I am becoming more familiar with it.'

She accepts the flattery. Alice enters to stand looking at us, like a melodrama child which has affected a reconciliation between its parents. She is almost smug. I laugh and ask her to light me a cigarette. She obeys with cheerful alacrity, placing an ashtray beside me. Lady Cromach's hand has not left mine. 'Are you trying to mollify me, Lady Cromach? Or do you plan to include me in this seduction?'

'You're straightforward,' she says.

'Perhaps it's the atmosphere of this place. Perhaps it is the fact that we may all soon be blown to bits.' I remove my jacket, then my waistcoat. Alice takes them from me. 'I'll bring some champagne,' she says. Lady Cromach's eyes have narrowed and her breathing has become rapid. A nerve twitches in her neck. 'Champagne,' she says. 'What else did the Princess have to tell you?'

'Very little.'

Alice returns with a tray of champagne and glasses. She puts the tray on the little bedside table and curls up beside Lady Cromach. 'She must have yelled herself hoarse!'

'I've promised to try to reason with you and then report back to her.' I accept the cold glass.

'And are you reasoning now?' Lady Cromach wants to know.

'In my own fashion. Or perhaps I'm bargaining.'

'You wish me to "give Alexandra up"?'

'You know I'm not so rigid. I have told her I will not object to her sleeping with other women, though I draw the line at other men. I'd like it understood, though, that my feelings must take priority with Alexandra.'

'That's surely up to Alexandra.' Lady Cromach raises an eyebrow at my girl.

145

Alice says in a small voice: 'I'll do what everyone thinks best.' Neither Lady Diana nor myself are even briefly convinced. 'I'm sure you will,' says Lady Cromach, fondling her head. 'Oh, well, I think it can all be arranged satisfactorily, Herr von Bek. This would not be the first time, eh?' We toast one another with our glasses.

Later I remark to Lady Cromach that she has one of the loveliest bodies I have known. It is like fucking a supple youth with a cunt. It is a rare pleasure. 'You are a pretty rare pleasure for me,' she responds sardonically. I get dressed. We have agreed I should pretend to Princess Poliakoff that I am persuading the women the affair is not possible. I will hint at my ability to blackmail one or both of them. But when I get to her rooms Princess Poliakoff has vanished. A maid at work on the stairs says she saw her go out half-an-hour ago. Downstairs, Trudi says the Princess left with a small hand-bag, in a cab. She did not say where she was going. Relieved at this, I return to my women. 'It's almost too good to be true.'

'She has her pride,' says Diana thoughtfully. 'But she also has a taste for revenge.'

I know. She is probably scheming vengeance in one of the empty hotels near the station. She is certainly not dead or planning to die. I clamber into bed. Later tonight I will sleep in Clara's room. In the morning we shall go to breakfast with Alice and Diana. There will be a slightly formal atmosphere until Clara produces her cocaine. Outside large flakes of snow will fall over Frau Schmetterling's garden. Alice will clap her hands. 'It's going to be the most marvellous Christmas!'

The next weeks at Rosenstrasse will be the happiest I shall ever experience. The intimacy between Alice, Rose, Diana and myself will grow. The affection will take on the nature of a family's and I shall fall cheerfully into my rôle of charming younger brother, ready for any sport, undemandingly co-operative. Who could fail to love such a man? We will scarcely notice the food growing poorer and sparser, or the brothel beginning to assume a run-down look. Frau Schmetterling, who will have taken charge of our rations and seen to it that doors and windows are properly barricaded, will not be quite so maternally self-possessed as usual. More and more young officers will attend the salon, and fewer civilians. One officer, young Captain Adolf Mencken, is now resident here. The brothel is an official telephone post.

The snow heals the scars on the city, softening the outlines of the fortifications, muting the sounds of distress. Mirenburg is visibly beginning to starve. There is no word from Germany. Holzhammer has strengthened his encirclement. The dribble of water in the river is brackish and filthy and reveals all kinds of horrors. These, too, the snow will cover. Sometimes in my imagination the brothel in Rosenstrasse will seem to be the only building still standing; the only security in a desolate and mutilated world. But then too often I will begin to notice the reality, the theadbare quality of the deception. Frau Schmetterling maintains it by her will alone. She once leaned easily on her cushions, controlling a universe of comfort, maintaining by moral strength and skill an illusion of absolute sanctuary, but now the effort is visibly draining her. 'Mister' has become more solicitous; her chow dogs can scarcely summon the energy to bark at the clients. She still dusts every piece of china in her vast dresser. Mirenburg is hungry. The meals at the brothel remain reasonable. We eat once a day. Nobody asks where 'Mister' finds his supplies. Nobody asks where the flowers come from.

We move, all four of us, in a web of reference where our needs and attitudes are the only ones worth considering. Alice, of course, is trapped in this more thoroughly than the rest, who at least know on one level that what they are doing can ultimately be self-destructive: we have conspired and chosen, she has merely accepted. Our games, our fantasies, our rituals become increasingly elaborate and abstract, yet we congratulate ourselves that they are 'humane'. So they are, I suppose, in this private world, and we would be impatient if we were forced to consider them in any different context. I am a woman amongst women; my perfume is their perfume; we share our clothes, our jewellery, our identities. Memory is floating scarlets and pinks shading into yellow and grey, the taste of sex, the sensation of being forever relaxed, forever in a state of heightened sensuality, forever alive. I can smell this paper: it has an old dusty odour, and the ink is bitter in my nostrils. After the War I spent a few months in Algeria, much of this time in a whorehouse having some of the atmosphere of Frau Schmetterling's, although it was a much rougher place. It was frequented by certain elements of the French Army. One of the girls, a pretty redheaded Russian called Marya, whose parents had been killed by the Bolsheviks and who had come here from Yalta, was dying by the hour. She was consumptive. She had a little cubicle off the main floor, where we sat on cushions and smoked hashish. On a certain night she had announced that it was 'free tonight, gentlemen'.

One by one the customers went to her as she called for champagne – a bottle with every man – standing in her door in a pink chemise which had brownish stains on it, challenging them to come, while the blood flowed down her lovely chin, and her delicate shoulders and beautiful little breasts shook as she coughed. 'This is a farewell performance.' But gradually even the coarsest of the soldiers began to hesitate and look to one another in the hope that someone would put a stop to the matter. The proprietor of the brothel, a half-Arab who wore a fez and a European suit, remained expressionless, watching Marya, watching the customers, perhaps curious himself to see how far it could all go. The soldiers took up their bottles of champagne and went into her cubicle, but none went very willingly or stayed very long. I still do not know why they went: I like to think it was out of respect for a dying and desperate girl. Perhaps she thought their bodies would bring her renewed life, or perhaps she hoped they would kill her. She died two days later, quietly, full of hashish.

Mirenburg huddles under the snow as if in a mixture of fear and pride. Her bells continue to chime; her lovely churches are crowded every day. There are no birds here now. They have all been caught and eaten. The factories are closed and every able-bodied man marches on the walls as part of his militia-duty. Holzhammer's armour squats not a quarter of a mile from our abandoned trenches on the other side of an expanse of almost unbroken snow. We have heard that German and Austrian diplomats quarrel over the Wäldenstein Question but no decision has yet been reached.

We expect the cannon to begin to fire again soon. Van Geest is still wearing his blanket-jacket. He talks to me one afternoon as we sit side by side on a couch in the gloom of the salon. 'I continue to associate this place with the funeral parlour where we took my mother. Isn't that peculiar? Yet the atmosphere seems exactly the same to me. It always has. Even before the siege began. It could be the dark drapery and the smell of incense. The potted palms. Is that all? The cause of the association is beyond me.' He sighs and lights his cigar. 'But I am comfortable here.' Over on the other side of the room, in the half-light, Frau Schmetterling sits at the piano, playing some mindless German song. As I get up to leave I hear a commotion in the vestibule and Thérèse comes storming in pointing behind her at the same porter who, a few weeks ago, complained about his wife's teeth. Thérèse is wearing a feather dressing-gown and mules. Only since the Siege have the girls been allowed to dress like this in public. She has lost all appearance of refinement. Her harsh gutter-Berlin rings out suddenly across the room. 'He's eaten Tiger! The horrible old bastard's eaten the cat!' Frau Schmetterling hurries from the piano. 'Not so loud, dear. What's the matter?' Thérèse points again. 'The cat. He said it was a rabbit.' She rounds on the man. 'And he offered me some if I'd doodle him. For a rabbit leg! Or a cat's leg, as it turned out. He's disgusting. Old swine! I'd rather eat *his* damned leg. Tiger was my only real friend.' She begins to weep, every so often pausing to glare at the bewildered porter. All he can say is: 'It wasn't Tiger. Somebody else got Tiger.' Frau Schmetterling tells him he is dismissed.

'One should try to draw the line at cats.' Captain Mencken,

all shaded eyes, colourless hair and sandy uniform, comes up to us and borrows a light from Van Geest. 'They are eating worse in the Moravia and Little Bohemia, I hear.' He looks down on us through smoked glasses, a sober lemur.

People seem to have become obsessed with what should and what should not be eaten. Yesterday I was in the kitchen while Frau Schmetterling discussed menus with her cook. Herr Ulric has always impressed me. He was a butcher in Steinbrucke twenty years ago, and he still retains something of the smell of the shambles about his coarse and enormously gentle body. His hands, when at rest, lie upon his thighs as if they grip an axe and his eyes contain that familiar sad tenderness of a betrayer of lambs and ewes. His old calling proves useful again. Herr Ulric was amused by Frau Schmetterling's insistence that the food be described simply as 'meat'. He agreed. 'So long as it isn't described as prime. That nag was hardly the finest horse in the cavalry, even when she was young!' Frau Schmetterling had nodded in that dismissive way she has when she does not wish to hear what is being said to her. Van Geest sighs. 'I feel like one of those dark weeds which grows in the deep sea, which never observes the light of the sky, is never exposed to the air. I wave in fathomless currents. I am moved by profound, slow forces; I am never attacked; I give a hiding place to both predator and prey, yet I am scarcely aware of them and never affected by them. Is this power, do you think?' Captain Mencken hands back the box of matches and looks to me for a reply, but I know Van Geest too well by now to bother to answer. Captain Mencken has little to do and frequently seems embarrassed to be here. He is courteous enough, but always distant. He is unhappy, he has confided to us, with a state of affairs in which our soldiers do battle with starving citizens in their own streets. There have been several terrible incidents. 'We should take the offensive,' he has said. 'That's my opinion. But we wait still for the Kaiser. And the Kaiser will not come. The only relief for Mirenburg depends on the actions of her soldiers. One good cavalry charge could take those positions. Or could have.' Now he moves away from us.

'The horses are growing too weak,' he says. 'Well, you know what's happening to them.'

He goes to the boarded-up window as if he hopes he will get some glimpse of the enemy. 'They're starving us rather successfully, aren't they?' He is one of the few Mirenburger soldiers to have seen active service. Frau Schmetterling returns and settles at her piano. Rakanaspya and Count Belozerski enter, speaking in low Russian voices. The Count has grown a thin pointed beard, and both men have become increasingly serious; they spend all their time together and appear to be discussing metaphysics. Count Belozerski's hair has been allowed to grow, too. It now touches his high fur collar, emphasising his Tartar blood and giving him a Mephisthophelean appearance completely at odds with his behaviour, which remains amiably courteous. He has been to see Caroline Vacarescu once or twice, though she is determinedly in pursuit of a rather nervous and flattered Captain Mencken, while granting her favours most frequently to Rudolph Stefanik. She is playing several hands at once. We have heard nothing at all of Princess Poliakoff except a vague rumour she has escaped the city and thrown herself on the mercy of her ex-lover Holzhammer. I enquired at every hotel and boarding-house I was able to find. I still fear she has guessed my perfidy and might by now have discovered who Alice really is. She would betray me if she could. She would betray us all. In the Town Hall a day or so ago a fire had been especially prepared for an emergency meeting. The business people of Mirenburg were to meet General von Landoff and his staff to discuss the situation. The big mediaeval hall, with its gilded gargoyles and elaborate flags, was full of loud voices and tobacco smoke. A number of old men were in contentious discourse near the fireplace. Everyone still wore their over-coats. No member of the military staff had yet arrived and merchants and bankers continued to represent themselves as experts in the business of War. There were rumours of an emissary from Holzhammer, of new peace-terms which General von Landoff had dismissed out of hand as 'quite

151

impossible'. One iron-master joked that he had it on good authority that all women under twenty were to be given up to the Bulgarians. 'My mistress was in tears when I got there last night. She knew that it was nonsense, of course, but was I suspect enjoying the melodrama. There is so little entertainment, these days. I told her the story was untrue but that I had made a private agreement with General von Landoff to give her up to his uses in return for my own safe-conduct.' No-one there knew anything of the Princess Poliakoff. 'You don't believe you're making sense, do you?' says Papadakis, uncorking a bottle of Chambertin. 'You're being foolish. What are you writing about? The girl? Because I won't listen any more, you're writing it down. Is that it?' Mirenburg is still alive. Her battlements have held off the Goth and the Hun and every empire Europe has known. 'She is indestructible.' Papadakis begins to pour the wine. 'Let it breathe!' I tell him. 'Let me breathe. Let us all breathe! God! You stink of disease. You are putrefying before my eyes. I can smell you night and day!' Clara joins me in the salon. She wears a sable coat, borrowed from Diana, and a matching muff and hat. We are going for one of our walks. Captain Mencken removes his smoked glasses and warns us to be cautious. His eyes have that pale, bloody look of dogs whose hair permanently covers their faces. 'The amount of crime in the city is prodigious . . . '

We laugh at him as we step into the path which has been cleared through the snow. The dismissed porter is close behind us, grumbling that it has become impossible to please anybody these days. He goes towards Rauchgasse while we turn in the opposite direction, to Papensgasse and the Botanical Gardens. The guards have stamped paths all over the gardens and we follow them. The smell of burning wood comes from near the Tropical Plant House. The white smoke rising over the snow adds to the haze. The sky is the colour of new steel and from the Moravia a score of belfries begin to peal. The people on that side are mostly Catholic. 'They pray four or five times a day now,' says Clara. She wants to investigate the source of the smoke, but I hold her back. 'It would be best not to find out what they are cooking,' I say. 'Have they become cannibals?' She makes to go on. 'There are rumours,' I say. She shivers and her eyes brighten. 'Oh!' She tries to find a remark and fails. 'How terrible,' she says finally, in a small voice. 'I wonder what would happen to me? Would they prefer to eat me or rape me, do you think?' We take the turning for the ornamental lake. 'Probably both,' I say. Most of the trees are down. They have been used for firewood. The unbroken snow covers their stumps, however, so that it is still possible to pretend the Siege does not exist and all is as it was in September. I walk slowly, savouring the sense of peace. I am a little light-headed from hunger. In the distance glass buildings are heavy with snow. Every other outline seems black. There is a strong smell of urine from the lake. Clara holds her nose. 'They must be using it as a cess-pit. I suppose they can't empty the sewage into the river any more, though I don't see what difference it makes.' A soup-kitchen has been set up in the Lugnerhoff. The line of people, many of them well-dressed, stretches the length of Korkziehiergasse and goes out of sight around the corner. I see an old acquaintance, Herr Prezant the tobacconist, and stop to talk to him. 'What's the soup like?' I ask him. 'It gets thinner every day,' he says, smiling. He is a grey ghost in astrakhan. 'Soon it will be only water, but we shall still go on queuing for it. By that time we shall not have noticed. It's as good a way as any of starving to death.' He seems to be quite serious. 'Relief will soon be here,' I say. He is fatalistic: 'There is nobody who would wish to help us in the current political climate. You must know that as well as I, Herr von Bek.'

'I am optimistic by nature, Herr Prezant. There's little point in being otherwise.' He offers me his hand and I shake it. It is all bone; yellow with the stains of his calling. Then he turns back into the line and stands there, his shoulders straight, his fingers toying with the brim of his Homburg hat. 'He is a brave little old fellow,' says Clara. 'But why are people so frequently passive in the face of misery and death? Have they been reconciled to it all their lives? So few of them seem surprised,

153

let alone outraged. Wouldn't you be angry?'

'I would not be in his position,' I tell her. 'But if I were I should probably behave very similarly. One makes choices, until there are no further choices to make. Then one accepts the results. His choices have led him to that queue. As have his circumstances, too, of course. My circumstances will never lead me to make Herr Prezant's choice. Let's count our blessings, Rose, my love.' There are no cabs. We must walk back. Black smoke floats towards the twilight. Fire has broken out in the Koenigsallee and has spread for several blocks. The hospital has been evacuated: the patients are lying on stretchers in the street until they can be removed to the Convent of the Poor Clares. The fire is said to be the work of incendiaries, of women patterning themselves after the communards of '71 and deciding it would be better to burn Mirenburg to the ground than to let it fall into the hands of the besiegers. The blaze is soon under control and several suspected 'petrolleuses' have been arrested. A crowd visits the burning buildings to warm itself and to loot whatever food might have survived. A few shots are fired in the dusk. A far less passive crowd rushes up Falfnersallee towards the Mirov Palace and is met by a fusillade. In the confusion some field-guns are discharged. We reach Rosenstrasse at dark, barely in time for curfew. Captain Mencken peers at us through the pools of his spectacles. 'You are safe, then?' Clara asks him what is happening. He tells us Holzhammer's agents have been creating dissension in the city. Those agents will soon be under arrest. I remark how hot it has become inside the house. Frau Schmetterling flusters through the door which leads down to the basement. 'He intends to burn us all up!' she says despairingly. 'Please help. It is 'Mister' and Chagani!' Captain Mencken and I go down to the furnace-room. The boiler is roaring so high it threatens to burst. Two men stand in the flickering darkness hurling log after log through its blinding mouth. 'He will not listen!' wails Frau Schmetterling. 'He continues to cram in fuel. You would think he was in Hell already!' 'Mister' stops suddenly. He is panting. He signs for his friend Chagani to continue their

154

work. He looks at us in surprise. He has an enthusiastic, boyish expression on his ruined face. He is sweating. 'Every room in the house is at tropical heat,' says Frau Schmetterling. Captain Mencken steps forward. 'I think this will do. We are supposed to be preserving fuel.' He speaks gently, even hesitantly. 'There is no point now,' says 'Mister'. 'Not now, sir. Why give them our firewood?'

'You think Holzhammer has won?'

'Holzhammer has won.' For the first time Chagani speaks. He does not look at us, but he drops the log he has been carrying. I recognise him. He sometimes entertains the girls with his monkey and his mimicry. Muscular and yet without strength, Chagani was an acrobat who destroyed his own judgement through self-demand and a lack of faith in his partners. This evening he has decided to wear his red, spangled costume. He steps back towards the boiler-room's outer door. The firelight shifts to silhouette him, frozen in loneliness, clinging to his pride as he might cling to the very sword which had killed him. 'Holzhammer was won. His troops will be here by morning.' In faded red and tarnished gold he stands stretching his calves, reaching back to a memory of his youth, obstinately continuing to identify the impatience he had then possessed with the subtler forms of optimism he has detected in others and yet been unable to comprehend. 'That's rubbish, Chagani,' I say. 'What on earth's your game? Why have you alarmed 'Mister'?'

Chagani laughs suddenly and springs into the depleted woodpile in the corner. He attempts a pirouette and lands on his back. The timber tumbles around him. He is still laughing. He is very drunk. 'Mister' goes to help him, his hands stretched. Frau Schmetterling says sharply: 'You are not to listen to him. He's always leading you into trouble. Why do you let him? Why do you get him the schnapps?' She crosses to the boiler and with a long iron rod taps and turns and slides until the thing is burning at a normal level again. She whirls around with the rod in her hand. 'Mister' has aided Chagani to regain his feet. The ex-acrobat flexes his upper arms. He is not

155

hurt. 'I still know how to fall,' he says. He glares at us. 'Which is more than any of you do. Can't you see it's over for you? Your luck has failed.' Frau Schmetterling threatens him with the black rod. He arches his back like a ballerina and, limping, allows 'Mister' to help him to the outer door. I watch him as he mounts the steps up to the garden. There are several cavalry-horses stabled there now. The cockatoos, the macaws, the parrot, all have gone, and there are no more orchids. Captain Mencken follows behind Chagani as the man is challenged by a guard. 'It's all right, Huyst.' And 'Mister' looks after his departing friend before descending the steps and tugging something out of his shirt. It is a half-empty stone bottle. Frau Schmetterling takes it, shaking her head, and drops the rod with a clang to the dusty flagstones. Mencken and I return upstairs. 'They are all going mad,' he says. 'It is hunger and alcohol, I suppose. Who can blame them?'

The four of us, out of choice, are dining most evenings off morphine, opium and cocaine. It is better than the food we have, and thanks to Clara the drugs are still plentiful. When we require warming, we drink old cognac. Wilke, summoned by a maid, stands at the top of the steps as we come back up. 'I thought we were on fire,' he says. 'And that was shooting earlier, wasn't it? I was asleep.' His big, passive head is drowsy and his voice is furred. He wears a red and white dressing gown; his feet are bare. 'What do you want me to do, chicken?' He addressed Frau Schmetterling. 'It is over,' she says. 'I am sorry you were woken up. 'Mister' lost control of the furnace.'

'Do you want me to have a look at it?' asks Wilke. 'It is all right now,' she says. 'Go back to bed.' She kisses him on the cheek as he turns obediently about. He is quite as loyal to her, I suspect, as 'Mister'. They are a strange pair of children. 'I thought the Bulgarians had arrived,' he says, almost to himself, 'and had set us on fire.'

'Could Chagani have some word?' I ask Captain Mencken. Behind his smoked glasses he is inscrutable. 'Hardly!' he says. 'A man like that? It would take much more than a day for Holzhammer to break through into the city. It was rubbish. He was drunk as a pig. Drunk as a pig.' I have sweat and grime all over my face. I go up to Clara's room to bathe. A maid fills the tub for me. We are gasping from the heat. 'Don't touch the radiators,' warns Clara. 'I have already burned myself.' She displays a red spot on the back of her hand. On her mirror she has laid out two thick lines of cocaine. 'Have one of those,' she says. 'It will spoil my appetite for dinner,' I tell her. 'Then have both,' she says with a laugh. She is wearing her Broderie Anglaise negligée. Her white body, with its firm breasts and big nipples, is beaded with perspiration. She sprays at herself with a cologne-bottle. 'Ugh! Who could have expected this? That Chagani is mad. I've always said so. He hates the human race. He'll burn us down, yet.'

'Wilke thought the Bulgarians had arrived.'

'He's not the only one. We're all on edge, Ricky, dear.'

After my bath I go to see my other ladies. They usually prefer to be together until mid-afternoon when they like to receive me. This arrangement suits Clara. She has her naps while I am away. Alice and Diana come to embrace me. They could almost be brother and sister. Twins. 'Oh, those guns again,' says Lady Cromach. 'My nerves! Did you hear them?'

'Nothing to worry about.'

'Why do men always say that to women and children?' Diana shakes her head and leads me towards the bedroom. 'And you seem so pleased with yourselves when you do it!'

'Aha. Perhaps we're talking *to* ourselves.'

'Perhaps you are, my dear.' Diana kisses me again. 'There is a child in all of us sometimes, who cries and must be comforted.'

Alice follows behind us. She has her hands together on her stomach. Diana and I stretch ourselves on the bed but Alice continues to stand. 'We've got to leave,' she says. Our Alice is drawing attention to herself. She is looking a little fatter and, as a result, even lovelier than usual. Her skin's lustre reminds me of pink pearls in the deep sea, still enlivened by the movement of the waters. Her hands press against glass. Behind the glass are shutters, nailed with boards on the outside, and only a few bars of yellow light shed by the houses opposite, enter through the gaps. Within the brothel we live almost entirely by artificial light. There is no more gas. Oil and candles are in short supply. She wears one of Clara's grey silk dressing-gowns and the remains of last night's theatrical make-up – we had turned her into a doll, a Coppelia. 'This is wretched.'

'There is absolutely nothing we can do, dear.' Diana strokes the linen of my arm. 'Where could we go?' She looks at me.

'They were shooting at civilians,' I tell Alice. 'It was a riot near the Mirov Palace. Clara and I were almost caught up in it, but it wasn't really dangerous.'

'What was Clara doing, letting you go out in that?' says Alice. 'Clara is a fool! Clara will get you killed. She looks for danger. She loves to be near death. It's the way she's made. You shouldn't go along with her silly schemes.'

'We were taking our usual stroll,' I say mildly, looking to Diana for an explanation. Diana gets up and goes into the other room to find her playing cards. Alice has pinched her cheeks together and juts her red lips at me. It is the expression she usually employs when she pretends to know somebody else's secret, or disbelieves a statement, or disapproves of an explanation. 'Don't do that,' I say. 'It makes you look ugly.' I will do almost anything to take that particular expression off her face. 'If you're frightened, then admit it. But you shouldn't try to turn your fear onto somebody else. Clara doesn't deserve that.' She is for the first time, however, thoroughly unreachable. She will not respond. The realisation gives me a physical shock. 'It isn't fair,' I add. But I am losing her. I can sense it. She needs me to give something which I do not have. I do not even know exactly what it is she wants. I would give it if I could. I hold back. Perhaps it is simply that she has used me up. Anything I say will be contrary to my interests. Alice is cold. 'You have changed,' she says. It is as if a judge has reached a verdict. 'You used to be so gay.' I am condemned and sentenced and still my crime is unknown to me. Diana returns. 'Shall we all go down to dinner tonight?' she says. She seems innocent. Has she been speaking about me to Alice? Or

158

against Clara? Nobody could do that unless Alice wanted it.

'Why not?' I reply. 'We'll have Horsemeat Surprise. Or perhaps tonight it will be Pouf-Pouf stew.' My joke falls flat. Alice cries: 'Oh, my God!' and begins to cry into her hands. Diana comforts her. Somehow I have compounded my crime.

'I'm very sorry,' I say.

'It isn't your fault.' Diana is grim. 'You'd better bring Clara here. This is getting out of proportion. At all costs we four must stick together.' Alice looks up. Snails seem to have crawled across her caked face. 'The pair of them are already against us. Can't you see that, Diana?' Lady Cromach puts on her dark dressing gown. 'I'll get Clara. You stay here with Ricky.' As soon as she has left Alice sniffs and stops crying. She glares at me. She goes to her dressing table and begins to wipe the cosmetics from her face. She has become much more skilled with her clothes and her make-up. 'We've got to get away from here, Ricky,' she says. 'We haven't been trying properly. We'll be like those Romans – those people in Pompei – still making love when the volcano went off. Diana and Clara must take their chances. You surely know of some means . . .' I am again shocked, both by her disloyalty and her volte-face. Why has she suddenly forgiven me? I am disturbed, yet flattered she should choose me as her conspirator against the others. 'We've got to get to Paris, Ricky.' The traces of tears are nearly gone. She begins to work on her hair, brushing rapidly. She leans into the mirror. 'It would be pointless to take Clara with us. She has no breeding. Well, you can't expect it from a whore, I suppose.'

I am angry on Clara's behalf, yet to defend her would be to lose my child. Alice has fired her warning shot.

'What about Diana?' I ask.

'She's too unimaginative. You and I are the only ones with imagination, Ricky. It is our bond. Remember?' She turns with a lovely little smile. 'Twin souls?'

I laugh. I recognise her motives and her techniques but I can't resist them. She is my muse, my alter-ego, my creation. 'Let's at least behave decently.' I attempt to save something of

159

my old standards. 'There's no need to condemn either of them just because we're tired of them. Let's just admit we want to get to Paris together.'

She is almost happy. She blows me a kiss from her reflection. 'All right. That's fair enough. What will you do?'

'I'll make enquiries. I know someone . . . There's a chance . . . ' This is empty reassurance, of course. She must hope. She must pin that hope on me. She has given me an ultimatum. To lose her would be to lose myself.

'I just want to be on our own again,' she says. 'In Paris. Or Vienna. Wherever you think. But we can't stay here, Ricky. There are too many dangers. Too many awful memories. I want to start afresh. I want to be your wife, as you promised.'

I am enormously elated as she embraces me; I have had a last-minute reprieve. But there are conditions. We hear Clara and Diana coming back. She whispers: 'Get us away.' And she continues with her toilet. 'She's much better now,' I say. 'It was the shooting and the heat. We're all relaxing again.' I laugh. I look at the two women I intend to deceive. They seem merely pleased emotions have settled. I see no reason to feel guilt. It will simply be Alice and me again. We shall finish where we began. Nobody will have lost. There have been no bargains made. But I am already lost; I refuse to consider what I will receive in place of love; or what I shall win to replace the pain and the beauty of worshipping a woman rather than a child. I shall become a coward. The future threatens me and I refuse to acknowledge it. The moment is all that matters. I might have ended my days with affectionate memories and all I shall actually have will be a litany of petty revenges and self-pity. I will come to deceive all women as wilfully as I now plan to deceive myself. I will exploit their romance as mine was exploited. I know all this but I am compelled to continue. Alice has begun to sing that old familiar parting song; finding faults, compiling lists of supposed slights so that she might justify her next decision. And what she can turn against these two friends she can as easily turn against me. I am in that state of disbelief which can sometimes last for days or weeks before the

160

fact of disaffection is accepted. I look away. When shall I be struck? In Paris? Before or after we are married? I will suffer that particular indignity. I will listen to lies about what we have done and distortions of the facts of our life together. I will not leave. I will not, as I should, let her sing that song alone. But all this knowledge is swamped by the tiniest hope that she will change: that what I see is not the truth.

Alexandra. You must not leave me. You must not change. From the triumph of eyes freshly-adult she will one day mock my misery. She will refuse the role which it will have suited her to play, which will no longer be useful to her. She will change her ambitions, but not her nature. I shall be hardly peripheral to her consideration when not long ago I should have been central. From a citadel of lace and velvet she will look down on a wretch. Now she flashes me a private smile. They are getting changed. They are chatting amongst themselves. They prepare themselves for the dinner. Then Clara and Diana leave me alone with Alice again. 'I must have your guarantee,' I tell her. 'I must know you will not betray me.' She hugs me. She kisses me warmly. 'How could I betray you, darling Ricky? You are my master!' I hold her to me, not daring to look at her face for fear I will see the deception too clearly. 'It's wrong to do this to Clara and Diana,' I say. She pulls away from me. 'That's stupid. What do we owe them?' I sit on the chair, my shoulders stooped. She offers me something in her gloved hand, palm outstretched as if to a pet. It is a little pill of opium. Wonderingly, I take it. She turns away. 'You know, Ricky, that I have no conception of your ideas of morality sometimes. We see things so differently. I don't plan to do any harm to either Diana or Clara. Do you think that?'

'No . . .'

'I love them both. They are wonderful. But you and I have something special. What purpose would be served in blurting everything out? It can only cause trouble – and pain to others.'

'I should have thought that we owed them – '

She comes to kneel beside me. 'We owe them nothing. That is our freedom.'

161

I listen to her as a disciple might listen to a holy man; striving to perceive the wisdom, the new attitude, the truth of what she says.

'They're not like Poliakoff,' she says. 'They won't hurt us.'

'We ought to tell them.'

'What's the point?'

As I rise to my feet my legs are trembling. I cannot fathom the changes which have taken place in her strange, dreaming, greedy brain. I am as much at a loss for an explanation as if I attempted to analyse the perceptions and nature of a household pet. Like a pet she is able to take on the colour of any master; to be obedient and passive for as long as it suits her, to respond to whatever desires or signals one might display. But now I disguise my desires, for fear of losing her. Have I therefore lost her to someone who offers her clearer signals? To someone who represents what she calls 'freedom'? At dinner I look suspiciously around the table, at the Russians, at Count Stefanik, at Caroline Vacarescu, even at honest Egon Wilke, chewing his food with as much relish as if it were the finest beef. And Alice is merry. Alice is the darling of the company. Everyone dotes on her. 'You cheer us all up, my dear,' says Frau Schmetterling. She has become much more tolerant of late. Will Frau Schmetterling somehow betray me? I am scarcely in control of myself, though I appear to be as relaxed and as good-tempered and as witty as always. And yet, has Clara taken on that peculiar, impressive dignity of an injured woman; that dignity which induces in any reasonably sensitive man a mixture of awe, guilt, respect, and sometimes envious anger? We drink too deeply. In bed together that night we tire easily and fall asleep. A terrible depression has overwhelmed me. The dream is lost. I am desperate to rediscover it. I get up from that tangle of women early and go to Clara's room to sleep. I help myself to her cocaine. I look through her books and her musical scores and I cannot rid myself of the thought that I have resisted as heartily as has Clara the thought that she might love me and I her. This scarcely affects my obsession with Alice. I want it to be as it was. 'In Paris,' I murmur to myself. 'It will come back in Paris.' And then I ask myself: 'What am I?' I am corrupted and I am revelling in my corruption. I am the victim of my imagination, trapped in a terrible fantasy of my own devising. I am still awake when, at dawn, the Holzhammer guns begin to fire on Mirenburg. She trembles. She cries out. The shells blow up the Café Schmidt and flesh scatters into the morning air; the statues of St Varoslav and St Ormond fall in a haze of white dust, crashing onto the shattered slabs of masonry below. The Liberty apartments, the baroque and romanesque churches, the domes and the steeples, are falling one by one at first and then in their hundreds. Mirenburg, that city of all cities, is being murdered. She is being murdered. And here is Lady Cromach, startled and anxious, asking if I have seen Alice. Clara is behind her. Have I seen Alice? She cannot have left. But she has taken a coat, a hat. I go out to look for her. The shells are relentless. I can see them going past; I hear their wailing and their thunder. I know her family church, near Nussbaumhof. It is still standing, though most of the other buildings are flattened. I am in time to find her coming down the wide steps, dressed inadequately in a silk tea-gown and a summer cloak. The mysterious vulnerability of her face is emphasised by the stooped set of her shoulders, her nervous eyes, as she recognises me and comes towards me for a few paces before pausing and looking back at others also emerging from the white Gothic arch. 'What were you looking for in there?' I ask. She begins to shiver. I go up to her and put my own coat around her. 'Comfort?' she says. 'Certainty? I don't know.' I try to lead her back to Rosenstrasse but she will not move. 'It's unlike you,' I say. 'What?' she asks. 'To risk so much danger.' She frowns. 'There wasn't any. The guns started later.' I smile, almost in relief. 'I must leave you,' she says. 'I must leave you all. I must be free.' I am sympathetic. 'So you shall be. You can do what you like. But first we must escape Mirenburg. Get to Paris. Come.'

'No.' She stands firm. I act as if I am dealing with a child. 'Very well.' I lift my hat and return down the steps, feeling

163

that I have somehow hurt her and myself at the same time. Her confusion is infectious. I stop and look back. She is staring at me from those blank eyes. She is staring. 'Come along, Alexandra.' I stretch out my hand. 'I can no longer afford to indulge myself in this fantasy of youthful infatuation. Either you come with me or I shall abandon you.'

'I want you to go.'

I return, one by one, up the steps. The shells are like a chorus of harpies all around us. 'But what of me?' I say. I am still hoping to appeal to her. 'What shall I be left with?'

She looks at me almost with contempt. 'Love and affection,' she says.

I cannot recover myself. Mirenburg is being destroyed. All my romance is being taken from me at once and there is no one I can blame. This desolation is too complete. She shrugs and joins me. Through all the yelling and all the death we walk slowly home to Rosenstrasse. 'You were lying to me,' she says. 'There is no means of getting to Paris.'

'I will find a way,' I promise. If only I can keep her with me, can get her free of all this terror, we can become calm again. She will love me again. She will know me for what I am, a decent, ordinary, kind-hearted man. In Rosenstrasse everyone is relieved to see us. Alice is put to bed. 'It is exhaustion,' says Lady Diana. 'She is only a child. She's in shock.' For twenty-four hours she hardly moves, although she is awake. We take turns sitting with her. 'Don't leave me, Ricky,' she says suddenly, in the depths of the night. I grasp her hand. I have begun to seek out a plan of Rosenstrasse's sewers; it has occurred to me that this could be our best means of escape. Some of the sewers must run outside the walls, or connect with the underground river. She is so weak. She is fading. Her temperature is alarmingly high. Clara assures me there is nothing seriously wrong with her. I am suspicious of Clara. One is always suspicious of those one deceives. I too am dying, I suppose. That must be why Papadakis humours me so readily, no longer refusing me wine or anything else I demand. He can afford to be charitable. There is never any snow here, only relentless blues and yellows and whites occasionally softened by mist or rain. I can see no green trees from my window. How can they give beauty to me so easily and then take it away just as thoughtlessly? Why should she wish to do that? She stands in the snow with shredded flags limp on her remaining turrets, like a captured heroine. Mirenburg is defeated, but Holzhammer, perhaps so there should be no physical monument to his bestiality, is relentless. Hour after hour the shells fall on the city and at night she is livelier than by day, for her fires are now inextinguishable; her broken silhouettes possess a nobility they lack under the light of the sun. Mirenburg is all but dead. She makes sad, fluttering sounds and little whimpers: the steady booming we hear is the triumphant beating of enemy hearts. If they rape her now, they shall have only the satisfaction of violating a creature which has already made its peace with death. She will give them no pleasure; she will put no curse upon them. They have damned themselves.

We are not allowed outside. Captain Mencken sits beside the telephone, waiting for the instrument to give him orders. In the street there is a horse and cart. We can see it through a hole in the boarded window. All the glass is broken. The horse is dead, from shrapnel. 'Mister' was bringing it back, with our provisions. 'Mister' was killed, too. His body was dragged inside. The cart has remained there for hours. At night its silhouette is thrown onto the blinds by any nearby explosion. 'That cart is the Devil's own carriage,' says Rakanaspya. 'It is waiting for one of us.' He laughs and pulls heavily on his brandy bottle. He is wearing an opera hat and cape. He has an ebony stick in his left hand, together with a pair of gloves. Captain Mencken wishes to know why the window is unprotected when all the others are boarded up. 'We needed some air,' says Rakanaspya. Frau Schmetterling has given shelter to a group of musicians. They are playing now. Their music is exotic, but its inspiration escapes me: there is an Oriental quality to it, though it follows the familiar form of a sonata. The musicians themselves have a slightly Asian cast to their features. Count Belozerski assures me they are not Russian. I have enquired the name of the composer, but I did not recognise it. They are still playing in the morning when I look through the blinds. I can smell the dead horse. In the half-light I see a young, naked child, squatting upon the carcass, picking with its claws at the tough, steaming meat, its own pink body seeming to merge into that of the dead beast, its black eyes hard and wary, like the eyes of a guilty crow. I once used to say that I had an ear for music, an eye for women and a strong distaste for death. While that little orchestra played and while I tortured myself over the question of Alexandra I came to doubt both former statements and to feel thoroughly reinforced in the latter. The whores do not bother to dress in their tasteful finery now. They make love in corners of the salon if they feel like it. Frau Schmetterling is hardly ever present. She has disappeared with Wilke. Only once did I hear her put her foot down in her old, firm way. It was when Inez, the Spanish girl, refused point blank to accompany Van Geest to the rocking-horse room. 'I will not do any of those things,' she had insisted. 'It is quite true,' Frau Schmetterling had said softly, 'that Inez is not required, Herr Van Geest, to visit the rocking-horse room. Perhaps Greta would oblige?' But Van Geest, lost in the depths of his own brain and very drunk, had insisted that he wanted Inez. 'You said nothing of the rocking-horse room when you asked for Inez or I should have told you, Herr Van Geest, that she was not available. There has always been an agreement, after all.' Van Geest offered to pay double. Inez had considered this and then again shaken her head. Van Geest had said angrily: 'In other establishments girls like you are severely punished. There are Houses in Amsterdam which specialise in taming stupid, disobedient young women.' Frau Schmetterling had pursed her lips. 'Then I suggest you wait until you can return to Amsterdam, Herr Van Geest.'

Van Geest had glared and then given up, stumbling back to his room. Inez had begun to giggle in relief. Frau Schmetterling had been disapproving. 'You should not have caused a scene,' she had said. But there have been other scenes since and she has not been present to make the peace. Sometimes, when I have been keeping vigil beside Alice's bed, I have had to go out into the corridor to beg people to be quiet. I have managed to get hold of the plans to the sewers. I have found a way of escape. When Alice murmurs to me and pleads for reassurance I tell her we are as good as free. All she has to do is to regain her strength. Soon she is a little better. I show her the plans. I describe the route we are going to take through the mountains to the border where we shall be able to get the train. She frowns. 'Is there no other way?' I shake my head. I begin to tell her how we shall drop into the sewers, what we can take with us, and what we shall tell the others. 'It's tiring.' She sinks again into semi-sleep. 'I'll leave it to you.' I am disturbed by this response. I have managed to do what she wants and she scarcely thanks me. I cannot fathom this sickness. Clara is certain it is a sickness of the spirit. We can only blame the shock of War. The horse is eventually freed from the shafts and what is left of it is butchered for meat. The naked child disappears. Four or five of our girls put on a tableau meant to take our minds off the relentless sound of shelling. Clara and I watch together, comfortable in each other's company. The tableau represents something Arcadian and employs a great many artificial flowers which, of course, the girls have in abundance. Since only three of them speak reasonable German and the others have only the most limited vocabularies the 'play' becomes quickly incomprehensible with the result that the actresses are soon laughing more than the audience. Clara and I applaud. I glance furtively at her to see if she knows anything of my plan. She seems innocent of suspicion tonight. At dawn I slip away to look for the entrance to the sewer. It is not far from here, joining with the underground river which runs beneath Rosenstrasse. The intense light of the winter day threatens my eyes. I should be glad of Captain Mencken's glasses. I manage to open the metal hatch beneath the archway of Papensgasse and I hear water running below, but it stinks. There can be no fresh water, other than melted snow, left in the whole of Mirenburg. I know that one can go from here to the main sewer, or get to it directly from the riverbed. I lower the hatch and walk down Papensgasse to inspect the river entrance to the sewer. Looking over the embankment wall from this side I can just see it, a murky hole rimmed with slime. It seems large enough. When the siege is lifted, I wonder, will they redirect the river to its old course or will it continue to follow the new one? There is a familiar whistling overhead. A Krupp shell begins to fall towards me. I run for the relative security of Papensgasse. I hear the shell but I have not heard the gun which fired it, either because it was so far away or because I am so used to the sound of cannon.

The shell falls not far from Rosenstrasse. Out of the dusty debris comes galloping a column of flying artillery. It stops in a flurry of hooves and steel on the embankment. The soldiers rush to position their guns so they point across the river at the Moravia. I slip back to the brothel and return to Clara. She stirs in her sleep. I am not sure she has noticed my absence. Since we all three take turns sitting with Alice Clara has become used to frequent comings and goings. Later that morning we both get dressed and go to see how the child is. To our considerable surprise she is not only up, she is eating cheese and drinking watered wine. Diana is full of joy. 'What a wonderful recovery.' Clara frowns.

I do my best to disguise my pleasure. Alice must be ready to travel. When Clara and Diana go downstairs together I hug my little girl. 'Are you ready for our next adventure?'

'Oh, yes!' she grins at me, a conspiratorial innocent. 'What's the plan?'

I tell her we shall leave separately tonight. I will wait for her at midnight in Papensgasse, round the corner from the archway. 'It might be easier than I thought. They've moved our guns up to the river. That probably means Holzhammer has broken through the defences and is in the Moravia already. We'll come out well behind his main lines. I'll buy horses, then it's a clear ride to the border and a train.' We hear sounds in the corridor. She says gently, with hesitant fingers on my arm:

168

'You don't think you'd be happier going with Clara?' I am taken aback. My heart sinks. 'Of course not. Why?' She makes a little movement with her lovely shoulders. 'Nothing.' The door opens. 'I'll be there.'

Clara enters. She seems distressed. Has she guessed? 'It's Van Geest,' she says. 'He's shot himself. God knows why. Downstairs is full of police and soldiers. They don't seriously think it's murder. But the building's now officially occupied. Soldiers are being billeted here. Temporarily, they say, because of the 'new emergency', whatever that is.' I return to the ground floor with her, so she will not get suspicious. I blow my smiling Alice a kiss as we leave. The vestibule is still hung with its many portraits of the French emperor whom Frau Schmetterling adored and who, some say, was her first lover. The soldiers show distaste for these pictures and seem discomfited by them. The officer in charge, Captain Kolovrat, attempts to order them removed from the walls. This Frau Schmetterling firmly refuses. She is the only one of us with any authority to resist them; my own choice is to pretend respect and to avoid them as much as I can. Unlike Mencken, these men are used to power and know how to gain it. A soldier must be broken in such a way as to make him wholly reliant upon his superiors, otherwise he cannot be controlled in battle. Most officers employ this knowledge in their dealings with women, first destroying their confidence, then supplying it themselves so that those they would command become entirely dependant upon them. I must admit to being nervous. They remind me of well-trained hounds: their natural ferocity, their terror of their own madness, contained and controlled almost entirely by their wills. Such personalities yearn for uniforms, for rituals. They demand them in others, for they must order a world they fear and thus will simplify themselves and those around them as much as they can. Captain Mencken is in conversation with a police inspector wearing a kepi and gold epaulettes on his maroon uniform. Captain Kolovrat, presumably senior to Mencken, struts about the salon inspecting its contents as if he were kicking his heels in a provincial

169

art-gallery. He has a Prussian-style helmet decorated in gold and silver, a black and white uniform, and a variety of medals. His hand sticks his sword out behind him like the extended tail of a scorpion. His little fat face is embellished by a waxed moustache and a monocle. He wheels around and marches towards me to be introduced by a defeated Frau Schmetterling, whose only victory has been the pictures. He salutes me. I bow my head. He clicks his heels and says: 'You must understand, sir, that every resident is now under military discipline. Your privileges, I regret, are at an end.'

'They were over when 'Mister' died,' says Frau Schmetterling softly. And then, to him: 'I hope you don't expect to find supplies here, Captain Kolovrat. We were living hand to mouth as it was.'

'We shall see,' he says. 'I shall want inventories. Anything we use will, of course, receive a receipt and you can claim full payment from the government after the War. Mencken? Inspector Serval?'

'Suicide without doubt,' says Serval. 'He was probably suffering from some form of delirium. Maybe bad meat, maybe drink, maybe a disease. The doctor will let us know. But he shot himself through the temple with his own revolver. A familiar situation at present.'

'Disease,' says Kolovrat, rubbing at his chubby chin. He rolls the word on his tongue and seems about to spit it out. 'Of course. There must be a medical inspection. I shall send to headquarters.'

Frau Schmetterling is offended. 'I assure you that the likelihood . . .'

'The likelihood is what a soldier must consider, madame.' He is fastidious and condescending. She falls silent, reconciled for the time being to this man's swaggering rudeness. Mencken seems embarrassed and apologetic. Clara, Diana and I go with the others, girls and clients, into the salon. Alice is mentioned and excused because she is unwell. I present her papers. Kolovrat has had a bureau placed in the middle of the floor. He sits at this now, making up a register. One by one we give our names and nationalities, showing him our identification cards. We are allowed to sit or to stand around the walls of the salon. Outside, the shells are constant and from time to time the whole building shakes or more glass crashes to the floor. Kolovrat's inquisition is frequently punctuated by the chiming of the chandelier over his head. One series of shots seems closer: I realise it is our own artillery, firing across the river. Kolovrat knows the sound, too, and looks up. I fail to read his fat little face. Eventually we are dismissed. Young soldiers stand to attention everywhere. Clara, Diana and myself are asked by Frau Schmetterling to accompany her to her kitchen. Whenever a shell lands nearby she jumps and looks at her shivering dresser, at her wonderful, rattling china. So far nothing is damaged. 'I am worried,' she says, 'about my daughter. With 'Mister' gone Elvira has no-one but me . . . ' She sits down at her long table. Trudi, smiling in the background, makes us something to drink. Outside, there is a lull in the bombardment and we can hear Herr Ulric the butcher-cook in the courtyard. His loud healthy voice rings and echoes. He is arguing with a young cavalryman: 'The horse is no good to you and no good to itself. It is dying of starvation!' The soldier is passionate. 'We shall die together!' he shouts. The butcher is reasonable: 'Go inside and fuck one of the girls. While you're at it I'll deal with the horse.'

'You are disgusting!'

The butcher drops his voice and so does the cavalryman. We hear no more and soon the shells are landing again. The building is scarcely ever still. It is as if an earthquake perpetually shakes it. Frau Schmetterling says to Lady Cromach: 'You have connections, I presume, in England. Could you get Elvira to school there? If anything happens to me.'

'Nothing will happen to you, Frau Schmetterling, and of course I'll do whatever I can. Do you wish me to recommend some schools, somewhere where Elvira could stay? I have an old nanny who still lives in London.'

'Yes,' says Frau Schmetterling. 'That's the sort of thing.'

She produces a notebook. 'Some names and addresses?'

Lady Diana makes an awkward, affectionate gesture. She frowns and then spells in English. When she has finished she says: 'If anything else comes to mind I'll let you know. You wish your daughter to leave soon?'

'Oh, yes, soon.' Frau Schmetterling's large bosom rises and falls. 'I must stay with my girls. Elvira . . . '

'We'll see that's she's safe,' says Diana. 'I promise.' Her voice is soft and comforting. It has lost most of that inflexion which makes almost every word seem sardonic. She squeezes Frau Schmetterling's shoulder. The madam sighs. 'Thank you, Lady Cromach.'

Our band has begun to play again in the salon. Presumably Captain Kolovrat has decided this will improve morale. The staccato, nervous quality of the tune becomes increasingly intrusive as we sit in silence round Frau Schmetterling's table, drinking spiced grog and getting a little drunk. The steady thumping of the guns, the shrieks and explosions, seem preferable to the music. Eventually, Frau Schmetterling rises and says she must speak to Ulric about lunch. She rings for the cook. He comes striding in, grinning widely. His leather apron is covered in blood. He bows to us. I envy him his insouciance as much as I envy him his sinewy arms, the strong veins standing out from the hard muscle. As we three leave the kitchen and return upstairs Diana remarks that I seem in unusually good spirits. We reach my door. Alice is sitting in the easy chair, reading a magazine. She kisses us, one by one. There is an air of excitement about her which amuses us all, even Clara. 'The shock has worn off as quickly as it came,' says my Rose.

'That, I suppose, is the nature of such complaints. Particularly in the very young.' Lady Diana thoughtfully strokes Alice's hair. Alice puts lips to her wrist. We decide we shall all lunch together so that Alice can meet the new Captain. 'That's splendid!' exclaims Alice. At lunch Rakanaspya and Count Belozerski eat in silence, perhaps in mourning for Van Geest. Caroline Vacarescu hangs on Count Stefanik's arm but at the same time spares a bright smile for Captain Kolovrat and another for Captain Mencken, both of whom dine with us. Trudi is helped at the table by a young, red-faced military orderly who sweats visibly and whose smell is almost as vile as the meat we are eating. Egon Wilke, at Frau Schmetterling's elbow, has an embarrassed air about him. He is presumably not comfortable sitting down to eat with so much Authority on either side of him. Kolovrat attempts to make a joke across the table, addressing Mencken. 'Well, here we are, the two oldest professions in the world sharing a table. I suppose that is only proper. What would you rather be, Frau Schmetterling, a whore or a soldier?'

'As a matter of fact, monsieur,' she says in French, 'I am neither. But I think I should rather be a whore. I see it as a superior calling.'

Kolovrat pretends to be amused, again seeking to catch Mencken's eye and being baffled by the expressionless smoked glasses. 'What? Why so, madame?'

'I think there is a considerable difference,' she says coolly, 'between those of us who kill for a living and those of us who fuck for a living.'

Frau Schmetterling has never used such a word in public before. But Kolovrat is the only one who does not realise it. Presumably he thinks the proprietress of a brothel capable of any language.

'In the first place,' he says, 'we do not willingly kill for a living. We are protecting the citizens of Mirenburg. And in the second place, what is sold here, surely is not honest fornication. This,' he waves a fork, 'this is death. This is corruption. The destruction of all true feeling. What has it to do with love? All you women have diseases. They kill my men, do they not? And turn them mad first, eh? Madame, I would prefer a bayonet in the stomach. That's a better death than one you purchase at a whorehouse!'

Frau Schmetterling is calm. 'The only death you will find here is the death of sentimental illusion. But even that . . . '

'There is a corpse still upstairs awaiting collection!' He

173

laughs and chews the butcher's latest prize. 'That's what I call death. And I say again: I'd rather have a bayonet in the stomach.'

Her smile is almost sweet. I have never seen her in this terrible, baiting mood, but Wilke, plainly, knows it well. He is privately amused. 'Monsieur,' she says, 'there is a wide variety of alternatives. One does not necessarily have a disease and one may not go so far as to stab or be stabbed in the stomach. The soldier takes risks with his life. So do we. But we do not set out to kill or to enforce our wills upon others. I believe that our profession is the better of the two and can more easily be justified in moral terms. I do not wish to kill you, monsieur. I would wish, if I were a whore, merely to satisfy your lust in exchange for a crown or two.' She stares directly into his little eyes and he again looks to Mencken, then frowns. Alice snorts behind her hand. Lady Cromach smiles and tries to silence her. The two of them are like older and younger sister today. I suddenly regret that our time together is over. I shall miss Diana almost as much as I shall my Rose. As we are finishing lunch, Albert Jirichek, a journalist for the *Weekly Gazette,* is granted a brief interview with Captain Kolovrat who is reluctant to speak in anything but the vaguest terms. It is true Holzhammer is in the Moravia, but it is not true he is making steady inroads. 'Our armour is keeping him pinned down and there is every chance he will be defeated by tomorrow.' As Kolovrat continues to speak, Jirichek opens his notebook and begins to scribble rapidly in shorthand. This causes Captain Mencken some amusement. 'Are you unaware, Herr Jirichek, that the *Gazette* was blown apart by shell-fire this morning? I doubt very much if we shall see another edition within the next few days.' It is evident he has no liking for the journal, which takes a mildly left-wing bias. Jirichek has not heard the news. He closes his notebook. He lifts his hand to one and all and departs the room in silence. Most of us laugh at this. I am relaxed, unwilling to leave the company too soon. I know I shall never experience this kind of comradeship again. By tomorrow Alice and I will be far away from the main fighting. By the day after we should have crossed the border into Saxony. From there it will be an easy matter to take the train to Paris. In less than three days we should have new wardrobes, a comfortable hotel and (delightful anticipation!) the finest food in the world. Alice and Diana decide to return upstairs because Alice says she feels faint. I am generous enough to want them to spend what time together they can. I tell myself that jealousy would be petty. Clara and I remain at the table, drinking brandy. Captain Kolovrat watches Alice leave. I feel sudden hatred of him. He begins to court me, because he desires her. His eyes follow her as he speaks to us. 'Yesterday was hard work. The Vlodinya prison was shelled. In the confusion half the jailbirds escaped. We did our best to round them up; we herded them like wild cows but a few honest people got mixed in with them. It was a relief to be sent here. I don't know why they wanted to escape. Those bastards were better off where they were!' He is pleased with his joke and repeats it.

Frau Schmetterling, still intent on baiting him, leans towards him. 'Have you ever been to prison, Captain Kolovrat?'

'Of course not, madame.'

'Has anyone else here been to prison?' Wilke alone lowers his eyes. The rest of us shake our heads.

'It destroys your personality,' she says. 'To maintain your morale you have to become a Top Dog. That means accepting all the ruthless conditions of prison life. You pay a high price by becoming inhuman and coarse. But if you do not become a hardened prisoner you go back into the world with no belief in yourself whatsoever. Prisons have little social benefit, Captain Kolovrat, save to lock a criminal away for a while. Their main task is to make us passive and malleable: whereupon they return us to persuasive friends who are usually outside the law and glad to suggest ways to easy wealth . . . Destroying the human spirit is not merely immoral. It is anti-social!'

I have never heard her speak so passionately. She has captured Rakanaspya's attention. He asks her, with deference, how she is so well-informed about prison. She shrugs. She has

175

known short spells in Berlin and in Odessa. She has talked to many people whose experience of prison was far worse than her own. 'You know me, gentlemen. I am a law-abiding citizen. I believe in peace and quiet; an orderly society. You will not find me taking up the cause of anarchy. However, I can say from the bottom of my heart that the whole conception of prison is disgusting to me.' With that she continues pecking at a tiny piece of stale cheese. She has brought silence to the company. Perhaps that was her intention. The table is shaken by another blast. Count Stefanik has undone his collar and unbuttoned his waistcoat. He is the kind of man who should wear loose, peasant clothes. Even then he would not seem entirely comfortable. He puts his hand under his beard and pushes it up towards his face. He is wary and thoughtful, as if he listens for Holzhammer's footsteps in the vestibule. He is wanted by the Austrians for more than one offence, including the scattering of nationalist leaflets from the skies above Prague. If Holzhammer arrests him he knows that he, himself, faces prison, if not death. He sighs a deep desolate sigh and rises, excusing himself. 'I feel sorry for him,' says Clara. Caroline Vacarescu makes to follow him, then returns to offer Captain Mencken all her attention. She has given up her hopes, it seems of balloon-escape. A little later he passes the open door of the salon to go out. He clears his throat and puts on his hat and overcoat. 'The man's a fool to walk the streets!' says Kolovrat dispassionately. 'Perhaps he'd rather be killed than captured,' says Rakanaspya. I am overwhelmed by a sudden depression, a fear of betrayal and loss. I excuse myself. I take Clara's hand and we go upstairs to her room where I insist on making slow, gentle love. She is warm. She is tender. She is womanly. I rise in agitation from the bed. I am disgusted with myself. Another shell explodes nearby. She is baffled by my behaviour. I silence her question with a gesture.

She sits up. 'This bombardment is getting on everyone's nerves. I'm almost praying for defeat now, for peace, even the peace of the grave. If the Bulgarians are allowed . . . ' She cannot finish.

'The house must be evacuated before that happens,' I say. 'Every effort must be made to get the girls out and split up. They must not be recognised for what they are. Frau Schmetterling won't keep this place going as a cheap soldier's bordello. It would destroy the point of it. She has always been clear on that.'

Clara frowns. 'True. But it will be up to the girls. They will be frightened. Are you leaving, Ricky?'

I ignore her question. 'You wouldn't stay here, would you? To service those pigs?'

She lowers her head. 'No,' she says, as if keeping her temper, as if I have insulted her. 'No, I would not.'

'That's good. That's good.' I am distracted. It is almost dusk. I look at my watch. My bag is packed and hidden. I assume Alice has also packed. The time is passing slowly. 'Let's have some cocaine,' I say. 'Then I think I'll go downstairs and see what's happening.' She begins to prepare the drug. 'Be careful,' she says, when I go.

In the dirty snow of the quays the soldiers stagger to their guns with shells from boxes stored for safety's sake behind sandbags on the other side of the street. I watch them through the murk. They are ham-fisted, filthy, worn out. Black smoke billows across the southern suburbs. It would appear Holzhammer has fired that entire section of the city. An officer, mounted on a skinny horse, peers through field-glasses and sees nothing. The smoke is oily, moving sluggishly. It is snowing fitfully again. Papadakis! The pain is coming back! It is like shrapnel in my belly! Oh, God, I need a woman here. But I have spent too long taking revenge on women. Now there are none to comfort me. When romance dies, cynicism replaces it, unless one is prepared to relinquish all the consolations of religion at a stroke. I could not. I fled into lies, flattery, deceitful conquest. I fled into mistrustful artifice. Even my wholesome lechery became tainted by fear and wary cunning. I lost my capacity to trust. Was I so dishonest and so hypocritically cruel before Mirenburg? Too much romance was destroyed at once, in the space of a few days. Mirenburg

177

crumbles. The twin spires of St-Maria-and-St-Maria are down. The Hotel Liverpool is obliterated. All the care and artistry of centuries, all the worship, the love, the genius, is ground up as if in a mortar and scattered on the wind. The museums and the galleries, the monasteries and the great houses, fall down before Holzhammer's insane ferocity. It is too late to parley. Holzhammer will not accept anything less than the absolute obliteration of the city. He wants no monuments to remind him of his crime. These are the actions of children, of wild beasts. Love and hope drown beneath the exploding iron. Clara is still in bed when I return. She stretches on her cushions, smoking a cigarette, looking at me with an expression I find unreadable, but which I fear is contempt. 'It is terrible out there,' I say. 'The whole southern side is burning. The Radota Bridge is destroyed and all the statues are down. The river is piled with corpses. Presumably they were trying to get away from the Bulgarians.'

Clara nods to herself and offers me a lighted cigarette which I take. 'Are we to expect them tonight, do you think?'

'Not tonight. But possibly tomorrow. At the latest the day after.'

'Then perhaps we should do something.'

'Yes,' I say. 'It would be a good idea. I have plans. I've some business this evening. I won't tell you about it now, not until I'm certain. But in the morning, everything should be clear.'

I detect a smile on her long lips. She stretches and yawns. I want to see Alice, to remind her exactly of the plan, to be certain that she knows what we are to do. But I console myself that it is simple enough. She will meet me in Papensgasse at midnight, slipping out unseen as I shall slip a little earlier.

'Shall we go to Alice and Diana, to see how the child is?' asks Clara. I dart her a look. 'Leave them. They said they wanted to rest.'

She shrugs. 'Just as you like.' Then she says: 'Come here, Ricky. I want to make love to you.'

I am disconcerted. Off-duty she is not normally so direct.

178

But I do as she orders. I undress. She is ferocious. She kisses every part of me. She sits astride me, shoving my penis into her cunt. The pleasure is astounding. It seems altogether fresh. I am exhausted. She throws herself off me, laughing. 'That wasn't fair. But I enjoyed it.'

I kiss her. 'What?' she says. 'You seem to be crying.' Of course I am not crying. Where is Papadakis? I need to piss and the pot is full. I am having trouble breathing. The lamp is flickering. There is not enough air in this room. The flowers are wilting.

As soon as Clara is asleep I get up carefully and go to the cupboard where I have hidden my bag. I dress and creep from the room. The house rocks and vibrates constantly. It will not be long before there is a direct hit. Half Rosenstrasse bears the marks of Krupp now. There is noise and music from the salon. No soldiers guard the door. I am out into the cold, into the darkness, shivering and suddenly very cowardly. I think to turn back, but it would be impossible. I move falteringly between the heaps of filthy snow, through the passage and into Papensgasse. There will be no military patrols tonight, I am sure, to enforce the curfew. I look at my watch. It is eleven-forty-five. I will not have long to wait. Soon Alice will be mine alone. Married. I shall be secure with her. She would not dare to betray me. But this will not stop us sharing further adventures – and in Paris! The very prospect warms me and makes me forget how cold I am. Firelight dances on the far river bank. Men are shouting. There is not much terror in their voices now. They are too weary. The guns fire. The guns reply. Love will come back to me. Alice is late. She will be having trouble getting away from Diana. We shall roll again in fresh linen, with great cups of newly-made coffee in the mornings, with delicate lunches in the restaurants of the Champs Elysees, with drives to Versailles, and in the summer we shall go south to Venice, and I will show her North Africa and bring joy to her exotic heart. But it is twelve-thirty. I hear voices whispering in Rosenstrasse. Has she been caught? Eventually I risk peering round into the street; it is too dark to

179

see anything. Then, at last, someone emerges from the archway and I grin to myself, full of the prospect of escape and further adventure. The woman wears a cloak with a cowl covering her head. I know immediately that it is Clara and I am filled with hatred for her. She has guessed! She has interfered. She lifts a hand to silence me. 'They went hours ago,' she says. 'I thought this might be what you were doing. They left before dark, Ricky.' I fall back against the wall, not fully understanding; not wishing to understand. 'What?'

'Diana and our Alice have gone together,' she says quietly. She takes my hand. 'You're very cold. You'd better come back.'

'No!' I think it is a trick. I pull free of her. 'There was an agreement, Clara. You should not be doing this. Where are they?'

'I don't know. You'll freeze to death, if a bullet doesn't kill you.'

'Where are they?'

'They were as secretive with me as with anyone. They could have joined Count Stefanik. It's my only guess.'

'Stefanik? His balloon?'

'A guess.'

'Where is his balloon?'

'I have no idea where he kept it. It's probably destroyed. It was a guess.'

I begin to run up Papensgasse and through the Botanical Gardens. There are fires everywhere. The soldiers ignore me. I get to Pushkinstrasse and I cannot recognise anything. There are no more buildings. I look up into the blazing night sky in the hope of seeing the airship. The Indian Quarter has vanished. The Customs House is a guttering cinder. Within an hour I am standing in the ruins of her church. The Yanokovski Promenade has become a mass of black rubble. I can see St-Maria-and-St-Maria on the hill, twin chimneys of light. Flames course through the cathedral, glowing from every window. She is roaring as if in pain and anger. And the shells continue. Holzhammer must surely have come to relish the

180

destruction for its own sake. We are at his mercy. And he is not merciful. Little Bohemia and the Synagogue are one hellish pyre. I reach down to pick up a piece of masonry. It is a small stone head, part of the motif above the left-hand column framing the central door: the face of a woman. It seems to me that she stares past my shoulder at a memory. The expression on her face is resigned. Has that expression always been there? For the three hundred years of her existence has she always known this would be her fate? There is no snow. The Theatre is an insubstantial outline of dancing red and orange. Everything is melting in the heat. Later I will hear that Prince Badehoff-Krasny had ordered the remains of the city to be fired. ('This is my Moscow'). Nobody will ever come to understand how Mirenburg fell, any more than they will really know how Magdeburg was destroyed or what led to the extinction of Troy. Man's greatest monuments, his architecture, never outlast his acts of aggression. At dawn I wade through fields of ash. I cannot find her. Thin sunlight attacks the drifting smoke. Little groups of people wander here and there, each with a bundle, none with any hope. They look at me, some of them, as I pass, but most trudge on with their heads bowed. There are fewer shells, now. They fall on ruins and pulverise them. As I pass it, the Casino collapses in on itself. There is hardly anything left for them to destroy. I cannot find her. Periodically, I inspect the sky. There is no ship there. I would like to think it has borne her up. In my mind's eye I can see the bright reds and golds of the balloon's canopy in contrast to the grey, misty luminousness of the morning. Dressed in his Chinese silk shirt and riding breeches, with a gaily-dressed woman on either side of him, the young Bohemian aviator lifts a strong arm to his valves. I can see the balloon rising higher and higher above the flattened wastes of our murdered city, as if Mirenburg's spirit goes free. I can see her smiling carelessly, merely enjoying the sensation of flight, forgetful of me and of everyone. She kisses the bearded cheek of Stefanik not from any particular affection but from simple, passing gratitude to the person who has given her this, her most recent, pleasure.

181

One should never attempt to possess a beautiful whore, or hold on to the soul of a child, nor assault an idea as fragile as Mirenburg. Alice. I shall never fully understand why you fled from me. I wish you had been able to tell me the truth. But, if I were ever to confront you, you would reply: 'You must have known.' and dismiss all responsibility for your deception. 'You must have known.' But when you deny my suspicions that is a deeper lie still. 'You must have known, that I deceived you. It is your fault for not admitting it.' Yet did I really ever guess? Was I not always too afraid of the true answer? They will build a new city along the fresh course of the river. It will be called Svitenburg as a sop to the nationalists who are soon, of course, to become Austrian subjects in all but name. It is still little more than an industrial village. Its most impressive buildings are its warehouses. Did Alexandra live to marry a well-to-do Swiss and give him little babies in Geneva? She could banish all the old shadows, the memories of a 'wicked past', and have forgotten a lifetime in a matter of hours. And Wäldenstein will become Svitavia again, a province of Bohemia, then a department of Czecho-Slovakia; forty years later that is what she remains, looking to Prague, such a poor imitation of Mirenburg, for her directions. Here in the yellow heat and ease I have spent the past eighteen years peering out at the world I came to fear. The Germans rise again and recover their wealth through patriotism, mysticism and a fascination with steel, as they will always do; the French continue to squabble and refer to past glories as solutions for the future; the English see their society collapsing all around them and find a panacea in American jazz; the Russians stir and dream again of Empire, having revived the methods and ambitions of Ivan the Terrible. And the Italians have conquered poverty, although they had to go to Abyssinia to do it. Wäldenstein, settled in the arms of her new Slavic mother, is left, at least, in peace. When I return to Rosenstrasse, Captain Kolovrat has galloped off about some other importance. The brothel is now almost the only whole building in the street. Captain Mencken commands the two or three soldiers left. He has no orders and he is drunk. The

182

smoked glasses fall down on his nose as he looks at me and offers a bottle. I shake my head. Thérèse and Renée, all lace and dark stockings, sit together on a couch singing a little song together. 'Your wife,' he says, 'is upstairs I believe.' He is perfectly grave. 'Do you speak,' he drinks again, 'Bulgarian by any chance?' He laughs. He appears to have fled into that familiar, self-protective dramatisation which is only one step away from hysteria. I am in no hurry to see Clara. I accept the offer of his bottle. 'We can abandon ourselves to War quite as readily as we can abandon ourselves to lust,' says Mencken, making an effort to hand up the bottle to me. 'And War's so much easier and less mystifying than sex, is it not?' He grins at me. 'I'm serious.' I do not doubt it. He lets his eye drift towards the ladies who are as drunk as he is and are giggling together. 'War doesn't whisper. It doesn't have shades of meaning. It demands courage, of course, and decisive action. It offers glory and threatens death. But lust offers pain and threatens us with life, eh?' He is pleased with this turn of phrase.

The sunlight begins to shine through the shattered boards and glass. I put the bottle back into his hands and with a sigh climb up to Clara and a reckoning. Holzhammer will become Governor Regent of Wäldenstein under the Austrians and will be blown to pieces by an Anarchist bomb in 1904. Clara is asleep. There is no confrontation. I feel vague disappointment. I leave her and return to my room, hoping to find a clue. My anger with Lady Cromach is growing. She has deceived me treacherously. And yet my actions were no less treacherous. It is different, I tell myself, but I know it is not. I cannot feel the same anger towards Alice. The room is strewn with all her abandoned finery, with half-packed trunks and bags. I pick up a pair of pale blue silk drawers. They still stink of her. There are no notes. But in a cupboard I find some crumpled sheets of violet notepaper with scraps of Alice's handwriting on them and little pictures of the sort a schoolgirl might draw when bored. I spread them on top of the Chinese dresser. There is a quotation from something: *It's a fine day. Let's go fishing said the worm to the man.* And another scrap: *He is not what I imagined him to be.* I am beginning to shake. 'You are a fool!' I say. 'For *you* could have become what I imagined you to be. You have ruined any possibility of that now. What a woman you might have been.' It is my failure. I feel it as a painter might experience a failure of creativity. It is as if half my own flesh has been torn from me, half my mind stolen. The guns batter my past into the dust and my future has run away into the ruins. I am so horribly betrayed. And it is my own doing. My anger comes on me suddenly and I begin to rip at her dresses, her underwear, her aigrettes, stamping on her little shoes, flinging silk and lace and feathers into the air until my tiredness causes me to collapse, sucking at a hand I have somehow cut, in the middle of the debris. I have tried to destroy everything which reminds me of her, which hurts me. I poured so much of myself into that valueless vessel. As I squat there, weeping and shaking, Clara enters the room. She is wearing a patterned tea-gown over her nightclothes. She moves here and there, replacing ornaments, clearing up broken china and glass. 'She's taken every piece of jewellery,' she says. I moan at her to go away. She stands looking down on me. 'Have you hurt yourself badly?'

'No.'

She closes the door behind her.

When, at length, I return to Clara's room she is asleep again with the sheets drawn over her head. I take off my jacket and my waistcoat and go to sit in the armchair near the window. I cannot sleep. Every time I close my eyes I am filled with bitter images, with a yearning for the recent past and all the happiness I have lost. Mirenburg is gone. Papadakis grumbles at me as he brings back the clean chamber pot. 'You've pissed in the bed again,' he says. 'I know it. I can smell it.'

He has made me stand, leaning on the table and trembling, while he gathers up the soiled linen. 'I'm going to bring the doctor in the morning.' Now the bed is clean. Through the open window comes the smell of hyacinths and the sea. Mirenburg no longer lives; she is a grey memory. She has been biding her time, hiding in a neurasthenic slumber while she waited for the best which would be offered to her: a kind of hibernation because she did not want to accept my offer but was afraid to refuse it, afraid to take any action. What had Diana promised? I doubt if it was anything than a more glamorous, if less realistic, plan of escape. Stefanik's balloon? I get out of the chair. My legs are weak. Clara turns, casting off her covering to hold out tolerant arms. Her face is full of controlled sympathy. How can she forgive me? Why do women do this to us? I begin to weep again. 'We are going away this evening,' she says. 'It is all arranged with Frau Schmetterling. We will take Elvira. Wilke will be with us. How did you plan to escape from the city?' Still snivelling, I tell her about the underground river and the sewers.' She pats my shoulder. 'Not bad. It could work.' Eventually I go to sleep. I am awakened by an explosion. From somewhere within the house I hear voices shouting and the crash of falling plaster. It is dark in the room. I lie on the bed and wait for the next shell. Instead the door opens and Clara stands there, an oil-lamp raised in her hand. Frau Schmetterling is with her. The madam holds something in her hands. It is a bloody, palpitating chow-dog. 'They have killed Pouf-Pouf,' she says flatly. 'And this poor little one is dying, too.'

Clara is already in her outdoor clothes: a black and grey tailor-made. Over this she draws a plain cloak of the sort peasant women wear. She points to a bundle at her feet. 'Here are some of 'Mister's' clothes. They should fit you. You'll have to leave your wardrobe behind, my dear.'

I have become pliable and obedient. The dog begins to groan. Frau Schmetterling whispers something to Clara and then returns downstairs. I receive a strange feeling of satisfaction as I pull on the rough garments; it is almost as if I shall wear sackcloth in mourning for Mirenburg and my slain imagination. 'I want reality so badly,' I tell Clara. 'She was won over by nothing more than a fantastic promise.'

'Very likely.' Clara helps me button the coat. 'Do you still have the map?'

I give it to her. 'We'll put Wilke in charge, I think,' she says. 'At least for the moment. Are you feeling any better?'

'I want reality,' I tell her.

'This is reality enough for anyone.' She is humorous. 'But I'm sure you'll find a way out of it. I trust your instincts for that. Lead the way, your lordship.'

We leave, the four of us, in the night. In Rosenstrasse we have to pass two soldiers who are still alive, though their bodies are dreadfully mutilated. They call out to us for help. 'I'll deal with them,' says Frau Schmetterling, hurrying us forward.

Wilke and I raise the cover of the manhole. He goes first, swinging the lamp we have brought with us. Our shadows slide this way and that on the moist stones of the shaft. The metal ladder leads us down into the old watercourse. Elvira is too small to keep her head above the water, so I raise her on my shoulders. Throughout this journey I will find a kind of delicate consolation in being allowed to tend to the child's needs and will catch myself occasionally using the same kind of words and gestures used by 'Mister' in his conversation with her. We wade through shit and corpses to some sort of liberty, emerging on the fringes of the Moravian inferno and joining lines of refugees stumbling towards the cleaner air of a countryside stripped of all its wealth. We walk steadily for two more days until we cross the Bohemian border and are able, with the gold Frau Schmetterling has given us, to get a train to Prague where we separate. Wilke will take Elvira to England. I still have no volition and allow Clara to make every decision. We go first by train to Berlin and the hospitality of my brother Wolfgang, who congratulates me on the charm and the breeding of my English fiancée. Within days, of course, we are taken up by Society. Everyone must hear of our experiences. I recover myself sufficiently to present at least an acceptable facade and I speak with authority of the suffering and destruction I have witnessed. I am asked to write the articles which become that silly book *The 100 Day Siege: A Personal Record of the Last Months of Mirenburg*. I mention nothing of any real importance to me, but for a while I become a hero.

186

Holzhammer's villainy is the subject of a thousand editorials. He is called the Butcher of Mirenburg and the perfidy of Austria-Hungary has shocked, we read, the entire civilised world. But Holzhammer rules and Badehoff-Krasny is exiled and the diplomats gradually do their seedy work so that the Peace of Europe is maintained for a few more years. And Mirenburg is gone. I hear many rumours, but there is no news of Alice. I will talk to anyone who has a grain of gossip. It is still hard for me to accept that so much beauty has vanished as a result of trivial political decisions. There will never be a brothel like Frau Schmetterling's in Rosenstrasse, for there will never be another Mirenburg, with its history and its charm. And psycho-analysis has made us too self-conscious. This is an age of great remedies; they seem to believe there is a cure for human greed. There is not. But neither should the greedy be condemned. They should merely be guarded against. Greed is not evil. What is evil is the manipulation of others in order to satisfy it; the quest for power. That is the crime. Do you hear me, Papadakis? He is still shuffling about in the shadows.

Will you read this, Alice, in your Geneva home? Or did you die with the others in Mirenburg? I could not find you. In London and Dublin we thought to discover news of Lady Cromach, but she had not returned. Someone said she had changed her name 'because of certain scandals' and might be living in Paris. But she was not in Paris. And as for Princess Poliakoff, all we heard of her was that she could have gone to India. They said that on Sunday, 19th December 1897, when Holzhammer's troops arrived at Rosenstrasse, Poliakoff had sat in her old lover's carriage and directed the mercenaries into the brothel. I can imagine with what pleasure the Bulgarians took our ladies ('All they found later was a pile of bloody lace'). Baby is crying, Lady Cromach used to say. Baby is angry. Rakanaspya was killed, probably by the Austrians. Count Belozerski was wounded but managed to return to Kiev where I believe he still lives, writing about factories. Baby is crying. We are lost. Deserted. That which comforts us grows old and dies. We long to recapture it; the security of childhood, the

187

attention of others. Clara was familiar with Lady Cromach's remarks. But she was not so tolerant of Baby. 'Sooner or later,' she said to me, 'that baby's crying becomes an irritant to our adult ears. It is then we have the right to turn upon the weak and with all due ruthlessness squeeze the life from a silly, mindless creature. If we are to survive, Baby must be destroyed.'

I was not to meet Frau Schmetterling for a long time, after Clara had despaired of my sniffing after Alice's non-existent trail and had returned to Germany alone. Clara said, as she waited on the platform for her train: 'I shall always love you, Ricky, for what you are, as well as what you could have become. But I know you are in love with an illusion, and it is a lost illusion at that. What would happen if you found her, if Mirenburg had not been destroyed? What would have happened if she had stayed with you? You have told me yourself. You know, but you refuse to act on your knowledge. And that is madness.' Now my honest Clara is gone and I am alone with an obsession which has taken up my life and drained from me what was not already drained by the treacherous Alice, who refused to be what I needed her to be. She was myself. The city is gone. She would be fifty-seven years old now. Frau Schmetterling was in Dresden, the proprietress of an ordinary boarding house catering to single middle-class gentlemen. I reminded her gently of our ordeal in Mirenburg. 'Yes,' she said, 'it was ghastly. Hardly a saucer remained of all that crockery I had collected over twenty years.'

I asked if she had heard anything of my Alice. 'No,' she said. 'Not unless she was the one who married the Swiss. I think she was killed, wasn't she? I hope those bastards didn't rape her.' Frau Schmetterling had attempted to protect her girls from the troops but she had eventually left Mirenburg with Renée and Trudi and joined Wilke in Brighton. They had gone to America for a little while, but had not been able to stay. Most of her girls had had no means of travelling so the house had rapidly become a common bordello used by the occupying army. The Bulgarians had been brutes. Everything of value had been stolen during the looting. 'I heard,' the old madam told me, 'that at least one of the girls was killed. Remember Dolly? Natalia told me. I met Natalia outside the theatre one evening, in Cologne. She was selling flowers. She dropped the whole basket to hug me!' Frau Schmetterling had laughed before she became serious again. 'She was the one who told me about Dolly. Those Bulgars destroyed everything that was delicate. They ruined everything beautiful. They didn't understand the rocking-horse room, so they simply ripped it apart. They killed the acrobat. That friend of 'Mister's'. *Laches!* He insulted an officer, apparently.'

Natalia had stayed on, she had told Frau Schmetterling, in the hope of filling the madam's place when things calmed down. Several of the whores had had the same idea. But Holzhammer had given the order to destroy every building left standing. 'They were lucky, in the end, to escape with the clothes still on their backs. Natalia left with a returning Bulgarian officer. He knocked her about. She got away from him in Buda-Pesht, she told me, while they were changing trains. She was married. She wasn't on hard times. Her husband had a big flower-business in Cologne. They had two little boys. And Caroline Vacarescu escaped. I don't know how. She married an American and went to live in Ohio, though I believe she's now in California. Elvira's at university, you know, in Munich. She still remembers you carrying her through that sewer.' Frau Schmetterling had winked at me with a trace of her old good humour. 'You'd like her. She's just your type.' I was able to laugh and tell her that I had lost interest in females under twenty-five when Mirenburg was destroyed. 'But what about the balloonist, that Czech?' She thought he had probably tried to get his airship up and had been shot down by Holzhammer's artillery. Much later I heard a rumour that, under an assumed name, he had been killed on the Eastern Front in 1915, flying a plane of his own design against the Austrians. Someone else said he had died with the Czech Legion in Siberia.

Frau Schmetterling had made me eat a huge dinner and had

introduced me to her new dogs, two pugs. When I had left she had kissed me and said that I should look after my health. 'It is a shame you'll never make a fool of yourself over a woman again. Your mistake was in refusing to believe that another woman could be a worthy rival. Men will do that.' I had shaken my head. 'I respected her insufficiently. And in my efforts to obscure my motives from her I lost her forever.' But Frau Schmetterling had been impatient with this. 'Interpret it any way you choose, Ricky. The fact was that you seduced a child and you paid the price for it.' She had shrugged. 'And she would always have been a child, probably, with men like you to look after her. She's a child now, if she married that Swiss. Enjoy youth when it's given to you. It's a mistake to try to imprison it, though. It's too greedy, Ricky. And it never works, my boy.' She is still in Dresden, I believe. We exchange postcards every couple of years. Prince Badehoff-Krasny lived not twenty miles from me, up the coast, until his death. Von Landoff replaced Holzhammer as Governor, after the assassination. Captain Mencken was killed in Papensgasse, firing a carbine at the Bulgarians as they swept round from the embankment. Had Princess Poliakoff died in Mirenburg? Frau Schmetterling wrote that she might have done. She could not remember if Poliakoff had been with Holzhammer when the Bulgarians took over the brothel, but she remembered the rumour. 'Personally, I think she died in the bombardment.'

Alice. My Alexandra. My little schoolgirl. Your soft body is no longer warm. Your perfume is faint. I see you in your red and gold balloon as it drifts up towards the silver sunshine. I wish it was my cheek you kiss as you lean over the rim of the gondola and see the spreading ash, the few remaining ruins, saying 'Look, there's the Radota Bridge! Isn't it terrible! And there's the Cathedral! And there's Rosenstrasse. Wave, Ricky!' It is so hard to write. The light is very dim for midday. I must tell Papadakis to turn on the gas. Clara married. She runs a restaurant in Liège and has done well for herself, though they say her husband is a drunk. She loved me. She told me she would always love me, but she had to look after herself. I understood. She had given me too much, I said. She had shaken her head. 'It would not have been too much if you had wanted it.' I spent so many cynical years in pursuit of my dream, in revenge on those I blamed for destroying it. And I never found her. She is washed away in that grisly tide. It is ash. She is a ghost. The twin spires glitter in the early afternoon sun. We look down past them towards the white walls. We are having a picnic. Falfnersallee and the Restaurant Schmidt. Waiting for her. I sip absinthe in the sunshine opposite the Radota Bridge. We visit the dress-shops and the jewellers. Deep in the luxury of the brothel. A riding crop rises and falls. A distant, excited scream. Lady Cromach's smile betrays the betrayer. Clara loved me. That last soft kiss. Alexandra. It was a blow to the groin. I can still feel the bruise. My right hand has started to tremble. Papadakis must bring me some more wine. The sea is too loud. The pain is nothing. I can return to Mirenburg whenever I wish.